COURTING JUSTICE

NEW YORK TIMES AND USA TODAY BESTSELLING AUTHOR

BRENDA JACKSON

COURTING JUSTICE

ARABESQUE®

Recycling programs
for this product may
not exist in your area.

COURTING JUSTICE

ISBN-13: 978-0-373-53473-9

Copyright © 2012 by Brenda Streater Jackson

All rights reserved. The reproduction, transmission or utilization
of this work in whole or in part in any form by any electronic, mechanical
or other means, now known or hereafter invented, including xerography,
photocopying and recording, or in any information storage or retrieval
system, is forbidden without written permission. For permission please
contact Kimani Press, 225 Duncan Mill Road, Toronto, Ontario M3B 3K9,
Canada.

This is a work of fiction. Names, characters, places and incidents are
either the product of the author's imagination or are used fictitiously,
and any resemblance to actual persons, living or dead, business
establishments, events or locales is entirely coincidental.

® and TM are trademarks. Trademarks indicated with ® are registered in
the United States Patent and Trademark Office, the Canadian Trade Marks
Office and/or other countries.

www.kimanipress.com

Printed in U.S.A.

To the love of my life, Gerald Jackson, Sr.
My one and only. Always. Happy 40th anniversary!
And I'm looking forward to many, many more!

To everyone who enjoys reading about the Madarises,
this one is especially for you.

THE MADARIS FAMILY

Milton Madaris, Sr. and Felicia Laverne Lee Madaris

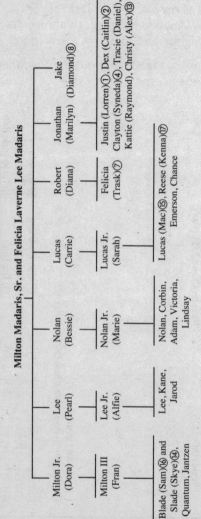

Milton Jr. (Dora)	Lee (Pearl)	Nolan (Bessie)	Lucas (Carrie)	Robert (Diana)	Jonathan (Marilyn)	Jake (Diamond)⑧

Milton III (Fran)

Lee Jr. (Alfie)

Nolan Jr. (Marie)

Lucas Jr. (Sarah)

Felicia (Trask)⑦

Justin (Lorren)①, Dex (Caitlin)②
Clayton (Syneda)④, Tracie (Daniel),
Kattie (Raymond), Christy (Alex)⑬

Blade (Sam)⑯ and
Slade (Skye)⑭,
Quantum, Jantzen

Lee, Kane,
Jarod

Nolan, Corbin,
Adam, Victoria,
Lindsay

Lucas (Mac)⑮, Reese (Kenna)⑰
Emerson, Chance

KEY:

( ) — denotes a spouse

◯ and number — denotes title of book for that couple's story

① Tonight and Forever	⑤ One Special Moment	⑨ True Love
② Whispered Promises	⑥ Fire and Desire	⑩ Surrender
③ Cupid's Bow	⑦ Truly Everlasting	⑪ The Best Man
④ Eternally Yours	⑧ Secret Love	⑫ The Midnight Hour

⑬ Unfinished Business	⑰ Inseparable
⑭ Slow Burn	
⑮ Taste of Passion	
⑯ Sensual Confessions	

THE MADARIS FRIENDS

Maurice and Stella Grant

Trevor (Corinthians)⑥,
Regina (Mitch)⑪

Angelique Hamilton Chenault

Sterling Hamilton (Colby)⑤,
Nicholas Chenault (Shayla)⑨

Kyle Garwood (Kimara)③

Nedwyn Lansing
(Diana)⑭

Drake Warren
(Tori)⑫

Trent Jordache
(Brenna)⑨

Ashton Sinclair
(Netherland)⑩

KEY:
( ) — denotes a spouse
◯ and number — denotes title of book for that couple's story

① Tonight and Forever
② Whispered Promises
③ Cupid's Bow
④ Eternally Yours
⑤ One Special Moment
⑥ Fire and Desire

⑦ Truly Everlasting
⑧ Secret Love
⑨ True Love

⑩ Surrender
⑪ The Best Man
⑫ The Midnight Hour

⑬ Unfinished Business
⑭ Slow Burn

Dear Reader,

I never imagined when I penned my first Madaris novel that I would still be going strong seventeen years later.

The Madaris family is special, not just because it is my first family series, but because over the years you've made them your family. I've often said that the Madaris men have become your heroes because they represent those things you desire— men whose looks not only take your breath away, but who have the ability to make you appreciate the fact that you're a woman.

I set the stage for *Courting Justice* in my last three Madaris novels. The hero and heroine, De Angelo Di Meglio and Peyton Mahoney, take center stage in a love story that will leave you breathless until the end.

I hope you enjoy reading *Courting Justice*, the eighteenth book in the Madaris Family and Friends series.

All the best,

Brenda Jackson

For none of us liveth to himself,
and no man dieth to himself.
—*Romans* 14:7

Chapter 1

"This is Martin Long reporting live from the steps of the U.S. District courthouse in lower Manhattan. We've just been told that a verdict has been reached in the federal case against Senator Ivan Russ. So far the headlines have been dominated by the prosecutor and the defense attorney in the case—a legal battle between two high-profile lawyers dubbed the "Thriller Maxilla" and the "Italian Hellion." According to sources, defense attorney DeAngelo Di Meglio has gotten his client, Senator Russ, acquitted on all charges. Government prosecutors, headed by Attorney Samuel Maxilla, were shocked when their key witness in the case broke down after only fifteen minutes on the stand under cross-examination from Di Meglio."

The reporter shifted the microphone to his other hand. *"Under relentless questioning by Di Meglio, Congresswoman Andrea Vermeil shocked everyone in the courtroom with her confession that she had framed Senator Russ in a conspiracy to embezzle over a half million dollars in campaign funds..."*

DeAngelo Di Meglio tuned out the reporters surrounding him and braced himself for the onslaught of media that would descend on him the moment he left the courthouse. This case was what he'd worked hard for his entire career, one that would make him a household name, one that would put him at the top and establish his legal reputation. And now at the ripe old age of thirty-four and after practicing law for ten years, he'd finally done it.

"Mr. Di Meglio, how did the case come together?"

"Why didn't the senator admit to the affair with the congresswoman to save himself?"

"Are you upset the senator wasn't truthful with you about everything?"

The reporters' questions came at him from every direction.

He'd had a gut feeling the moment Congresswoman Vermeil had taken the stand, and his instincts made him push her in his cross-examination. Maybe it was the "I'm about to hang you by the balls" look she'd given his client, Senator Russ, who denied having an affair with the congresswoman and was willing to risk prison time to keep the affair from his wife, who was terminally ill. DeAngelo shook his head. Ivan Russ had actually believed that it was better for his dying wife to believe he was an embezzler rather than find out he was unfaithful.

The reporters continued to bombard him with more questions despite his response of "no comment."

"How do you feel about breaking this case?"

"What do you think about the federal prosecutors and how they handled the case?"

The scene outside the courthouse reminded De-Angelo of the very first time he'd lost a case and how he'd felt then. He remembered the advice his parents, both of whom were lawyers, had given him: *If you can't say anything nice about somebody, then don't say anything at all.*

He looked straight into the TV camera pointed in his face and said in a direct, confident voice, "No comment for now. We'll answer questions at the press conference."

A short while later he was back in his office, surrounded by family, friends, associates and the law firm staff. They had all dropped by his office to congratulate him on winning a case many had thought would last for weeks or months. In fact, a few had even assumed there was only a snowball's chance in hell of winning the case. The federal prosecutors had boasted that they had an airtight case against the senator, and when they found a briefcase filled with half a million dollars buried in his backyard, many assumed he was guilty.

Although the evidence had been damaging, for some reason DeAngelo had believed Senator Russ's claims of innocence. But DeAngelo *had* suspected the senator wasn't being truthful when he'd asked him if he knew of anyone who would want to frame him. DeAngelo got the sense that Senator Russ was trying to hide something, trying to protect someone. But no matter how he'd tried, he couldn't get Ivan Russ to tell him anything other than that he didn't plant the money in his backyard.

Momentarily distracted, DeAngelo blinked when his father snapped a finger in front of his face.

"Daydreaming, son? If you are, then you're entitled. That case has consumed you for months now, and I speak on behalf of this entire firm in saying that you made us proud today."

"You most certainly did, Angelo," his mother chimed in with a huge smile on her face.

Coming from his parents, it meant a lot. He'd always appreciated their opinions—even at times when he didn't want to hear them. "Thanks, Dad, Mom."

His mother and father had always been his heroes. The two were highly respected attorneys who'd made a name for themselves and the Di Meglio law firm in Manhattan. The family firm had been established generations ago by his great-great-grandfather, and now included his parents, his father's two brothers—Federico and Leandro—and their sons, Maddox and Damon. They were all Di Meglios, and had made a name for themselves representing the rich and famous. The only person who wasn't part of the law firm was his younger sister, Samari. She was a partner in two law firms—one in Houston and another in Oklahoma City—and she had called moments ago to congratulate him and to tell him how proud she was of him.

"Same here, Angelo," his uncles chimed in, as they grinned from ear to ear. "We want you to take some time off. You deserve it," his uncle Leandro, the eldest of the three Di Meglio brothers, said. "Besides, you need to prepare to take on all those interviews and book offers that will be coming your way. The case not only made national headlines, it even made news overseas. Winning this case makes you one of the hottest lawyers around."

"Hey, but don't get the big-head," his cousin Maddox warned.

"If you do, then we'll have to take you down a peg or two," his cousin Damon threatened. Both tried to look serious, but Angelo saw the amusement lurking behind their dark eyes.

He was about to tell both of them—who he thought of more like brothers than cousins—to kiss him where the sun don't shine when he remembered his parents and uncles were still in the room. Instead he glanced over at his uncle Leandro. "I doubt things will go that far, Uncle Andro. I may be news today, but history tomorrow."

"Don't be too sure of that, Angelo," his uncle Federico warned. Fed—as everyone called him—was the middle Di Meglio brother, and the uncle who was the most fun to be around. He was the Di Meglio who'd covered for Angelo and his cousins over the years when they'd gotten into trouble.

Over the next three hours, DeAngelo's uncle's warning was born out when his phone kept ringing nonstop. It seemed that winning a high-profile case had not only given a boost to his career but also to his love life. In reality, he'd stopped considering himself a "ladies' man" a while ago. These days he dated just for fun, and always let the women he went out with know beforehand that there was no chance of emotional involvement. That had been deliberate on his part once he'd decided just what his future was.

He paused a second after locking his office door and glanced around. Everyone had left hours ago, but he and his two cousins had stayed late to celebrate some more. He had begged off Maddox's invitation to go back to his place to party and have a good time. Back in the day he would have gone along with the kind of partying Maddox had in mind—beautiful women and lots of champagne—but not now.

He knew his cousins were wondering just what the hell was wrong with him since for the past couple of years his wild bachelor lifestyle had begun winding down. They accused him of no longer being any fun—

like tonight. No doubt Maddox and Damon had hooked up with some hot women and had plans for an outrageous night.

Bidding good-night to the firm's security guards, Angelo left the office and caught the elevator to the parking garage. He had received lots of calls that day. Some he'd preferred not to have received. There were the morning talk shows that called to get an interview and several well-known publishers offering book deals. Tomorrow, he decided, he would hire someone to handle all the press.

Then there were the calls from women he hadn't dated in months—deliberately. Evidently they hadn't gotten the hint since most of their calls made it seem as if they were still his flavor of the month, and would enjoy being by his side in the spotlight. He thought to himself, that wouldn't be happening.

He fished his car keys out of his coat pocket. He opened the door to his two-seater Mercedes sports car and slid in. Whether his admirers knew it or not, his absence hadn't been by accident. He had stopped seeing them for a reason. It seemed that lately one woman in particular seemed to dominate his thoughts.

After buckling his seat belt, he pulled out his cell phone and checked his messages. He would have to clear some of them out, he thought as texts and voice mails nearly totaled a hundred. He frowned as he realized the one call he had wanted most wasn't among them. He had expected her call if for no other reason than because he was her best friend's brother and he'd won an important case. Since she was a lawyer herself, she would know what that meant and how it felt.

Even now he remembered the first time he'd met her, the first time his sister Sam had brought her two best friends from law school—Mackenzie Standfield and Peyton Mahoney—home to spend the holidays with the Di Meglio family at their Long Island estate. Both women had been lookers, but there had been something special about Peyton that held his interest, if only for a moment. It was easy enough to see that she had issues. For starters, he sensed that she was uncomfortable surrounded by the Di Meglios' wealth. She'd had a chip on her shoulder the size of the Rock of Gibraltar. Later, he'd found out why when he heard about the hard life she'd had growing up on Chicago's South Side. He couldn't help but admire her.

Although he rarely saw her, over the years he'd come to realize that he was attracted to her. It was subtle—and sexual, or so he thought—but his interest increased whenever he saw her. At first, he chalked it up to her being different. But then things changed when he made a surprise visit to his sister in Oklahoma, only to find she was away on a business trip in Florida for several days. At the time, Peyton wouldn't hear of him staying at a hotel and had invited him to crash at her place until Sam returned to town.

It was during those five days that he'd gotten a chance to really know Peyton Mahoney and see a side of her she probably reserved for only those closest to her. With him, she let her guard down. And in doing so, he found her even more intriguing. She hadn't been as unapproachable as he'd thought she was. During that time he'd discovered just how compassionate and loyal she was and that she didn't have a pretentious bone in her body. Those five days had been special. And it was during those days, as unlikely as it might seem, that he had become totally enamored with her, although he'd done a good job of hiding it and ignoring his feelings. The man who could have any woman he wanted was hot and heavy for a woman who probably didn't want anything to do with him, even if she knew how he felt.

He was about to slide his cell phone back into his pocket when it rang. He glanced at the caller ID and when he saw it was an Oklahoma number, he heaved a sigh of relief. He felt a twinge that sent a fluttery feeling through his body. He'd been waiting for this call. He pressed the key to connect the call. "This is Angelo."

"Hey, this is Peyton. I don't want to take up much of your time, but I just had to call to congratulate you. I've been keeping up with the trial and you were simply fantastic."

The first thought that ran through his mind was that she could never take up too much of his time. And the second, a compliment coming from her meant everything. "Thanks, Peyton. I appreciate you calling. It was difficult at times."

"I can imagine. I'm involved in a messy case now myself. I go to trial in a couple of weeks, so wish me luck. I want some of that Di Meglio courtroom magic to rub off on me."

He smiled, thinking that the Di Meglio good fortune wasn't the only thing he wanted to rub off on her. The thought of his hands touching her skin sent shivers of desire down his spine.

"Well, I'll let you go, Angelo. I don't want to hold up The Man."

She'd always referred to him as that: The Man. Now he was beginning to wonder what it took to go from The Man to her man. "You're not holding me up. Besides, I'm on my way home from the office. I've got nothing better to do tonight."

"Yeah. Right."

He could tell from her voice that she didn't believe him. She still thought he was that skirt-chasing Di Meglio who enjoyed adding notches to his bedpost. He rolled down the car window to let in the summer breeze as he drove toward his place in Long Island. His parents had invited him to drop by their house, but he'd wanted to go home.

"I mean it. I don't have anything better to do tonight." *Anything I'd rather do than talk to you,* he thought silently. He wondered where she was. At the office? Home? "I enjoy talking to you," he added.

"Thanks for being sweet and saying that, but I can't indulge you, at least not tonight. I have to be back in court first thing in the morning. The attorney for the plaintiff is trying to play games, and I'm not in a playing mood. Gotta go, Angelo. It was good talking to you. Congratulations."

He couldn't imagine her taking a break. In all the years he'd known Peyton, he'd never seen her let her hair down and just enjoy life. She usually worked from sunup to sundown on her cases, and when she did take a break from the office he knew that she usually headed back home to Chicago to do pro bono work in the community. She probably didn't know the meaning of relaxing, or pampering herself, or just plain chilling.

"Well, don't celebrate too much tonight."

He chuckled. If only she knew that was the last thing he intended to do. He would go home, shower, retire early and lie in bed savoring her phone call. "I won't and I hope you have a good day in court tomorrow."

"Hey, thanks. I'm going to need it. Next time I see you I hope you're willing to share your secrets. You've won so many cases this year and I'd like to know how you do it."

The answer to that question was easy. *By staying focused and understanding what I really want out of life*, he thought to himself. "Yes, next time we see each other I'll be more than happy to share my secrets with you."

He could hear her laughter and the sound was more sensuous than anything he'd heard in a while. Goose bumps pricked his skin and stoked his libido in a way that only she could do. She didn't have a clue just how sexy he thought she was.

"Good night, Angelo."

"Same to you, Peyton."

After disconnecting the call, he was exhilarated yet felt a sense of longing. As the breeze blowing through the window floated across his face, he decided it was time to finally put his plan into action. There had to be some reason why he was so attracted to her, why he sought her out whenever they attended parties or family functions together and why he got jealous of any man who dared try and talk to her.

It was time for him to discover what it was about Peyton that had him fighting feelings he wasn't accustomed to. When he got home, he would call his sister Samari, who had voiced her suspicions that he had a thing for her best friend. She'd known it and no telling how many others did as well—except for the lady herself.

Tonight he was going to enlist his sister Sam's help in orchestrating his plan. His sister had been the first one to notice the attraction. And of course he had denied it, mostly because at the time he hadn't been sure just what his feelings were. All he knew was that he was intensely attracted to Peyton.

As he drove along the expressway toward home, he couldn't help but smile. There was a feeling of peace and tranquility that flowed through him. His friends and family had nicknamed him "Smooth Operator." And because of his courtroom success, the media had dubbed him the "Italian Hellion."

Right now, the only thing he wanted to be successful at, the only thing he wanted to be known as, was the man who conquered Peyton Mahoney.

Two weeks later...

Peyton stared across the table at the two women who had been her best friends since law school—Samari and Mackenzie Madaris. She looked down again at the early birthday gift they'd given her—a gift certificate for two weeks at Dunwoody Cove, the exclusive five-star, singles-only resort on a private island in the Bahamas.

Knowing the cost of a stay at the posh resort, her eyes widened. She glanced up and a smile touched her lips. "Have I been so much of a bitch lately that the two of you felt you needed to get rid of me?"

Of course it was Sam who smiled sweetly and said, "Your being a bitch we can handle. But a horny bitch is a little too much for anyone to have to deal with, Pey."

Mackenzie gave Samari a playful punch on the shoulder. "Hey, Sam, did you have to go for the jugular?"

Peyton ignored the jab as she stuffed the tissue paper back into the gift bag and grinned. "Sticks and stones may break my bones but—"

"But that's exactly what you need, Peyton—bones," Sam interjected. "You need some fine man's bones to jump. Then maybe that'll get you out of this funk you've been in lately."

Peyton didn't say anything, because Sam was right. They knew the source of her bad attitude lately. It was just weeks before her thirtieth birthday, and she was still single with no love life to speak of. Her two best friends, however—Sam and Mac—were not only married to drop-dead gorgeous men who happened to be cousins, but both were mothers to two beautiful babies. Mac had a three-month-old son named after her husband, Luke, and Sam had a beautiful little girl named Blair, who would be celebrating her first birthday in a few months.

"You're going to the resort for two weeks, aren't you?"

Peyton glanced at Mac. Her friends, who were genuinely concerned, didn't know the half of it. Although the part about her being horny was up for discussion, she was never one to constantly need male companionship. But what she did need was a break from Oklahoma and from her caseload.

She'd won her last case a few days before, but it hadn't been easy. Opposing counsel had tried to play hardball, but she'd shown them that when pushed, she could take things to a whole new level. She had proven when provoked, she could go toe-to-toe with anyone in the courtroom.

She was glad the case was over and wasn't ready to take on another one. She just needed some time away from work, and it would be nice to go somewhere other than Chicago. Although she liked going home, since her grandmother who'd raised her had died a few years ago, the South Side hadn't been the same.

She met Mac and Sam's expectant gazes. "Yes, I'm definitely going," she said, inhaling deeply.

"Hallelujah!"

Peyton knew that what she really needed to do was figure out the reason why she'd recently begun thinking about things she'd never considered before—like settling down, getting married and making some babies. She could very easily attribute it to Mac and Sam. Lately, they'd been all smiley-faced.

Sam had a huge smile on her face now. "That means we get to go shopping," she said.

"For what?" Peyton said.

"For some lingerie."

"I'm going to the resort to rest, Sam, not necessarily to get laid. Besides, I have lingerie."

"It's a singles resort, kiddo. Of course you're going there to get laid," Sam said, giving her a pointed look as Mac leaned back in her chair and grinned.

"And we're talking about sexy lingerie, Peyton. There's no way you're going to the Dunwoody taking that granny-panties underwear you have," Sam added.

Peyton rolled her eyes knowing not to take offense at Sam's comment and feel insulted. Been there, done that. And with Sam it was only a waste of time. Sam was Sam and there was no changing her. In law school, they had gotten off to a bad start, mainly because they'd come from two totally different backgrounds. She'd seen Sam as a spoiled little rich kid and Sam had seen her as the tough South Side of Chicago girl who still had a chip on her shoulder because she came from the wrong side of the tracks. It was one of the reasons Peyton still believed in defending the little guy.

Thanks to Mac, who'd always been the peacemaker, the three of them had come to an understanding and their friendship had survived the test of time, including some of Sam's exorbitant shopping sprees. The woman could spend money like she had her own personal mint, while Peyton still watched her pennies, something she'd always done. She had grown up not knowing where her next meal was coming from or when it would get there.

Besides, both Sam and Mac knew that when it came to sharing her bed, she was as picky as hell.

"So what time do you want to meet us at Sylvia's tomorrow?"

Peyton immediately held up her hand. "Whoa! Back up! I will not go shopping for anything at that place again."

The last time Sam had talked her into going to Sylvia's to shop, what she'd spent on a nightgown could have fed the entire block of the housing project where she grew up. She enjoyed nice things like anyone else, but the prices at Sylvia's were utterly ridiculous. Personally, she didn't think the lingerie looked any better than what she'd bought at Victoria's Secret.

"Okay, we'll go to Diana's Boutique then."

Peyton rolled her eyes. The prices at Diana's were just as bad, but she decided that now was not the time to argue with Sam or things could get ugly. And she didn't want that. Especially after the wonderful gift they'd given her. She was not particularly outgoing, so it would be hard at first for her to socialize with a bunch of strangers at a resort. But she would try.

Although she, Mac and Sam still did things together, it wasn't the same. Now they set their watches to get home to their hubbies and babies in time. She couldn't much blame them and was happy for them, really. But she still remembered those times when they would work hard during the day and head over to Cello's for dinner and to party. Now those days were long gone.

"Okay, so it's all set. Tomorrow we'll meet in town at noon at Diana's."

Peyton opened her mouth to argue then closed it. She glanced over at Mac who gave her a playful wink, and she couldn't help but chuckle. She didn't have a fighting chance against these two. Somehow she would get through this or she would end up killing Sam.

Chapter 2

Angelo entered the huge ballroom and glanced around. It was "Getting to Know You" night and the place was filled wall-to-wall with people, mostly women. All of them appeared ready, willing and available. After all, this was a singles resort. There was a time when a scene like this would have excited every sexual bone in Angelo's body. And the Di Meglio nose—which could detect a woman a mile away—would be sniffing like crazy, zeroing in on his next conquest.

It had been three weeks since he'd won the Russ case, and women were still throwing themselves at him. He'd told them that his playboy days were over, but they still didn't believe him. Some thought that tempting him with sexual favors would do the trick. And he was still shaking his head at the number of brazen propositions that had recently come his way.

As he perused his way around the ballroom, he was

very much aware of the eyes that turned to follow him. But while they were watching him, he was scanning the room for someone else. Tonight his focus was on finding one particular woman. Thursday was her birthday, and he intended to help her celebrate. In fact, whether she knew it or not, he intended to spend all of his time with her, if that's what it took. He was determined that by the time they left Dunwoody Cove their relationship would have moved to a whole new level—sexual, that is. She would no longer see him as the brother of one of her closest friends. Instead, he planned on being a whole lot more.

He suddenly heard that throaty laughter of hers and his head spun around in that direction. Even in dim light his gaze focused on Peyton sitting on a stool at the bar with several men standing around her. Already she'd acquired a fan club. She had been at the resort two days before he'd arrived and that might have been two days too many, he thought. But he would remedy that very soon.

Now that he'd arrived he wouldn't waste any time staking his claim…but subtly. He wouldn't rush her, but he intended to be thorough in his pursuit. Two weeks would just be the start of things—the groundbreaking for their relationship, so to speak. He had decided that the best approach was to get her away from her life in Oklahoma—here, unsuspecting, alone and with him.

First he had to gain her trust, though there was no reason for her not to trust him. After all, he was Samari Di Meglio Madaris's brother. She had known him close to seven years and seemed comfortable with the friendship they'd forged. He wanted her to see him not just as a friend, but as something more. He wanted her to take the blinders off and finally see what others had been seeing for years. It went deeper than just the physical attraction, but he was willing to stoke the sexual chemistry first.

Peyton being here at Dunwoody Cove was his idea. Getting Mac and Sam to go along with his plan hadn't been easy. After all, Peyton was their best friend and they knew of his reputation when it came to women. Convincing them he wanted more out of a relationship with her had been difficult, and they had questioned his motives. Nevertheless, he took it in stride since he'd made up his mind to go after Peyton with or without their help. And once he made up his mind about something, there was no stopping him. But there was a nagging question: why was he so determined to have her?

Peyton was sitting on a barstool in a slinky black cocktail dress with a split up the side that displayed nearly every inch of her thigh and gorgeous leg. She looked absolutely stunning, the way the thickness of her dreadlocks swept across her shoulders. She hadn't seen him yet, which gave him a chance to observe her unnoticed. Although she usually came off tough as nails, there was a softness that showed in her face. Her lips were full and sexy, and the reason why he had laid in bed so many times thinking about how it would feel to taste them. Her coffee-colored skin framed her dark eyes. And a pair of gold chandelier earrings dangled from her earlobes, giving her an exotic, sensual look.

She shifted in her seat, revealing a bit more of her thigh, and a spasm of desire coursed through him. He couldn't see much of her dress. But from what he could see, it covered just enough to make him fantasize about the rest of her.

The men standing around her were eagerly hanging on her every word. They reminded him of predators circling their prey, ready to pounce at the first chance. And he intended to make sure they didn't. They may have put her at the top of the food chain, but he was going to have her on his menu for her entire stay.

Peyton laughed again, throwing her head back and accentuating her long graceful neck. She sat there looking simply gorgeous and more dazzling than any other woman in the room. This wasn't the first time he'd seen her look so jaw-droppingly beautiful. There had been times they'd run into each other at weddings and family gatherings. And she always managed to garner more than enough attention, just like now.

When she laughed again, he figured she had started the party without him and it was time to make his presence known, especially when one of the men continued refilling her cocktail as another placed his hand in the center of her back, touching her bare skin.

Not on his watch.

Ignoring the women looking in his direction, he moved toward the bar where Peyton sat entertaining her audience. He frowned the closer he got. It seemed one guy in particular intended to make her his for the night, the one who kept refreshing her cocktail.

She was talkative, more than he'd ever seen before. When he was in her line of sight, she blinked. Seconds later, a huge smile spread across her lips, from corner to corner. "Angelo! What on earth are you doing here?"

Angelo smiled warmly at her as he moved past the men encircling her and came to a stop in front of her. He heard the slight slur in her voice, which meant she'd had one drink too many. "Maybe I should be asking you the same thing, Pey," he said, intentionally using her nickname to convey his familiarity as he gently pried the glass out of her hand and placed it on the counter.

Angelo knew that Peyton wasn't a drinker, seldom

touched the stuff. She wasn't completely sloshed yet, but a few more would get her there. "What are you drinking?" he asked her.

She shrugged her shoulders. "Scotch and water. I don't drink much."

Angelo nodded. "I know." He glanced at the glass. It was more Scotch than water.

"I'm celebrating my birthday. It's this week, and I'll be thirty."

He heard the excitement in her voice. "I know that," he said, "and an early happy birthday to you."

"Thanks. These guys are helping me celebrate," she said, motioning to the men standing around her.

"Umm, you don't say." Angelo stared at them, taking a hard look at each one of them. A few had the decency to look away, probably to shield the guilty looks on their faces. He knew just how they had intended to help her celebrate.

"Yes, wasn't that nice of them?"

She really didn't want to know what he truly thought of them, so instead of answering, he slid onto the stool opposite her. "How can you be turning thirty when you don't look a day over twenty-five?"

She reached out and patted his cheek. "You're so sweet, Angelo."

"Hey, evidently you don't know the rules around here," the man who'd had a heavy hand in refreshing her drink said gruffly, moving to stand closer to Peyton's side.

Angelo gave the man a hard look. "No, I think you're the one who doesn't know the rules, especially with the amount of Scotch you've been giving her," he said, glancing back at Peyton, and seeing the glassy look in her eyes.

"He was just being nice, Angelo," she said softly, smiling. "I'm here to have a good time, right?"

"Right, but I think you've had too much of a good time for now."

She nodded slowly. "Yes, I think so, too." Then she leaned in closer. He ignored how good she smelled and listened attentively when she whispered, "I'm beginning to feel sick."

"Then, let me get you to your room," he said, standing.

"Hey, look here, buddy," the man said angrily.

Angelo turned stony eyes on him. "No, you look," he said in a steely voice, trying to keep it down so as not to cause a scene. But if he had to, he would. "You were deliberately trying to get her drunk. Now, I suggest you haul ass before I kick yours."

The man was about to open his mouth to say something when one of the resort's well-dressed, no-nonsense security men approached. "Is there a problem, Mr. Di Meglio?"

Angelo glanced over at the resort's security manager whose name was Saul. "No problem."

He reached out and took Peyton's hand and gently tugged her off the barstool to bring her to his side. "I'm escorting Ms. Mahoney to her room. You might want to go over the rules of the resort with these guys, regarding taking advantage of guests by getting them drunk."

With Peyton nestled close to his side, he began shouldering his way through the crowd. Behind him he heard the man ask Saul in a pissed-off voice, "Just who the hell does he think he is?"

Saul's response was short and direct. "He's one of the owners."

* * *

"Do you need me to help you undress?"

If Angelo had meant to snap her out of her tipsy state he certainly succeeded with that question, Peyton thought, drawing in a quick breath and glancing across the room at him.

She'd just stepped out of the bathroom, after voiding her stomach of the Scotch she'd drank earlier. She'd stayed in the bathroom a few minutes longer, wiping a warm cloth across her face, brushing her teeth and gargling. She felt a little better, but not a whole lot, and knew that in the morning she would probably have a doozy of a headache.

What on earth had made her drink that much when she knew she couldn't handle it? She'd always known her limits. Overindulging had never been her thing, and she would get upset at anyone who did.

"Peyton?"

It was then that she realized she hadn't responded to Angelo's bizarre question. And maybe it wasn't so bizarre considering how sick she'd been moments ago in the bathroom. There was no doubt he'd heard it and probably figured she'd almost died in the bathroom.

"No thanks, I can manage," she said, entering the room on wobbly legs and dropping down in the nearest chair.

Mac and Sam hadn't just given her a room at Dunwoody Cove. They had given her the mother of all luxury suites. She could have probably fit her modest-size apartment in here. She couldn't believe the view she had of the ocean from her balcony, as well as how expensive the furniture looked. And the closets were big enough to accommodate a family of four.

"You sure?"

Rubbing her temples as she already felt a headache coming on, she met his gaze. "Positive. But thanks for asking."

"You're welcome."

A few seconds passed, and then he said, "All right then. Do you want to talk about it?"

She dropped her hand down in her lap and couldn't help the smile that touched her lips. Sam would always tell them how whenever she got in trouble about anything, Angelo would begin their discussion by asking that question. *Do you want to talk about it?*

"There's really nothing to discuss, Angelo." Bottom line, she'd made a fool of herself tonight. No big deal. No harm done. She drew in a deep breath knowing that it *was* a big deal since it was so unlike her. She glanced down at herself and decided to blame it on the dress.

She had found enough courage to wear one of the outfits she'd bought shopping with Mac and Sam last week. For once, she had let Sam talk her into buying a couple of things she normally wouldn't have purchased.

She wasn't vain, but she had to admit the dress looked pretty damn good on her. When she had walked into the ballroom and noticed the attention several men had given her, her head had swelled a little. She couldn't remember the last time she'd worn something that had turned a man's head, mainly because she couldn't remember the last time she'd gone out of her way to impress anyone. That wasn't her style.

She could only assume the reason the attention had gotten to her was because she was going through this almost-over-the-hill, turning-thirty crisis. She was enjoying her last few days in her twenties, and it had been pretty heady stuff to draw the attention away from women a few years younger than she was.

"You are aware that that man was deliberately trying to get you drunk?"

Yes, she knew and would have eventually called him out on it. But dammit, she had enjoyed being the center of attention. And the Scotch had brought her out of her shell and made the never-have-anything-to-say-except-in-the-courtroom Peyton Mahoney more sociable. Besides, she figured she could handle the amount of Scotch he'd been giving her. She hadn't expected her system to react so adversely, so soon.

"You're not falling asleep on me, are you, Peyton?"

She chuckled at the thought and rested her head back against the sofa cushions. What woman in her right mind would fall asleep on DeAngelo Antonio Di Meglio, the "Italian Hellion," and one of the most gorgeous men to walk the face of the earth?

"No, I'm wide-awake," she said, glancing over at him.

He was still standing, and she couldn't help the way her gaze scanned him up and down. He was amazingly tall and so well-built that when he walked into a room, women did a double take before going slack-jawed and drooling. She'd done that very thing the first time Sam had taken her and Mac home for the holidays. As soon as she'd seen Angelo, she'd immediately thought that Sam had one fine brother. The Di Meglio cousins, Damon and Maddox, were eye candy as well, but there had been something about Angelo that had managed to swoosh air from her lungs whenever she saw him. The man was so incredibly handsome it made her eyes hurt just looking at him.

It might have been the beautiful, even tone of his chestnut-colored skin, or the gorgeous dark eyes that could hypnotize anyone. Or it could be the sharp angle of his nose, which bore his Italian ancestry, or his luscious-looking lips. His face was clean-shaven and his hair was cut low in the front but longer in the back so that the silky strands of his hair grazed the collar of his shirt. Tonight his hair had a rugged, unkempt look that made him appear even sexier. And last but not least, there was that diamond stud in his ear.

"Maybe I need to undress you, after all, and get you in the bed."

She swallowed, knowing he hadn't meant it the way it had sounded. He was playing the big brother role and quite naturally, since she was Sam's friend, it would extend to her. It wouldn't be the first time. She chuckled as she remembered when she, Sam and Mac had gone partying in Manhattan one year and had gotten plastered.

"I'm glad one of us can find humor in tonight, Peyton."

She wiped the smile off her face. "Lay off, Angelo," she said, straightening herself in the chair. "I told you I'm fine. So please forget about the big brother role. I can manage. Thanks for seeing me to my room."

"You're welcome."

"But you never did answer my question about what you're doing here."

He paused a moment. "I come here often."

She nodded. And why wouldn't he, with so many beautiful, single women in one place? Angelo was extremely rich just as he was extremely handsome. He would be a good catch for any woman.

Even if he didn't work a day in his life, he could still live off the trust fund he'd inherited once he turned thirty. Since she was one of Sam's best friends she knew all about it. She knew that his paternal great-grandparents had come to this country from Sicily with little more than the clothes on their backs. They had worked hard, educated their sons and were proud when they went into practice together, opening the first Di Meglio law firm in the Bronx office above their father's little Italian restaurant so many years ago. One of Angelo's cousins still owned and operated the restaurant today.

The Di Meglio brothers made a name for themselves and pretty soon had made enough money to open an office in Manhattan and build the twenty-five-story Di Meglio Building. It was widely suspected that his family had had ties to the Mafia, especially since they were Sicilians—every last one of them. And they had money and plenty of it. Peyton had always thought the family spent money frivolously, especially when you considered the people who didn't have any.

"It's a nice place," she said, deciding to keep the conversation going. The room suddenly felt hot and stuffy, which was odd since the air-conditioning was on full blast.

"I think so, too. Hopefully, you can see more of it tomorrow."

She frowned, not sure what that meant. She might decide to sleep off the hangover she'd probably have. She blinked when he walked over and eased down into the chair across from her in a move that was ultra-sexy. She couldn't help noticing how the fabric of his slacks stretched across his taut thighs when he did so. She'd always thought he had a way about him that was smooth and ultra-cool.

"Can I get you anything?" he asked.

Her eyes moved from his thighs back to his face.

"No, I'm fine."

When he just sat there and stared at her, she suddenly felt her entire body heat up. What on earth was wrong with her? She had gotten over her stupid crush on Angelo ages ago, she was sure of it. She'd stopped getting those funny butterflies in her stomach whenever he came within ten feet of her years ago. So why was her composure—the little she had left—weakening around him now? And what was this hot rush of desire that was overtaking her, prickling her skin, stroking her insides?

She cleared her throat. "Aren't you leaving?"

"Not until you answer my question."

She frowned. *What question was that?* Then she remembered. "No, I don't want to talk about it." She'd almost made a major blunder by celebrating too much. It happened. She realized that some men were still assholes who would try to take advantage of a woman if given the chance.

And then, because she felt a little put out by Angelo's presence, by the way his being here was making her feel, she all but snapped. "And you don't have to babysit me. I'm not Sam. You're *her* brother, not mine."

Evidently her words hadn't offended him, if the smile that suddenly curved his luscious-looking lips was anything to go by. "Yes, you're right. You aren't Sam, and I am not your brother."

Peyton blinked. She might be wrong, but it seemed as if he was reiterating her statement for a reason. "Good. I'm glad we understand each other, Angelo. I'm here to have a good time. It's my birthday present from Mac and Sam. I hadn't expected to run into you here, but that's fine. Although I appreciate your making sure I got to my room tonight before I threw up all over the place, the last thing I want is for you to play the big brother."

He threw his head back and chuckled. "Trust me, I don't intend to play the role of big brother to you, Peyton. I had a reason for coming here."

She nodded and didn't have to think twice about what that reason was. This was a singles resort, and the women outnumbered the men two to one. She'd heard from Sam that the media had dubbed him the new legal boy wonder. His name was now an everyday word on the lips of many…mostly women. She was surprised he wasn't reveling in the publicity, milking his newfound popularity and fame for all it was worth.

"Glad to hear it," she heard herself say.

"So, as you can see, you have nothing to worry about, Peyton."

He slowly rose from the chair as her gaze followed his every move. Damn, he did everything with the smoothness of a man who had it goin' on and was comfortable in his own skin. And speaking of skin, she thought his coloring—the perfect blend of his Italian father and African-American mother—was simply beautiful. His features were all Italian, except for the fullness of his lips. They had to be the sexiest pair she'd ever seen on a man.

For some reason she had always been a woman drawn to a man's lips and believed they could tell a lot about him. She'd heard that a man with full lips, like the ones Angelo had, meant that he was extremely sensual and sexually demonstrative. Men with full lips were into physical pleasure, had high-energy and stamina when it came to passion and liked to keep their sex lives interesting. She could believe that about him after hearing for years about all his sex-capades from Sam.

"I would ask you to walk me to the door, but I'm not sure you'll be able to make it without falling flat on your face."

Peyton couldn't help but smile. "Hey, it's not that bad."

He chuckled. "Tell me that in the morning. I have a feeling you're going to wake up with a hell of a head-ache."

"Like I said, I'm here for my birthday and I plan to enjoy myself and have a good time."

"And I want you to enjoy yourself and have a good time as well."

He had come to stand in front of her and surprised her when he reached out his hand to her, especially since he'd acknowledged earlier that she was in no shape to walk him to the door.

She took his hand and stood. She felt a moment of light-headedness and reached out and flattened her hands against his chest. "Sorry, I guess I'm not as steady on my feet as I thought I was."

"That's fine. I've got you and I won't let you go."

It wasn't so much what he said, but the sensual tone she heard in his voice that made her lift her gaze to his. And then, at that moment, her breath was nearly snatched from her throat and the very air she was breath-ing was suddenly suffused with heat of the most in-tense kind.

She figured that it had to be the Scotch that was still in her system. Because, at that moment, when she stared up into his eyes, she could have sworn she saw hot-blooded passion in his gaze—intense, simmering heat. And the sight of it was torching her insides, churning de-sire through her veins and playing havoc with her senses.

She swallowed as his gaze held hers, and seconds later she could barely breathe. She tried breaking eye contact with him but she couldn't move. It was as if her gaze refused to cooperate and was glued to him. At that moment she became even more aware of the power in his masculine frame as he took a step closer, bringing his body next to hers.

Was it his hardened erection she felt that made the nipples of her breasts rigid in response and caused her to take on a whole new breathing pattern? She blinked and quickly concluded that yes, it was definitely an erection—an arousal of the most intense kind. And instinctively, her body seemed to inch closer. She felt the hot throbbing at the juncture of her legs, and thanks to the thin material of the dress she was wearing, she suddenly felt like a naked body plastered to him.

She shivered. *Oh, God.* She felt a pang as if she'd been stunned. Another sensuous tremor jolted her, making her shiver again.

"Are you cold, Peyton?"

He must have felt her quivering. She bit down on her lips to bite back the feelings of shock. His erection meant he was attracted to her. *Why?* Sam had teased her about the dress drawing male attention. *But arousing the likes of Angelo Di Meglio? Come on? Really?*

She shook her head, knowing she was way off base. There had to be another reason he had a hard-on. "No, I'm not cold," she said, aware that her denial hadn't sounded convincing.

He tightened his arms around her anyway, and the warmth of his touch was almost startling, and definitely unexpected. There had to be a reason she was reacting to Angelo this way. She quickly figured out that since she hadn't had a real serious date in months, her body must be starved for attention and affection. Yes, that had to be it.

She leaned back and glanced up at him. "Angelo?"
"Yes?"

He'd only responded with that one word. Why did he

have to sound so mouthwateringly sexy when he'd said it? Why did her breath continue to catch that way? And why had he suddenly moved his hands to rest in the center of her bare back? And why had a warm rush of desire trickled over her skin the moment he'd touched her?

She wanted to ask him what was going on. Why were they embracing in what seemed like a sensual cocoon? Instead she replied, "Nothing."

Peyton was tempted to close her eyes and wrap herself up in the sensations that were overtaking her like a summer breeze on a hot July night. But she knew she had to keep her eyes open and try to figure out what was happening to her. Why had the palms of her hands, which were flattened against his chest, lifted of their own accord and wrapped themselves around his neck?

"Peyton?"

He said her name and for the life of her, even though she was staring into his face, she didn't see his lips move. "Yes?"

"Think about what you said moments ago."

What had she said? She couldn't remember. It was as if her mind had suddenly gone blank and the only thing she was focused on was him. Peyton couldn't say that she was seeing him in a whole new light, because she'd always been aware of just how overpoweringly sexy he was—how breathtakingly handsome. But she was confused about her reaction to him—her deep-in-the-belly kind of attraction. Of course she had been drawn to him years ago when they'd first met. What woman wouldn't be drawn to such a sexy hunk?

But that had been more than seven years ago and the attraction had quickly worn off when she'd known she was way out of his league. Sam had already told them about her brother. Peyton had known about the revolving door to his bedroom and about the women who threw themselves at him. She hadn't wanted to be one of them, figured she didn't have a chance even if she'd wanted to.

Besides, she'd never fit into his world and preferred her own life anyway, thank you very much. She'd been proud of her humble beginnings in the South Side of Chicago. Times had been hard, and she'd had to be tough. But growing up with very little had taught her how to appreciate much. She didn't need a lot of money to be content.

And speaking of content, why did it feel so good being in his arms this way? Why was she in his arms anyway? Thinking she needed to come to her senses and quick, she made a move to step back, but his hands on her back tightened, making it impossible to retreat.

"DeAngelo?" And why did she feel it necessary to call him by his first name and not the shorter version she usually used? And why did doing so sound so right at that moment?

"Yes?"

His single-word response packed a wallop, and she drew in another deep gulp of air. "What did I say? I can't remember. And just what is going on here?"

She'd tried sounding a little annoyed, but the feeling truly wasn't there. She was overwhelmed by sudden feelings of lust and yearnings that she hadn't indulged in in a long time. She felt warm, and her body was getting hotter by the second. He had opened the French doors to the balcony and the gentle June breeze was coming through but was doing nothing to cool her off.

Her brain was warring with competing emotions. One side kept reminding her that this was Angelo, Sam's outrageously sexy brother—the one who made her do a double take the first time she'd met him. But then the other side of her brain, the one that had a few screws loose on occasion, reminded her where she was and why. This was a singles resort, and she was here to celebrate her birthday. If she was going to get buck-wild, then shouldn't it be with someone she knew?

Peyton blinked when he reached out with his thumb and touched her bottom lip moments before he leaned in close to her—so close she could feel the warmth of his breath on her mouth.

"I can show you what's going on here, a whole hell of a lot better than I can tell you, Peyton," he said, his voice dropping an octave to a sensuous low.

And then, before she could draw another breath, his mouth slanted across hers.

Angelo hadn't known just how much he wanted Peyton until he got his first taste of her, and then it was on. He wasted no time kissing the confused look right off her lips. It was obvious she hadn't expected it, but she would find out soon enough that he was full of surprises.

Now it was time to take the kiss to the next level.

She stiffened only for a second when he slid his tongue into her mouth and began devouring her with all the heated desire that had been bottled up inside of him for some time now—a couple of years in fact. During those two years he'd wondered how she tasted. Now he was finding out firsthand. Caught off guard, Peyton began returning his kiss. She didn't have a choice, particularly when his tongue became more demanding and probing, exploring her mouth with a persistence and greed that he felt everywhere, especially in his groin.

Initially, he had thought about being gentle. After all, this was their first kiss and he intended for there to be plenty more. But the more his mouth plundered hers, the greedier he became. Whether she knew it or not, she was the one he wanted. The one woman he wanted to make love to.

Maddox and Damon thought he'd lost his mind, but they just didn't understand. He hadn't understood at first either, but now he did. His grandfather had always warned him things would be this way when he found the woman who was his soul mate.

For years, he hadn't accepted such a thing was possible. At least he hadn't wanted to believe it, considering he was having so much fun being single. But then the bachelor life had begun losing some of its allure and the thought of just being with one woman had begun to appeal to him.

He knew Peyton had had everything to do with his change of heart. She lived in Oklahoma, and he lived in New York. Sometimes he found the distance between them almost unbearable. In the past two years he had found excuse after excuse to visit his sister in Oklahoma. But now that Sam lived in Houston most of the time, he couldn't rely on that as an excuse. That's when he'd made the decision to do something about the woman he wanted in his love life.

When she leaned closer into him, he instinctively deepened the kiss. His tongue feasted on hers, staking a claim like he had every right to do so.

He wanted to just pick her up in his arms and carry her to the bedroom and make love to her, but he couldn't. He had waited a long time, and so he wanted to do things right.

She suddenly broke off the kiss, and he watched her draw in a deep breath. Her lips were wet, and he wanted to taste them again. But the frown that marred her features let him know that wouldn't be happening.

"What did you do that for?" she asked angrily.

He smiled when she unconsciously licked her top lip where his taste still lingered. "This is Dunwoody Cove," he said. "Everyone who comes here does so for a reason, Peyton. And as you reminded me, you might be close to my family but you are *not* my sister. And I don't intend to play the role of big brother to you—in fact, far from it."

He leaned down and swiped a quick kiss from her lips. "Get some rest, and I'll see you tomorrow."

As he headed for the door, he knew without looking that she was standing there stunned. But she would have plenty of time to figure things out because starting tomorrow, he was taking off the kid gloves and Peyton Mahoney wouldn't know what hit her until it was too late.

Chapter 3

Peyton opened her eyes then closed them when the insistent throbbing in her head became almost unbearable. It had been years since she'd had a serious hangover. Not since her college days, and this one was off the charts.

She kept her eyes closed as snippets of the previous night slowly began coming together in her mind. She recalled having a little more to drink than she'd intended. And then Angelo had appeared out of nowhere, and the next thing she knew he walked her back to her room where she'd rushed to the bathroom to throw up. She vaguely recalled what happened after she'd come out of the bathroom, and suddenly her eyes sprang open when she remembered that Angelo had kissed her. She reached out and touched her lips. Had he really kissed her or had she just dreamt it? She turned her body and stared up at the ceiling. Ignoring the deep pounding in her head, she tried to recall everything that had happened in the hotel room last night once she'd stepped out of the bathroom. They had been talking about nothing much, and he had gotten ready to leave. He had walked over to her, pulled her off her feet and into his arms and…

She shook her head. No, she had to be imagining things. There was no way Sam's sexy-and-handsome-as-sin brother would have kissed her. It had to be the side-effects of last night's drinking binge that had her brain mushy.

But if that was the case, then why was the memory of being locked in Angelo's arms so vividly clear? *They did kiss*, she thought. And then there was his touch. She remembered his hands grazing her spine, which was exposed in her backless dress. There had been the feel of her body plastered close to his, and even now she could feel the solid wall of muscles pressed against her.

Peyton closed her eyes, unsure whether her memories were reality or fantasy. At that moment, the only thing she was absolutely sure of was the persistent pounding in her head. That, combined with the memory of being held and kissed by Angelo, made her brain feel as if it was in overdrive. She tried clearing her head and found it nearly impossible to do so. The pounding and memories continued. And moments later she was pulled into another deep sleep.

Angelo leaned back in his chair, sipped his coffee and smiled. His kiss had taken Peyton by surprise last night—probably shocked the living daylights out of her. That was good, and it was something she might as well get used to, he thought.

He knew there was a possibility that she wouldn't remember anything about last night. That was okay since at some point today he intended to make his desire for her quite obvious. He had two weeks, and he intended to use them wisely. He'd never pursued a woman before. But then he'd never tried either. But he planned to do so with a purpose and a resolve like no other.

"Why am I not surprised to see you here DeAngelo?"

He glanced up and wished he hadn't. Lela Stillwell, the woman who had been a thorn in Sam's side throughout high school. For some reason the two of them always butted heads and had never gotten along. He later found out why. Lela always put herself on a pedestal, especially with the help of an over-indulgent father, who happened to be one of Angelo's father's clients.

Lela had come into the office several times with her old man some years ago, and Angelo had once even considered having an affair with her. But that was before she had accused a pro football player of attempted rape. The authorities weren't buying it and had detected holes in her story. Angelo's father had gotten her to drop the charges, and she later admitted that she had falsely accused the athlete when he had brushed off her advances. Luckily he didn't press charges against Lela, but that was only after her father reached an out-of-court settlement with the accused athlete. Her father had sent her to Paris for a year or so until the scandal died down. Evidently she was back.

"How are you, Lela?"

She slid into the seat across from him uninvited. "I'm doing fine now that I see that you're here, Angelo."

He gave her a smile that didn't quite reach his eyes. "I don't see why my presence would make a difference."

"Don't you?"

"Quite frankly, no," he said, checking his watch. It was close to noon. If Peyton wasn't up yet, then it was time for him to wake her up.

"I'm sure you know I've always been interested in you."

"Have you?"

"Yes, and I think you've been interested in me as well. That unfortunate incident last year with Kevin Swank wasn't my fault."

He wondered how she could say that. When she had shown up at Swank's home, security cameras had captured the entire incident. It hadn't been hard to figure out who had been pursuing whom. There hadn't been any inappropriate behavior on Kevin Swank's part as Lela had claimed. She had nearly ruined his career and reputation with her allegations, which ultimately forced her father to fork over a hefty settlement to avoid a countersuit.

"I've been hearing a lot about you lately, Angelo," she said, interrupting his thoughts. "Your name has been all in the news."

"Really?"

"Yes, and you need the right woman by your side to help you handle all that media attention—one who is refined, elegant and poised."

He looked over at her and couldn't help but smile. The one thing Lela hadn't mentioned was honest. That was definitely something she was not.

"Thanks for the suggestion," he said, standing. "Now if you'll excuse me, there's someplace I need to be."

Ignoring her, he took one last sip of coffee before walking off.

"Peyton."

Her name sounded like a whisper uttered from the deep, husky voice that infiltrated the recesses of her deep sleep. She slowly opened her eyes, looked up and immediately connected with the most gorgeous and intense dark orbs staring down at her.

Her heart kicked up a beat when she thought back to the time she'd first been ensnared by Angelo's eyes. She hadn't been in the Di Meglio's humongous house in the Hamptons for more than a few hours when Sam's tall, gorgeous and handsome-as-sin brother walked through the door.

Bringing her thoughts back to the present, Peyton's gaze shifted from his eyes to his mouth, and for a spellbinding moment she was mesmerized by the shape of his full and sensuous lips. They had kissed her last night and practically devoured her lips. *Why?* If he had been in the kissing mood, she was sure there were plenty of women at the resort who would have eagerly obliged. But then, she hadn't resisted either.

Now she was questioning her own actions last night, especially since she was no longer the starry-eyed twenty-two-year-old who'd had a crush on him. She was twenty-nine and looking at thirty too soon to suit her. But there was nothing she could do about it. "Angelo? What are you doing here?" she heard herself asking.

"I wanted to check in on you before leaving to play tennis."

Rubbing a hand down her face to wipe the sleep from her eyes, she sat up in bed, careful to keep the sheet covering her in place. She had very little on, which was normally how she slept—usually in a top but rarely any bottoms. "What time is it?"

"A little past noon."

"Noon!" she said in shock.

"Yes."

Peyton rubbed another hand across her face. She usually was an early riser and had never slept this late before. But then she usually didn't drink much either, and the pounding in her head reminded her that she'd started celebrating her birthday early.

"Here, I think you can use this."

He handed her a cup of coffee. "I made it just the way you like."

She took the cup and was about to ask how he knew the way she liked her coffee and then she remembered. He had stayed at her place a couple of years ago when Sam had been out of town and had probably become aware of her habits. *But not all of them.* He'd never known how much she'd lusted after him during those five days. She'd confided in Sam and Mac, and they'd all had a good laugh about it later, specifically about how many times she'd been tempted to jump his bones.

She took a sip of her coffee. He was right. It was just the way she liked with just the right amount of cream and sugar. "The housekeeper let you in?" she asked. The one thing the resort prided itself on was its security.

"No, I kept the key you gave me last night. I checked on you earlier this morning and you were sleeping soundly."

She blinked. "You came into my room while I was sleeping?"

"Yes."

The thought that he had come into her room when she'd been unaware annoyed her a little. She hoped it hadn't been one of those times she had kicked the covers off her body or he would have seen more than he had needed to.

Evidently it hadn't been one of those times. At least she could only assume it hadn't been since he was acting normal. But then he had kissed her, and he was acting normal about that as well. She reminded herself that this was a man who had his pick of women, and she was certain a lot of them had a better looking body than hers and could probably kiss a whole lot better. Seeing her partially naked on top of the covers and kissing her the way he had probably hadn't done anything for him.

"I figured when you did wake up you'd have a hangover and would need the coffee," he said, interrupting her thoughts.

She did, and it certainly hit the spot. She took another sip and studied him when he moved away from the bed. He was dressed in a pair of jeans and a white shirt and was sexy as sin.

"So what are your plans today, Peyton?"

He'd almost caught her staring when he turned to look at her. She shrugged. "I've slept a good bit of it away. I plan to shower, dress and then go downstairs to get something to eat."

She took another sip. She appreciated him thinking enough to make her coffee, but why was he hanging around? This was a singles resort. Certainly he had more important things to do. "Is something wrong, Angelo?" she asked. Was he uncomfortable with the thought that he'd actually kissed her last night? Should she let him know it hadn't been a big deal?

He opened his mouth to say something then stopped, and as if he'd made his mind up about something, he said, "I need to ask a favor of you. If you can't do it, I understand."

She raised a brow, wondering what kind of favor he needed. "What is it?"

"I ran into someone I wish weren't here," he said.

She chuckled. "Um, let me guess. An old girlfriend?"

"Hardly. She and I never dated. She was a former

client of my father's and has a tendency to make a nuisance of herself at times."

Peyton looked at him, clearly confused. "This is a singles resort," she reminded him. "The single women here are looking for single men. Last I heard you're still single."

He leaned back against her dresser. "Yes, but I'm not looking for anyone. I came here to get away. Escape the media, so to speak, to relax."

She shook her head and laughed. "Relax? *You* at a singles retreat? And you actually thought you would relax?"

He chuckled. "I could only hope. Things have been crazy for me since winning that case."

"So I heard. I also heard that one of those reality stars has been trying to grab your attention. I'm surprised you're not breaking your neck giving in to her. Most men would."

"I'm not like most men."

She took a sip as her gaze scanned his body. Yes, she'd definitely agree that he wasn't like most men. At least he wasn't like any she'd ever encountered. "So what's the favor?"

"For the next couple of days I'd like us to pretend that we're lovers. I know it might cramp your style since you're single and undoubtedly came here looking for single men."

She laughed. "No, I didn't come here looking for single men. This is a birthday gift from Mac and Sam, and God knows I need a break. That last case I worked on was a doozy."

"So you didn't come here looking for a man like I didn't come looking for a woman."

"Yes, that sounds about right."

"Then you won't have any problem pretending to be my lover."

She held up her hand. "Whoa, wait a minute, I didn't say that. I'm not good at pretending and especially about something like that."

"It will be easy. All you have to do is follow my lead."

Follow his lead.

And that was what she was afraid of, if the kiss last night was anything to go by. She had followed his lead and experienced something she'd never felt before. Evidently he'd forgotten their kiss since he hadn't brought it up. But then she really hadn't thought it meant anything to him anyway. Why would it have?

"I need to think about it, Angelo. Although I didn't come here looking for a man, I want to have fun. Besides, I met a couple of nice guys last night."

"They were jerks trying to get you drunk."

She'd figured as much, but still. Okay, what happened wasn't very smart on her part. She should have known better and acted responsibly. That dress had been asking for trouble. Instead of drawing the attention of nice guys, she'd caught the interest of a few less-than-desirables.

"I guess I'm going to have to deal with Lela Stillwell on my own."

Peyton's attention was captured. "Lela Stillwell? Isn't that the woman who Sam doesn't get along with—the woman who falsely accused that NFL player of forcing himself on her when it was actually the other way around?"

"Yes, she's the one."

"And she's here?" she asked.

"Yes, she's here."

Peyton had never met Lela Stillwell, but Sam had mentioned her often enough and none of it had been positive. According to Sam, Lela Stillwell had been after Angelo for years and had blamed Sam for Angelo not reciprocating Lela's interest. Peyton also remembered Sam saying that Lela had added salt to the wound on what was to have been Sam's wedding day to a guy named Guy Carrington. Lela had spread rumors about how things had gone down that were as far from the truth as they could get.

"Will you at least think about it?"

His question interrupted Peyton's thoughts, and she glanced over at him. "Okay, I'll do that, but I'm not making any promises."

He smiled. "Thanks, and I appreciate it."

Peyton felt a surge of warmth settle in the pit of her stomach. She tilted her head back to glance up at him. "Now I need you to leave so I can get up and get dressed."

"Are you coming down to participate in the activities lined up for today?" he asked.

"Not sure how many activities I'll get to. But then I don't plan on hanging around in this room for the rest of the day either. Sam and Mac paid too much money for me to not have fun. Besides, I'm hungry and want to grab something at that restaurant downstairs."

"Well, if you need anything, let me know. I'm on this floor."

She arched her brows. "You are?"

"Yes."

He smiled again before turning to leave. Her cheeks burned when she realized just how long she'd stared at his backside before hearing the door close behind him. It was only then that she thought about his proposition to avoid Lela Stillwell.

Truth be told, she couldn't imagine pretending to be

his lover, although it was a tempting idea. But then, she thought as she eased out of bed, how much pretending would she have to do to be enamored with Angelo? She didn't have a thing for him now, but she could easily see herself getting into character and that was one of the things that bothered her. She had felt something for him at one time. And although it had quickly passed once reality had set in, the feelings were still there. Was it possible that her feelings for Angelo could be rekindled?

She pushed such thoughts from her mind. That had been years ago. A lot had happened in her life since then. Although she no longer resented those who were wealthy, she still couldn't get past the fact that sometimes Sam reminded Peyton that she still walked around with a chip on her shoulder, as if she was holding a grudge against anyone lucky enough to be born with a silver spoon in his mouth.

Her thoughts shifted to the likes of the man-hungry, snooty-as-hell Lela Stillwell. At least the Di Meglios with all their money never came across as a family who thought they were better than anyone else. Whenever she spent time with them they had always made her feel welcome, like part of the family. And no one had looked down their ultra-rich nose at her. She had appreciated it, because heaven knows the situation was different than that first time she'd felt like a fish out of water.

Her thoughts returned to Angelo and his ridiculous proposal as she walked toward the bathroom, pulling down her top to hide the missing bottom. She was hungry, and she couldn't think on an empty stomach. Peyton wasn't sure why the thought of what he'd asked her to do intrigued her, but it did. Maybe it was the possibility that going along with his plan meant she might get another kiss out of it, or maybe it was something else.

Chapter 4

The corners of Angelo's lips were still smiling when he entered his own room moments later. As he closed the door behind him, his mind was already contemplating his next move.

If anyone would have told him a few years ago that he, DeAngelo Antonio Di Meglio, would be in hot pursuit of any woman he would have thought they were crazy. But here he was, at a singles resort filled with women, and he was chomping at the bit for just one. But she wasn't just any woman. He decided two years ago that she was the woman he wanted. Peyton was the one he intended to spend the rest of his life with. Now if he could only get her to thinking along those same lines.

Now, for his plan.

He didn't consider himself manipulative—far from it. But at this stage of his life he was calculating and determined, and he planned to use every opportunity he could to sway Peyton. Convincing her to go along with his romantic ruse was the first move. If that didn't work, it was on to Plan B.

He exhaled and couldn't help the sly grin that touched his lips. Lela's presence was a godsend. He of all people knew how close Mac, Sam and Peyton were. So it was obvious that if Sam didn't care for the woman, Peyton wouldn't either. Peyton and Sam might disagree on a lot of things, but their friendship and loyalty to one another was rock solid.

He glanced around his suite thinking that being one of the partners in the resort had its perks. The humongous room was divided into a small kitchen with a bar, a living room and a huge bedroom with a balcony that overlooked the beautiful blue waters of the Atlantic Ocean. He was a Di Meglio so he was used to the finer things in life. Still, it was nice to just take time to appreciate all the things he'd been blessed to have come his way.

A few years before, an escaped convict—hell-bent on getting even with Angelo's father—decided to turn his attention to Angelo. He'd never forget the night the man had finally made good on his threats and had forced Angelo off the road.

Luckily, he had survived. But it had taken coming that close to death to open his eyes and make him realize that tomorrow wasn't promised, and that there was more to life than partying and women. His cousins couldn't understand how he could walk away from both. After all, he was only in his mid-thirties and what his cousins called the prime of his bachelorhood. Now his focus had changed. Recently, he along with several businessmen—including his brother-in-law's cousin, Lee Madaris—had invested in several resorts around the world. In addition to Dunwoody Cove, they also had resorts in London and Paris.

Being an attorney was his career, but he didn't intend on making it his life. He hoped his investments would make it possible for him to retire by his fortieth birthday. The last thing he wanted to do was follow in his parents' footsteps and still be practicing law until his retirement. Although his parents still enjoyed practicing law and were still sharp as tacks, he believed there was a life outside of the Di Meglio law firm. He was content with how things were now, but was already planning his future, and heading the list was Peyton Mahoney.

Angelo kicked off his shoes and was about to stroll into his kitchen to grab a bottle of water out of the refrigerator when his cell phone rang. He rolled his eyes when he saw it was Sam on his caller ID.

He connected the call. "This had better be good, Samari."

He heard his sister's soft chuckle. "Mac's here in the office with me, and we want to know how Peyton is doing."

He dropped down on the sofa. Didn't his sister and Mac have law cases to work on? Babies to take care of? Husbands to keep happy? "And how is she supposed to be doing? I just got here last night."

And just in time, he thought, although he wasn't going to mention anything to Mac and Sam about Peyton almost being taken advantage of. They probably wouldn't have believed him, knowing Peyton would never let her guard down. Though he was hoping she would continue to let loose, but only with him.

"Well, just to let you know, we're beginning to have second thoughts about helping you win over Peyton."

He rubbed the back of his neck, refusing to let the

tension settle there. It was too late for them to have second thoughts now, but he was curious as to why. "Is there a reason for this change of heart?"

"An article in today's paper might have something to do with it."

He lifted his brow. "What article?"

"Some woman is claiming the two of you are in a hot and heavy affair, but you asked her to keep it secret. She says she has phone records to prove it."

"Bring 'em on." Angelo glanced across the room at the clock to check the time. "When did you start believing everything you read, Sam?"

"I don't. We just don't want Peyton caught up in your madness."

He drew in a deep breath, knowing that by *we* his sister meant both she and Mac. "It's nothing more than a publicity stunt, Sam. You and Mac should know that."

"We do. However, we figure that's just the beginning, and we'd prefer sparing Peyton any such foolishness."

He tensed a bit. He needed his sister and Mac as allies. Wavering support from them was the last thing he needed. He had been upfront with them about his feelings for Peyton and the two hadn't seemed particularly surprised. He had only confirmed what they had already thought, and like him, they figured it was time to finally let her know how he felt. Because they knew Peyton better than anyone, they thought a subtle approach was better than being more direct.

He didn't expect Peyton to suddenly fall head over heels for him in the next two weeks, but he did intend to get something going that would continue after they left the Bahamas. That would give them both time to build the type of relationship that was solid and one that could endure just about anything, especially claims like the one that appeared in the newspaper today.

The thought of a long-distance romance didn't bother him since he had made it a point to visit Oklahoma often before Sam moved to Houston. And he could visit his good friend Frederick Damon Rowe—nicknamed FDR—another attorney who had worked in their family law firm, had married and moved to Oklahoma.

"I gave you and Mac my word that everything would work out fine in the end. The two of you are going to have to trust me on this, Sam."

There was a pause on the other end, and he understood why. The three had been best of friends since law school and were very protective of each other. Then Sam said in a threatening tone, "I swear, Angelo, if you hurt her in any way, you're going to have hell to pay when you deal with me and Mac."

"Okay, I hear you. Now let me and Peyton have the next two weeks in peace without any more calls from you two. From here on out, I take care of Peyton. And I would never hurt her."

There was another pause. "You do care for her, don't you?" his sister asked, in a voice that sounded like it had finally dawned on her just how much.

"Yes, I do. More than you know. Now goodbye."

He disconnected the phone. Angelo couldn't recall exactly when he'd fallen for Peyton. He just knew that he had. He began to realize it during his stay with her in Oklahoma, but it had taken him a few years after that to accept what his feelings meant.

And then it was that kiss they'd shared the night before, a kiss he couldn't stop thinking about. He sat down and rested his head against the sofa cushion and closed his eyes. Images of Peyton filtered through his mind, how he would stand on the sidelines at parties and family events and watch her. Now was the time to act on that desire.

And he had just two weeks to get the wheels in motion.

Chapter 5

Peyton felt a little uncomfortable standing by herself in the elevator as other women gossiped about men they'd checked out since arriving. She would never have imagined herself coming here on her own, but would have definitely enjoyed it with Mac and Sam. But that was before the husbands and babies. Now they didn't live the same lifestyle nor have the same freedom they'd had before they were married. Their priorities had changed and understandably so. And although they went out of their way to still include her in most things, it wasn't the same. They were no longer a part of each other's lives the way they once were. She knew that and figured they knew it as well.

"Girl, have you seen that fine brother walking around here? The one they say is part Italian—the same one whose name has been in the news a lot lately after winning that high-profile political corruption case?"

Peyton's ears perked up when she heard the woman whispering about Angelo.

"Yeah, I saw him today at breakfast. He's fine, fine, fine. I couldn't eat for checking him out. I wouldn't mind him being my baby's daddy."

The other women in the group giggled, and Peyton could only shake her head. She understood the women going gaga at the sight of Angelo. Hadn't she done the same thing herself the first time she'd seen him? But seriously—Angelo being some baby's daddy? He would undoubtedly be a great catch for any woman, but she didn't think he was ready to take on a wife or fatherhood.

She shrugged. *Seriously.* None of that was any of her business. Angelo was a big boy, and she was certain that he could handle the likes of any wannabe-baby-mamas. Then why had he asked her to help him avoid a certain woman?

Peyton figured he wasn't dealing with just any woman. He was dealing with Lela Stillwell. And from the horror stories Sam had painted, the woman could take the description of spoiled, selfish and hellish to a whole other level.

The elevator reached the lobby, and Peyton waited for the other women to get off. They hurried on their way, probably to enjoy the fun that awaited them.

Dunwoody Cove was a huge place with lots of activities, if the brochure she'd been given upon arriving was anything to go by. She hadn't signed up to take part in any special activities, but she planned to attend the nightly parties. And the next time around she would keep her eye out for guys who were trying to take advantage of her.

Her stomach growled, and she increased her steps

to make it to the restaurant. There were other places to eat, but she liked this one. The items on the menu were simple, and she wasn't tempted to purchase anything she might not like. Upon reaching the café, she glanced around, grateful it wasn't crowded and that there were several empty tables. She would grab something to eat and then walk around a bit and check things out. Since she liked to swim she thought about hitting the pool later.

When she moved toward an empty table, a guy passed by her and met her gaze, but then quickly turned away, seemingly picking up his pace as he walked out of the café. She realized they'd met just last night. He'd been the one trying to get her drunk. She wondered if he was in such a hurry because he thought she was going to confront him about last night. Well, he was wrong if he thought so. She was just as much to blame. But like she'd told Angelo, she had come here to have a good time.

She was studying the menu when a sudden rush of heat suffused her. She glanced up. "Angelo."

He slid in the chair across from her. "Glad you finally came down to grab something to eat. And I forgot to mention that I like your new hairstyle."

A wave of pleasure skimmed across her skin at the sound of his deep, husky voice. She had just seen him a few hours ago, so why was she reacting to him this way? She was convinced it had everything to do with that kiss from last night, and it was a kiss that she was still trying to figure out.

She shifted in her chair and slid her fingers through her hair. Usually she wore her dreadlocked hair down her shoulders, but for the trip she had gotten them done up in lush curls that brought out its fullness, body and gloss. She had gotten a lot of compliments and had to admit she liked the style as well.

"Thanks. The hairstyle was Sam's idea."

He chuckled as he pulled a menu out of the rack on the table. "Now why doesn't that surprise me?"

"It shouldn't. You know your sister. She jumps at the chance to give anyone a makeover."

"Yes, and was the dress last night her idea as well?"

Peyton smiled. "Yes. But I have to admit I like it."

"So do I. You looked good in it." He leaned over the table. "But between us, you looked pretty darn good even before Sam's makeover."

"Thanks." She tried to fight back how her heartbeat had quickened with his compliment. She took a sip of the water the waitress had placed on the table and then glanced over at him. She could actually breathe in his scent. Whatever cologne he was wearing had his name on it.

"Angelo?"

He glanced over his menu and his gaze met hers. "Hmm?"

She thought he sounded good. Even his *hmm* had a sexiness that made her shift in her chair and cross her legs. "All this isn't necessary, you know," she said.

An innocent-looking expression appeared on his face. And was there a little mole on the side of his nose? Why hadn't she noticed it before? Why on earth was she noticing it now?

"What isn't necessary?" he asked.

"Telling me how nice my hair looks and complimenting me on the dress I wore last night, especially since I know you barely had a chance to notice it before whisking me off to my room. And saying I looked good even before my makeover was really pushing it."

"I take it you don't believe I was sincere in what I said."

She leaned over closer toward him. "Look, this is Peyton and not some woman you feel you have to impress. Not sure what's going on with you but—"

"What do you mean you're not sure what's going on with me?" he asked, before taking a sip of his water.

She shrugged. "I think you feel that by being here you need to practice your player lines. You're trying to steer clear of Lela, and you think I'm safe. Good old safe and reliable Peyton Mahoney."

He set his glass down and leaned back in his chair. "Is that what you think?"

She decided to come clean. "Honestly, I don't know what to think. But I believe whatever is going on here started with that kiss last night."

A smooth smile touched his lips. "No, it all started when you said you wanted me to remember you weren't Sam."

His words should have kick-started her memory of last night and what she'd said but they didn't. "I don't understand."

"And you have no idea what that kiss was all about?"

She frowned, trying to recall if there was any part of last night she had forgotten. She swallowed deeply before saying, "Please tell me that in my delirious state I didn't come on to you or something."

He chuckled. "Or something?"

She frowned at him. "You know what I mean."

He placed his menu back on the table. "No, you didn't come on to me, but evidently you think I came on to you."

No, she really didn't think that. But they had shared a kiss, and she needed to know why. "I really don't know what to think," she said, deliberately keeping her voice low when she saw one of the groups of women from the elevator walking in and taking a table not far away. They gave her a surprised look, as if it was hard to believe someone who looked like Angelo would be spending time with her. She might not be all dolled up like they were, but she didn't look bad.

She glanced back over at Angelo and a thought suddenly entered her mind. Maybe the kiss hadn't been all that hot and heavy like she assumed it had been. Maybe it was nothing more than a brotherly peck, and she had dreamt that it was something else.

"What's going on in that pretty little head of yours, Peyton?"

Pretty little head? Boy, he was full of compliments today. She held up her hand to cut off any further words from him. "Let's just forget it."

"Forget what? The kiss, or your thinking that I have ulterior motives for complimenting you?"

"Doesn't matter. Have you forgotten about Lela Stillwell and what you asked me to do?"

"No."

"Okay, then," she said, deciding that now they were finally getting somewhere.

"Will you do it?"

Peyton hesitated. She was certain she had fully slept off her hangover, so why had her head begun spinning again? She wondered if she should let Angelo know he was practically making her dizzy. "I've given it some thought."

"But you haven't made up your mind."

Actually, she had. She wouldn't do it since she wasn't sure if she could keep her infatuation with him from resurfacing. It had been bad enough two years ago when he'd stayed at her place those few days. She had told him to make himself comfortable and feel right at home. He'd done just that. He had thought nothing of walking around shirtless and letting her see him in just his pajama bottoms.

"Actually, I have. I don't think doing something like that will work. Who in their right mind would believe we have something going on?"

He glanced over at her, seeming surprised that she would say such a thing. "Why wouldn't they?"

She rolled her eyes. "Trust me, nobody would think of us as a couple."

"I disagree." He glanced around the café. "There's not a woman in here who I could imagine myself with besides you."

Following his gaze she glanced around the room, too, studying the various groups of women. Not surprisingly, the majority of them were staring right back at them. They were probably wondering why he was sitting with her instead of them.

She returned her gaze to Angelo and her heart rate increased when she saw he was staring intently at her. "Not that I think I'm chopped liver or anything, but look at them."

"I did."

"And what do you see?"

"Women—plenty of them with their faces made up, their hair in place and their nails done. And every last one of them with I'll-eat-you-alive-if-given-the-chance looks on their faces," he said.

She lifted a brow. "And that's a bad thing?"

"For me it is. I told you why I'm here. And the thought that anyone wouldn't think we're a couple is simply crazy. You are better for me than any other woman in this room, hands down."

Was that irritation she heard in his voice? She fought back a laugh that he would waste his time being annoyed at such a thing. "Hands down, huh?" she said, deciding to make light of their conversation.

He leaned in closer and the look in his eyes told her he wasn't making polite conversation. "So what do you think, Peyton?"

If he thought he had answered all her questions, she had news for him. "Why me, Angelo?"

Their gazes held, and the look in his eyes had her heart pumping like crazy. She bit her bottom lip, feeling a sudden flutter in the pit of her stomach. For whatever reason, it appeared he was still annoyed with her.

"You've known me longer than anyone here, so I can trust you," he finally said. "With you I don't have to worry about your interest in me being purely financial or because of my newfound fame."

His words were actually a compliment—kind of. And she couldn't help the sensation that made her chest swell or the undercurrents that were making the tips of her nipples harden under her blouse. "I thought men who weren't serious about women didn't care one way or the other, as long as they were on top of their game."

He shrugged his massive shoulders. "Maybe for some, but I've outgrown that."

She waved off his words. "Whatever."

"You don't believe me."

She rolled her eyes. "Honestly, Angelo? No. But does it matter what I believe?"

He was spared from answering when the waitress came to take their order. Just as well, Peyton thought. He had told her more than enough fairy tales today anyway.

* * *

Angelo shifted in his chair thinking that every muscle in his body was feeling Peyton's presence. Conversation for them had ceased for the moment while they enjoyed their meal.

She had ordered a lot, and he was surprised she ate it all. Since he'd eaten breakfast and lunch, all he wanted was something light and decided a bowl of soup would be enough, or so he'd thought. But more than once he swiped a French fry off her plate.

He slowly chewed on the fry thinking he could feel the connection between them even if she couldn't. Did she even sense what was taking place? Had she caught on that he was laying the groundwork for what was to come? What would eventually happen between them?

More than once he saw her glance at the group of women sitting at a table across the room. He was very much aware that the women were staring at them and had been doing so for quite a while. He wondered if that's what was bothering Peyton and decided to ask.

He glanced over at her and before he could speak his eyes devoured her, taking in the smooth, creamy brown texture of her skin, her dark eyes that preferred studying the food on her plate rather than him, and the way her mouth was curved in a pout.

He lifted a brow. "Would you like to tell me what's wrong, Peyton?"

She glanced up, met his gaze, held it and was about to move her mouth to speak when they both noticed a presence at their table. He lifted his gaze and stared into the face of Lela Stillwell.

Where the hell had she come from? And why had she chosen just that precise moment to appear? And what right did she have to glare at him like he'd been caught doing something wrong?

"Lela?" he said, acknowledging her presence.

"I've been looking for you," Lela said in that syrupy voice that made him cringe. Then she had the audacity to reach out and place her hand over his. Now she was being disrespectful to Peyton, and he wasn't going to put up with it. He reached out and removed her hand from his.

"You were looking for me for what reason?"

"I thought we could spend the afternoon together."

He gave her a smile that he knew didn't quite reach his eyes. Then he glanced over to Peyton. "I'm sure Lela somehow forgot her manners, so let me make the introductions. Peyton, this is Lela Stillwell. Lela, this is Peyton Mahoney." The two women glanced at each other, but neither extended their hands, nor did they exchange pleasantries.

In fact, as if dismissing Peyton altogether, Lela turned her attention back to him and said, "Well, are you ready?"

He lifted a brow. "Ready for what?"

"For us to spend the afternoon together. Didn't you read the brochure you were given when you checked in?"

He had to remind himself that standing before him was a woman who could take the words *spoiled, selfish* and *narcissistic* to a whole new level. "Evidently I didn't. What did it say?" he asked.

She smiled. "Tonight the resort is hosting the couples' ball, and it would be best to claim your date early."

He stared at her for a moment and then just to make sure he understood what she was insinuating, he said, "So you're claiming me?"

She smiled brightly. "Of course."

Sometimes people simply amazed him, especially women, and at that moment, particularly Lela. She had been born with a silver spoon in her mouth; had attended some of the best schools; had been introduced to all the finer things in life. But when it came to substance—namely manners and respecting others—she might as well have been raised by a pack of wild dogs. Especially compared to Peyton—who had been raised by her grandmother in a less than desirable part of Chicago, rarely saw her mother growing up, didn't know her father and had to pay her own way through college and law school but still possessed the kind of class and grace that money couldn't buy. If the two women were pitted against one another, Peyton was the winner hands down.

He held Lela's gaze and was about to open his mouth to tell Lela that it would be a cold day in hell before he would allow her to claim him for anything, when he heard Peyton's soft chuckle.

He glanced across the table in time to hear her say to Lela, "Sorry, Ms. What's-Your-Name, but you're a tad too late. Angelo might not have read the brochure, but I did. And he's already been claimed—by me."

Chapter 6

The coffee machine in Peyton's suite was taking too long to brew and the steady slow drip was driving her crazy. It wouldn't have been so bad if Angelo hadn't been standing across the room watching her every move.

After putting Lela in her place and watching her stomp away like the spoiled brat she was, Peyton had finished her coffee. Angelo had had the good sense to keep quiet while she did so. Telling him she'd see him later, she'd left the restaurant. To her surprise, when she passed the group of women from the elevator, they smiled and gave her the thumbs-up. Evidently they had witnessed Lela Stillwell's behavior from across the room and were glad she had been put in her place.

Peyton had met a lot of rude people during her lifetime, but she was convinced Lela took the icing off the cake. It wasn't what she said, but how she had said it, like she had every right to talk down to people. Who had made her queen? How dare Lela assume that even though Angelo was having lunch with Peyton, that she was insignificant and that Lela could make a play for him right in front of her and show her disrespect. Anger raced through her body.

The nerve of that hussy, she thought.

"I hope that coffee you're brewing is for drinking and not to throw on me."

She looked back at Angelo over her shoulder. She had let him in a few moments before, and he was still there standing with his back against the closed door, as if trying to decide whether it was safe to stay. "I don't know what I plan to do just yet," she said, still fuming inside.

"Why are you angry at me? It's not my fault Lela is the way she is."

He was right, it wasn't his fault. But still, why was he like a magnet for some of the most ill-mannered, obnoxious women around? Why?

She turned around and glared at him. "I hope you know that I had made up my mind not to get involved with you and that woman. You're a grown-ass man who should be able to fight off unwanted advances on your own. However, Lela Stillwell takes the damn cake. That heifer had the nerve, the damn audacity, to stand there and act like I wasn't there, like I was no better than the friggin' ketchup bottle on the table. Who in the hell gave her the right to ignore me that way? As if I was insignificant!"

"Definitely not me."

Peyton glared at him for a moment and then shook her head as the rich aroma of brewing coffee filled the air. There was an unreadable expression on his face and she couldn't help wondering if he'd found the situation amusing at her expense. The thought practically had steam coming out of her ears.

She studied his features—saw the way his chiseled jaw had tightened—as the angry lines around his lips matched the unmistakable glacial look in his eyes. No, he wasn't amused. Apparently he was just as pissed as she was.

She crossed her arms over her chest and lifted her chin. "Level with me, Angelo. Have you and Lela ever had an affair, and am I being used as a pawn to make her jealous or something?"

He walked toward her with a stride that was sexy as sin as well as measured and decisive. When he came to a stop in front of her, he glanced around, surveying the room instead of looking directly at her. She had a feeling he was merely trying to get his temper under control before he responded.

He glanced back at her and held her gaze. "No. Hell no! I've never been involved with Lela, although on countless occasions she made it her business to let me know she hoped otherwise."

He paused a moment. "There was a time when I thought about getting involved with her just to get it over with. It was going to be nothing more than a one-night stand. But luckily the controversy with Kevin Swank came up before I made a move. Although I felt bad for the guy, I was glad it was him and not me. After the scandal, Lela's father sent her out of the country. Now she's back, and she figures she can pick up where she left off trying to get me in her bed. And I don't trust her one bit."

He crossed his arms over his own chest. "You're right. I am a grown man, and trust me when I say I can handle my business. Maybe I didn't have the right to ask you to get involved by pretending there's something going on between us. But I figured if Lela saw me with another woman, she'd get the message that I'm not interested. Evidently I was wrong about that."

Peyton sighed. "Yes, Angelo, you were. There are plenty of women like Lela, who think just because they have money they can say or do whatever the hell they want, without considering others. All I can say is that she better be glad she's dealing with the classy, new Peyton Mahoney. If I was the same person I was ten years ago, I would have used her to clean the damn floor."

A smile touched the corners of his lips. She glared at him. "And just what's so funny?"

"Your attitude. You remind me of what I heard my mother used to be like back in the day. According to my father she was something else."

Peyton lifted a brow. "Your mother's family had money, too, Angelo."

He shrugged. "Not really. Although her father was a lawyer and her mother was a teacher, according to Mom, there wasn't always a lot of money. There were four of them, and her parents made sacrifices to educate their kids and help them fulfill their dreams."

Peyton drew in a deep breath, believing what she'd said was still true. Relatively speaking, his mother had money—at least compared to how things were for her growing up in Chicago. She still remembered how her grandmother took on several jobs to make ends meet. When Edith Mahoney should have been looking toward retirement, she'd had a six-month-old baby dumped in her lap. Instead of turning Peyton over to social services, her grandmother had raised her. Luckily they had good neighbors who had looked after her while her grandmother worked three jobs.

"Getting back to Lela, I ran into her when I left the restaurant, and I had a talk with her after you left. And I don't think you'll have to worry about her doing—"

Peyton raised her hand to cut him off. "I hope you don't think your little lecture or me speaking up is going to be the end of it. Get real, Angelo, you are a challenge to her. With your fame and good looks, you're a prize. She's not going to back off because of anything either of us might say. In fact, she's probably going to be even more persistent. Trust me, you aren't someone she plans on letting get away. So if you thought coming to the resort would give you time to relax and unwind, then you're wrong."

She could tell her words had him thinking as he continued rubbing his hand across his chin. "Okay, so what do you suggest?"

"I'm willing to reconsider your offer. Granted, Lela will try my patience and yours. But it's time she learned that she can't always have what she wants."

He dropped his hands to his sides. "And what will you get out of all this?"

She drew in a deep breath as she mulled over her answer. "On the way back to my room a couple of guys hit on me. And like I said, I'm not in the mood for that kind of attention. Although your sister and Mac have the best of intentions, I'm not as hard up for a man as they think. I want to rest, relax and have a good time. And having a good time doesn't necessarily mean I want guys to think I'm ready and willing."

She paused for a second. "However, I do want to celebrate my birthday on Thursday, and I'd prefer to do so with you rather than with any other man I've met so far. So what do you say?"

For a moment, Angelo didn't know just what to say.

He thought Lela had blown it for him. Instead, her little scene in the restaurant might have worked in his favor. But he'd been truthful about what he'd told Peyton. He did have a talk with Lela and had told her he wasn't interested in her. He thought he'd handled the situation. But Peyton had a point. Some women just didn't know when to give up, and unfortunately Lela was one of them.

"Angelo?"

He looked at her, really looked at her, and what he saw touched him so much that he almost reached out and pulled her into his arms. He was tempted. Lord, how he was tempted. He thought about telling her how he had convinced Mac and Sam to surprise her with a trip to the resort for her birthday, and how he had concocted a plan to make sure that they spent time together. Even with the complications created by Lela, it seemed his plan was falling into place quite nicely. Everything was turning out just right, so he wasn't about to look a gift horse in the mouth. He wanted her to get to know him—the real DeAngelo Di Meglio—in a way no other woman ever had.

After a long pause, he finally responded. "Yes?"

"So what do you think?"

He smiled. "I think that if you're right about Lela, then in order to pull this off, we're going to have to be exclusive. I know this is a singles' resort, and the idea is to date other people, but that's not going to work."

She chuckled. "So we're going to have to break the singles-resort rules? But then what can they do? Ask us to leave?"

Angelo reached behind her to grab a couple of coffee cups and shifted his body so that he was propped against the counter next to her. As he lifted the pot to pour the coffee, his hands seemed to tremble a little when Peyton came to stand beside him. He handed her a cup of coffee, took a sip from his own cup.

"No. They wouldn't dare, especially since I'm one of the owners."

She coughed, nearly choking on the coffee. "You are?"

"Yes." He figured she should at least know that since it might come up, and she'd wonder why he hadn't told her before. "I'm just a minority partner. In fact, I have less than twenty percent ownership in the resort. I got involved mainly for the tax write-offs, but decided it was a pretty nice place to visit every now and then."

"I'm sure it is. Single women walking all over the place... This place is probably right up your alley."

He chuckled. "Yes, but that was before I decided that I needed to change some things."

She took another sip of coffee and studied him. He felt warm under the scrutiny of her gaze. "And when exactly did you make this decision?"

"A couple of years ago.... In fact, it wasn't long after I got back from visiting Oklahoma when Sam was out of town."

He wondered if she would put the pieces together. He glanced over at her, and thought—not for the first time—that she was a beautiful woman.

"Why?"

"It was something I felt I should do. If you remember, I came to Oklahoma to lick my wounds after having just lost a case. Hell, I even thought about quitting practicing law."

She blinked. "You did?"

"Yes. But instead I decided to keep practicing law, but to make some changes in my personal life."

"And giving up women was one of them?"

"Pretty much," he said quietly. There was no need to explain any more.

"Um…" She looked down into her coffee cup. "This is delicious."

And so is she, he thought. Hell, he knew he had to be patient, but it had been two years already—two years since he'd realized he wanted her, and badly. She had begun invading his dreams, occupying his thoughts at times when he should have been concentrating on other things. That was what had made him decide it was time to make a move.

"Are you a good actor?"

Her words interrupted his thoughts. "Excuse me?"

"I asked if you're an actor. We need to be really convincing."

"And you don't think we can be?" he asked.

"You tell me. We'll have to engage in public displays of affection, kissing, whispering sweet nothings in my ear."

He smiled. "I can handle all of that. Can you?"

She seemed to mull over his question for a moment and then met his gaze. "Yes, as long as we both know it's nothing serious."

His gaze ran over her features again. "Fine."

"Good." She looked at her watch and then placed the coffee cup down. "Now it seems as if I'm going to have to ask you to leave for the second time today. I want to grab a nap before getting dressed for the party tonight."

He set his coffee cup down beside hers and grinned. "I know when I'm not wanted." He moved toward the door.

"Pouting doesn't become you, Angelo," she said, following a few paces behind him.

He opened the door and glanced over his shoulder. She was right there. He hadn't realized she was so close. Once again he was tempted to reach out and pull her into his arms and make the kiss they'd shared last night seem like child's play. "I'll be back around seven."

"I'll be ready."

He closed the door behind him and thought to himself, *so will I.*

Chapter 7

Three hours later, Peyton was well-rested when she opened the door to her suite to greet Angelo. For a moment, he just stood there staring at her, as she regarded him hopefully after twirling around. "Well, how do I look?"

She had to admit she was excited. She was wearing another dress she had purchased on her shopping spree with Mac and Sam, but this particular cocktail dress was one she had picked out herself. Even though it was more modestly priced than the other one, Sam had approved.

When Angelo didn't say anything and kept staring at her, she gave him an impatient look, placing her hands on her hips. "Well?"

He blinked. "You look absolutely gorgeous."

His compliment made her smile and boosted her ego a notch. Even if he was exaggerating a bit, she still needed to hear it. "Thanks. I was hoping you would like it."

"I do."

"It's not too much?" she asked.

He cocked his head to the side before throwing it back to laugh. "Sweetheart, if anything, it's not enough."

She laughed, too, and glanced down at herself. He was right. The dress was shorter than usual—much shorter. And the dress was backless and draped all the way to her waist. She was glad her breasts were firm and full and that she didn't really need to wear a bra, although she always did—just not tonight. She'd decided to pull out all the stops, figuring Lela wouldn't be playing fair either. She would probably be wearing something provocative. So it made Peyton feel good knowing she had already beaten Lela to the punch.

"Come in for a minute, I just need to grab my wrap."

"All right."

She hurried into the bedroom and paused in front of the mirror for a moment to take a deep breath. She couldn't help it. She had a thing for a man in formal attire—and Angelo looked so good in his white dinner jacket. He even smelled good. She swallowed hard. Why was she feeling butterflies in the pit of her stomach and why was there this intense heat settling right at the juncture of her thighs? It had to have something to do with the way he had looked at her when she'd opened the door. He probably hadn't expected to see her dressed in such revealing attire—a short, black, almost sheer, body-hugging backless design.

She smiled. This was the second night at the resort that she had captured a man's attention, and for some reason she felt giddy that the man was Angelo. The very thought was scary *and* exciting. She kept reminding herself not to get too carried away. But there was just something about being the center of attention where Angelo was concerned that had her melting inside.

Was it real or was he play-acting already?

Granted she didn't think she was his type, but just about any man would react to what she was wearing. *Um, that might be something worth exploring later.*

An imaginary slap brushed the side of her cheek, bringing her back to reality. Somewhere in the back of her mind her subconscious said, *Don't act crazy, Mahoney. You might be attracted to him and there might be a slim chance that he's attracted to you, but what of it? He's definitely a hottie. But he's also a Di Meglio—Sam's brother—a real player, even though he claims he's turned over a new leaf. Yeah, right.*

"Are you okay in there?"

His voice sounded deep, husky and sexy, and seemed to float into the bedroom. "Yes, I'm okay. I'll be out in a minute."

She had to pull herself together before facing him again. "I'm going to use the ladies' room one last time before we leave."

Taking in another deep breath, she rushed into the bathroom.

Angelo glanced at his watch, annoyed with himself that he was feeling agitated. Hell, he needed to get out of Peyton's suite and fast before he did something he might regret—like following her into the bathroom and taking her against the wall. How was he supposed to get through the night with her wearing something like that? When she'd opened the door and he saw her standing there, he'd nearly swallowed his tongue.

That black dress showed off every curve and angle—enticingly so. He could tell that her breasts were full, firm, and her nipples were taut and puckered—something that was easily detected through the fabric of her dress. The moment he noticed them, heat surged to his groin and a low moan barely escaped his lips. He imagined what it would be like to reach out and cup her breasts in his hand—to feel them, to lean down and taste them. Never had he wanted a woman the way he wanted her. And if he didn't regain control, he would try like hell to touch her tonight—before they even left the room.

He rubbed his hands down his face, thinking there had to be an easier way to win her over—one where he wouldn't lose his sanity in the process. He closed his eyes and then wished he hadn't when all kinds of erotic images raced through his mind, tempting him to no end.

"I'm ready for real this time, Angelo. Sorry I kept you waiting."

He slowly turned, and his gaze raked over her, making it difficult to suppress the urge to make love to her where she stood. It wouldn't take much to release himself, to lift her already short dress and slide right into her and keep going and going all the way to the hilt and then…

"Angelo? Are you all right?"

Her words startled him and he realized he'd been standing there staring at her. "Yes, I'm fine." He had to stop staring at her. "You're ready, right?" he asked.

Instead of responding, she nodded with a wary look in her eye. He didn't bother saying anything for fear she would give him a response he didn't want. There were some things a man just couldn't hide, and he knew his desire for her had to be pretty damn obvious.

"Then let's go," he said.

"Okay." She quickly headed toward the door, and he followed.

* * *

Peyton scanned the crowd the moment she and Angelo walked into the room. She might have imagined things but it seemed practically everyone turned to stare at them and she knew why. Together they made an eye-catching couple.

She caught a glimpse of them in the mirrored walls of the elevator and the sight had nearly taken her breath away. As he stood by her side, there had been something about his dashingly handsome looks that had complimented hers. Even the couple who had shared the elevator ride with them had kept saying how good they looked together. In retrospect, she really shouldn't have been surprised. Angelo brought out the best in any woman he was with.

"Our table is over this way," Angelo whispered, as he leaned toward her ear and placed his hand in the middle of her bare back. A shiver rushed up her spine as her stomach muscles clenched at his touch. All it had taken was a brush of his hand to her skin and desire immediately flared through every part of her body.

He paused briefly as he walked and glanced down at her. "You okay?"

She met his gaze and nodded. "Yes, why do you ask?"

"You're shivering."

She already felt the goose bumps on her skin. And if that wasn't bad enough, her nipples suddenly felt sensitive. With a great deal of effort she tried driving the sensations away. When they reached the table he pulled the chair out for her. "Thanks, Angelo."

"You're welcome."

She watched as he slid his muscular body in the chair opposite hers. For a moment she just stared, watching how the dim lights seemed to highlight his features. Everything about him seemed to cast a glow—the Rolex watch on his wrist, his gold cuff links and the diamond stud in his ear. It was as if he were lit for a movie set.

"What do you want to drink?"

She noticed his lips move and belatedly realized what he had asked her. "A glass of white wine would be nice."

"You got it."

He grabbed a passing waiter and ordered their drinks, then quickly turned back to her. "You look incredible, Peyton."

"Thanks." She felt tightness in her chest, and glanced around, very much aware that he was still looking at her. She couldn't help wondering what he was thinking and why he was looking at her like he wanted to devour her. Did the dress really look that good on her? Is that why he was staring at her? But then she asked herself, why was she staring at him as well?

"There are a lot of couples here tonight."

She glanced around and then over at him. "So I see. Do you think Lela will be here?"

He shrugged. "Not sure, and frankly I don't care."

She wondered how he could say that when Lela was the reason they were there. She was about to remind him of that fact when the waiter returned with their order. She quickly took a sip, feeling she definitely needed it to calm her nerves. His voice was deep and throaty and sent heat sizzling all over her.

"Good?"

She glanced up at him and smiled. "Yes. Really delicious."

She knew he thought she was talking about the wine, but in reality she was voicing her opinion of him. He glanced toward where the musicians were assembling, which gave her a chance to study him again without being obvious. Her gaze shifted to his own wineglass and focused on his long, strong-looking fingers. His hands were big—big, beautiful hands. Hands she figured could stroke a woman into an orgasm.

She almost choked on her wine and waited for the sting she was certain would touch her face, and when it never happened she wondered where a good slap of common sense was when she needed it. Why was she thinking about orgasms of all things?

"You hungry?"

She lifted her gaze from his hands back to his face. *Starving,* she thought. "Not really, I'm fine," she said.

"Well, I need something. I guess my stomach is like a bottomless pit."

His comment made her remember she had glanced at him below the waist before they'd left her room. He'd had an erection, she was sure of it. When she came back into the living room suite, he had turned around, and voila, it had been there, straining hard against the zipper of his pants. It was pretty damn obvious. She'd bit back the temptation to ask where the heck it had come from, and what had he been thinking about to make such a thing happen?

"So, where do you go after leaving the resort?"

She took another sip of her wine. "Back home for a couple of weeks. I have some important appointments at the office that I don't want to miss. Then I'm off to Chicago for a few weeks to visit friends. Then I'm in Oklahoma but not back at work for a while. I'm taking another month off. I need it."

"I know what you mean. I'm not looking forward to returning to work," he said, swirling the wine around in the glass. "In fact, I've got another couple of months off, and I plan to enjoy them. I might be coming to Oklahoma to visit everyone."

"I'm sure Sam will like that." She didn't want to make it seem personal, but she'd like to see him as well.

The waiter came by again, and Angelo ordered some appetizers that he coaxed her into sharing while they talked about movies, politics and what their favorite television shows were. The group of women from the elevator passed their table and paused long enough to greet them before moving on. She figured they weren't so bad and weren't really all that different from her, Mac and Sam whenever they got together.

"You know them, Peyton?"

She glanced over at Angelo. "Not personally. We were in the elevator together this morning. They were talking about this hot-looking guy they've been checking out here." There was no need to tell him he'd been the hunk under discussion.

"I think this would have been a place that Mac, Sam and I would have loved to come to…before they got married and had babies."

Something in her tone must have shed light on her inner feelings. "Was that a little resentment I heard?" he asked.

She shook her head. "No, not resentment—just reality. Things aren't the same with the three of us. But I'm happy for them. I truly am."

"You can have the same things for yourself, you know," he said in a low voice.

She didn't bother looking over at him. Instead she took another sip of her wine. "A husband? Babies? Me?" She chuckled. "No way."

"And why not?"

She shrugged. "Not interested, at least not at the moment. Maybe later, years from now. Please, I'm trying to get a grip on turning thirty."

"You don't look like you're about to turn thirty. You can still pass for twenty-one."

She reached across the table and patted his cheek. "Oh, Mr. Di Meglio, you're so sweet."

"Isn't this a touching scene?"

She glanced up. Lela had stopped at their table, and, as expected, her dress made a statement. It was almost see-through in the light. Men were staring and salivating. Women were gasping. If Lela's goal tonight was to get attention, then Peyton had to hand it to her, she had achieved it hands down.

"Yes, we think it's touching," Angelo said, reaching out and taking Peyton's hand in his. "Is there anything you wanted, Lela?"

The woman tossed her head back, which made her breasts tilt upward even higher. A man at the table beside theirs could be heard breathing. "Yes, there is something I want, DeAngelo. I was hoping we could talk for a minute," Lela said in a soft, seductive voice.

"About what?"

Lela looked annoyed that he would ask. "It's personal, and I prefer that we speak privately."

Angelo sighed before saying, "Maybe later, not now. You do remember Peyton, don't you?"

Lela tossed Peyton a dismissive glance. "Yes, I remember Peyton."

Peyton smiled at Lela as she inched closer to Angelo, entwining her arms with his. "Yes, and I also remember Lela. The woman who has no manners."

The woman glared at her and tightened her fingers around the designer clutch in her hand. Instead of responding to Peyton, Lela shifted her gaze back to Angelo. "But we will talk later, won't we, DeAngelo?"

She'd stated it as if it was a foregone conclusion. The look Angelo gave Lela was pretty damn cold to Peyton, and it clearly indicated they would be doing nothing of the sort. A part of her thought the woman should probably back off and do so now.

"Like I said, Lela, I don't know what we have to talk about. Besides, I intend to spend the entire evening with Peyton," he said, leaning over and placing a kiss on Peyton's lips.

To Peyton's way of thinking, that should have sent a message to the woman that Angelo wasn't interested in her and to move on, but Lela was persistent, if not real smart. She asked in an annoyed voice, "What about tomorrow, DeAngelo?"

Angelo smiled and leaned over and placed another kiss on Peyton's lips. The contact sent sensations whirling around inside of her. "I intend to spend tomorrow with Peyton as well. In fact, I don't see myself having any free time for a while."

Peyton thought it couldn't get any plainer than that, but from the look on Lela's face, she knew the woman still refused to accept that Angelo just wasn't interested. And Angelo wasn't sugarcoating anything. He was clearly letting her know he wasn't interested. Since Lela had decided to confront Angelo at the party, they had an audience.

Peyton found it amusing that Lela had intended to embarrass her. And it was obvious from the look on her face that Lela didn't like the turn of events. Lela shifted her gaze from Angelo to Peyton, and if looks could kill, Peyton thought, then she'd be six feet under.

Lela glanced back to Angelo. "I'll be here for a while

so eventually we will have a chance to talk." Then, without waiting for Angelo to respond, she walked away, as every man in the room watched and drooled.

Peyton glanced over at Angelo and whispered, "She doesn't plan on giving up, you know."

He smiled, and she realized just how close together they were. "I'm not worried. Eventually she'll come to her senses."

Peyton tried to move back, putting some distance between them. But Angelo reached out and placed a hand on her arm. "Stay close to me. She might come back."

Although it was highly unlikely, she stayed put. "All right."

At that moment the waiter returned. "Would the two of you like to order dinner now, Mr. Di Meglio?"

Angelo nodded. "Yes. Just give us a few moments to decide."

He glanced over at her when the waiter walked off. "Do you know what you want?"

An erotic image flashed through her mind of a naked Angelo mounting her on the large dining table in her suite. She suddenly felt heated embarrassment in her cheeks that she would even imagine such a thing. Truth be told, that's what she wanted.

"Peyton?"

She lifted her gaze to him, glad that he didn't have the ability to get inside her head. But since she would never share those thoughts with him, what was the harm. The main question she should've been asking herself is why was she having those thoughts in the first place? Why was everything about him suddenly becoming sexual? She, of all people, should know better when it came to a man like Angelo.

She didn't have a problem with the game they were

playing with Lela—the woman deserved it. And hopefully it would teach her a lesson about crossing the line when it came to making a nuisance of herself and going after someone else's man.

Peyton knew she had to remember that Angelo wasn't really her man, not by a long shot. But she definitely wanted to add him to her birthday wish list.

"I hate that we didn't get a chance to dance together tonight," Angelo said as he walked Peyton back to her room hours later.

She laughed and glanced over at him. "We did dance together. Why do you think my feet are killing me?"

"But we really didn't get a chance to dance together. Line dancing doesn't count." He had wanted to hold her in his arms up close and dance to some slow music. But each time a slow song came on, she would find some excuse to get off the dance floor. It was as if she was afraid of him holding her in his arms.

"But it was worth it if the look on Lela's face was anything to go by," she said. "Maybe she's finally getting it," Peyton said, coming to a stop in front of her door.

"I guess there's hope." He wanted to ask her to invite him in but decided not to rush things. The last thing he wanted was for her to think his interest in her was only sexual, although the thought of making love to her was constantly on his mind. Besides, she'd said on the elevator up to their floor that she was tired and couldn't wait to get to her room and go to bed.

"So what are your plans for tomorrow?" he asked her.

"Umm, not sure. I plan to sleep in late again, but once I get up and have breakfast…or lunch…whatever the case might be, I'll check to see what activities are going on for tomorrow."

He nodded. "I understand you're taking riding lessons." Then he watched how her lips twisted into a mischievous smile.

"They might be taking me…right to the bank. I have the best instructor at Luke's school, other than Luke himself, and I can't seem to move beyond level one. Believe it or not, I'm still stuck in the group of beginners."

The image of her standing, waiting her turn to ride a horse among a group of little kids, made him laugh out loud. Sam had mentioned she had gotten a slow start, but he hadn't thought things were *that* bad.

"Glad I was able to provide you with some comic relief, Angelo."

He wiped the laughter off his face but retained a smile. "Sorry. I tell you what. They are giving riding lessons here as well. That way you can continue to practice."

She shook her head. "I'll pass."

He lifted his brow. "I never took you for a coward."

"I'm not a coward."

"Prove it then." He barely managed to keep from laughing out loud again when her frown turned into a full-blown glare.

"I don't have to prove anything to you."

He shrugged. "You're right. You don't." Angelo knew his easy assent probably pissed her off even more.

"You're right, I don't." When he didn't say anything, one way or the other, she tightened her lips. "You think I'm afraid, don't you."

"I did, which is why I called you a coward. But you've set me straight when you said you weren't."

"But you still think I'm afraid?" she countered.

"I didn't say that."

"But you think it, Angelo."

"I didn't say that."

She didn't say anything for a moment and then she leaned in close to him, so close that their noses were almost touching. "But you're thinking it."

Little did she know that the only thing he was thinking about at that moment was that it wouldn't take much for him to move just a tad closer and lick her lips, nibble them a few times, slide his tongue inside her mouth and capture her tongue and feed on it with the hunger he was feeling. Instead he asked her, "When did you become a mind reader, Peyton?"

She didn't answer. It was as if she'd suddenly realized their positions—how close they were standing and the proximity of her mouth to his. She drew in a sharp breath before slowly easing a safe distance back against the door.

"Fine, DeAngelo Di Meglio, I think I'll take a riding lesson tomorrow, after all."

He chuckled. "This I've got to see."

She gave him a pointed look. "You do that."

"I will. Now go inside and go to bed. I want you well-rested when that horse kicks your butt tomorrow."

"Go to hell, Angelo," she threw over her shoulder as she opened her door.

"Um, not before I can see how you handle a horse."

She went inside and closed the door in his face as he stood there a moment, laughing and thinking he hadn't laughed this much in a long time. And it felt good.

Chapter 8

"Why is it every time I open the door you just stand there and stare before saying anything? A girl can develop a complex from that sort of thing," Peyton said, opening the door and stepping aside for Angelo to enter.

If anything, she should be the one staring. No man had any business looking this good before ten in the morning. He was wearing jeans and a pullover shirt. She'd seen him in jeans before but for some reason he looked so, so luscious. And the darkened area around his chin meant he hadn't bothered to shave this morning, which made him look even sexier, and just plain naughty.

"I don't want you to develop a complex," he said, dropping down on the sofa. "Take it for the compliment it is. I just happen to like your outfit."

She glanced down at herself. Like him, she was wearing jeans and a pullover top. "Why? It's nothing more than a pair of jeans and a top."

He smiled up at her. "Yes, but you look good in them."

She shook her head as she crossed the room to pour him a cup of freshly brewed coffee. "Don't try it, Angelo. Compliments won't get you anywhere this morning. I won't forget the mean things you said to me last night about some horse kicking my butt."

"Don't tell me that you're still holding a grudge. Didn't you get a good night's sleep?"

To be quite honest, she hadn't. There had to be something about spending the last two days in Angelo's presence. Now she was thinking about him at night—while she slept. And that wasn't good. "I could have gotten a better night's sleep," she said truthfully.

He tilted his head, studying her for a moment, and she saw concern in his eyes. "Something bothering you?"

If only you knew. Instead of saying anything, she waved him off. "The only thing bothering me is you and your lack of confidence in my horseback riding."

He laughed. "Hey, I wasn't the one who admitted to still being in the beginners' class."

She walked over to the sofa to hand him a cup of coffee. "Um, do you know how easy it would be to suddenly get clumsy? Just think of where this hot coffee would land if I were to accidentally drop it in your lap."

The widening of his eyes and the way his mouth dropped open was priceless. She saw his throat move when he inhaled a deep, fearful breath. "You wouldn't."

She stood there with the coffee in her hand while raising an arched brow. "I wouldn't?"

"Hell, I hope not."

She smiled. "That would be a surefire way to keep Lela away from you, if I were to damage your tools."

He tried shifting back a little and when she raised her brow a bit higher she figured he'd reach the conclusion that it would be in his best interest to stay put. "If you do that, I'll sue you for everything you've got," he warned.

She laughed out loud. "You won't be getting much. At least not compared to what you already have."

"Hey, stop laughing, Peyton. Your hand's shaking."

She looked at her hand and saw it was. "Oops."

Deciding she had scared him enough, she kept a steady hand on the coffee cup while she slowly stepped back. "Okay, Angelo, I won't scald you this time, but don't ever make fun of me again."

She saw he'd made sure he was out of harm's way before standing and saying in a warning growl, "I'm going to get you for that."

If only he would, she thought smiling.

"You didn't do so bad," Angelo said a few hours later after Peyton had finished her riding lesson and was walking toward him. "In fact, you did better than I thought you would."

He couldn't stop his gaze from roaming appreciatively over her body. She looked damn good in her jeans, top and boots. And as he'd watched her ride the horse, he couldn't help imagining her riding him that way—holding on tight, moving her hips and thighs up and down in time with his motion and flanking her thighs tight around him to keep him in place.

She shrugged her shoulders as they began walking to the stable where the horses were kept. "I don't know whether to thank you or not."

He chuckled. "Go ahead and thank me, even if it kills you."

She waved him away. "Not in the mood. I still feel I have a lot to learn."

"And you do. But at least you're trying."

"Yeah, but Mac and Sam are so good at it."

"From years of practice, trust me. Mac was all but born in a saddle. And as for Sam and I, our parents had us taking riding lessons before our third birthday. During the summers we spent a lot of time in the Hamptons, being spectators at the polo matches at the Seven Oaks Farm. We took riding lessons there as well."

"Must have been nice."

Although she uttered her comment in a low voice, he'd still heard the sarcasm. "Yes, it was nice," he said, not feeling he had to apologize for his family's wealth or feel guilty about it. Sam didn't have to warn him that in his pursuit of Peyton, money would be the bone of contention. Every once in a while she would rage about the inequities between the haves and the have-nots. But anyone who knew the Di Meglios was well aware of their struggles in the early years. He glanced down at her as they continued walking. "Tell me about your childhood." He'd heard about how tough she'd had it growing up from Sam, but wanted to hear about it from Peyton.

She glanced up at him. "Why?"

"Curious."

She didn't say anything for a while, as if pondering his request. "I never knew my father, although I heard rumors about him during my childhood."

He stopped walking and cocked his head to the side and studied her. Now that was something he hadn't known. "Really?"

She shrugged and continued to walk on. "Yes, really."

He picked up his pace again and eased in stride beside her. "Was he a married man?" he asked.

"Not at the time, at least that's what I was told. He was some big-shot politician, and my birth was an embarrassment to him. So was his affair with my mother. When she got pregnant, he gave her money for an abortion. She took the money, left town and returned a year later, just long enough to drop me off at my grandmother's house and keep going. I haven't seen her since."

"Never?"

She shook her head. "No. We heard she died years ago. There was never a body, so I can't say whether it's true or not. I can only assume."

He heard the impassive tone of her voice, and in a way he understood her lack of empathy. How could a woman give birth to a child and then drop her off and never see her again? He could just imagine how Peyton felt knowing she'd been abandoned.

"And your grandmother raised you?" he asked. Although he'd posed it as a question, he already knew the answer. Sam had told him just how close Peyton was to her grandmother, who'd died the year before she started law school. According to Sam, it had always been Peyton's grandmother's dream for Peyton to attend law school, and she had. After law school she had returned to Chicago to work as an attorney for a South Side neighborhood economic development agency.

She paused at the gate that led to the resort's beautiful flower gardens. This was one of the things that had captured his attention when he'd been given a tour of the grounds at the time he'd contemplated becoming a partner. Another had been the layout of the resort and its architecture. Spacious and natural, the resort was spread out over a hundred acres and sat on a hill above the Atlantic Ocean. He figured it would be a great place to get away and imagined singles enjoying the scenery and having fun.

"This is just my third day, but I love it here."

He glanced down at her as he followed her gaze around the garden. "What do you like about it?"

"The peace and quiet—at least it's peaceful in this part of the resort. I especially like secluded places where there aren't a lot of people around. And I like that the resort restricts the number of people who check in and are so concerned with making sure the guests have a good time. There are rules and regulations in place to ensure guests behave appropriately. I can see the potential for some women to get territorial when they have no right to be."

She glanced up at him. "Like Lela. I'm surprised she hasn't hunted you down by now."

In truth, she had. But there was no reason to mention it to Peyton. Lela had knocked on his door before eight this morning and invited him to breakfast. Of course, he declined. She'd tried her best to get inside his room. But he wasn't having it, and told her if she kept making a nuisance of herself he would report her to security.

Angelo was glad when his conversation with Peyton was interrupted by the group of women who'd stopped by their table last night. Official introductions were made. Although they looked nothing alike, the three were triplets from Charleston. They had signed up for riding lessons as well.

"They're nice," Peyton said moments later when the women walked off toward the stable stalls where the horses were. "Although the one named Tessa couldn't stop checking you out."

He smiled at her as he opened the door for them to enter the building. "Was she? I hadn't noticed."

"You wouldn't. All men are alike."

He chuckled. "Are we? In what way?"

"You're acutely aware of the effect you have on women and then pretend that you're clueless."

He led her over to the elevator and was glad they were the only couple in the car. Once the elevator door closed, he asked, "Are you in a man-hating mood today?"

"Is that what you think?" she asked, trying to temper her anger.

"I think that's how you sound. And if I didn't know better, I'd think you were a little put out that you saw another woman checking me out."

She gave him a pointed look. "See what I mean? Why do men think so highly of themselves?"

"You think that's what I'm doing?"

He could tell that he was beginning to annoy the hell out of her, but he didn't care. He was peeved that she was grouping him with other men, those she deemed less than desirable.

When she didn't respond, it bothered him. Why not move on to another subject? Why not talk about the weather, politics, religion—anything that wouldn't fire her up? But he couldn't let it go. He couldn't ignore the fact that the woman he was hot behind the zipper for had insinuated that he invited female attention.

"You know it works both ways, too."

The elevator came to a stop on their floor, and he waited for her to exit before following behind her.

"What are you talking about?" she asked, tossing the question over her shoulder.

"Women are also aware of what they do to men. They do it for the hell of it and then feign innocence."

She stopped in front of the door to her room. "I can't believe you said that."

He smiled and placed a hand gently on her arm. "That's my theory, and I'm sticking to it."

He reached into his pocket and pulled out her door key—the extra key he had yet to return to her. She didn't ask for it, and he didn't volunteer it. She probably would have asked for it back if his statement had not thrown her off kilter. It didn't take much to see what he'd said had gotten her angry—big-time.

"Are you talking about all women or some?" she asked in a voice that let him know she was more than ready to go head-to-head with him.

He shrugged as he opened the door to her room. "I don't know. Were you talking about all men or just some?"

Her glower deepened, and it took all his restraint to keep from grinning. This was serious business to her, but to him it was just a matter of setting the record straight.

He watched as she crossed the room and went straight to the counter and turned on the coffeemaker. He'd noticed that Peyton seemed to be able to drink coffee at any time of day. He quickly remembered that last episode with her and the cup of coffee and decided that to be on the safe side he probably needed to steer clear of the coffeepot.

"You have anything cold in the refrigerator?" he asked.

She glanced back over at him. "Yes, but the hotel keeps a tab on that stuff."

He lifted a brow. "Pardon me?"

"Anything from the minibar goes on your bill."

He frowned, thinking that's usually how it worked. After a brief pause, he said, "And you have a problem with that?"

He saw her nostrils flare. "Yes, I do, although I'm sure you probably don't. I have no desire to pay three times the cost for a little, itsy-bitsy bottle of water, wine or anything else in here. What they charge for a small bag of M&Ms is five times what I'd pay for a four-pound bag at the store. That's totally ridiculous. But since you're part owner of the resort, I don't expect you to sweat over it."

He shook his head thinking she was really on a roll, and all because…why? "You want to talk about it?"

From the look on her face, he must have pushed some now-you've-really-pissed-me-off button. She put her hands on her hips. "I told you I'm not Sam."

"Didn't say you were."

Dropping her hands to her sides, she moved over to the window to look out. "That's how you start off conversations with Sam when you're trying to get all into her business."

Was it? He'd never noticed. "I've said before that I'm well aware you aren't Sam." Even after the kiss the first night, she still had such foolish ideas embedded in that gorgeous head of hers?

He studied her for a second, saw the stiffening of her shoulders and the tilt of her chin. She was ready for battle. But there was also the way she was nervously licking her bottom lip with her tongue, tapping her fingers against her jeans. She was pissed and on edge. He could understand why she thought she should be upset with him, but where did the edginess come from? Did his presence make her tense? Why?

"You think I've been treating you like a sister?" he asked her.

She licked her lips again. "No."

He quirked a brow. "Then what is it?"

She didn't say anything. A few moments passed before he concluded she really didn't need to respond. If she was attracted to him the same way he was attracted to her and was trying to fight it, then he could understand why she seemed prickly.

She shook her head and rubbed the back of her neck as she moved away from the window. "I don't know. I honestly don't know."

He crossed the room toward her. "Um, maybe I do."

Chapter 9

Peyton watched as Angelo moved toward her with a purposeful stride. She knew she was in trouble, although she didn't really know why or to what extent. All she knew was that he was looking at her with that same look in his eyes that was there right before they'd kissed a couple of nights ago.

Did that mean...

No, that wasn't it. He was not going to kiss her again. If anything he was going to try and shake some sense into her—nothing more, nothing less. If she truly believed that then why was she backing up with his advance? Why was her heart racing a thousand miles a minute?

She stopped backing up when the back of her leg touched the sofa. She swallowed deeply. "What is wrong with you?"

He smiled that smile that sent everything inside of her haywire. The man was so incredibly sensuous it was a shame. He had way too much charisma. And she of all people should not succumb to his alluring charm. She knew better and had heard all the stories about him. She knew he liked to play games when it came to women. He didn't have a serious bone in his body.

"What's wrong with you, Angelo?"

He pushed a curl out of her face. "What makes you think something is wrong?"

She narrowed her gaze suspiciously. "You're acting funny."

"Funny in what way?"

His expression was so innocent, she was beginning to wonder whether she'd imagined that look in his eyes seconds ago. She drew in a deep breath and held up her hand. "Look, Angelo, I don't know what game you're playing, but I'm not in the mood."

He reached out and took hold of her fingers and pulled them to his lips and placed a kiss on the back of her hand, before turning it over and kissing the palm. Her insides started to sizzle. The juncture between her thighs was tingling with excitement, like a firecracker on the Fourth of July.

Still holding her hand in his, he said, "I'm not playing a game."

"Yes, you are," she countered in a voice that didn't quite sound like her own.

He shook his head. "No, I'm not. What makes you think I am?"

She had to get a grip on her things. Kissing her hand with his lips was way too much. Why was she suddenly feeling hot and sexually needy? "Come on, Angelo. This is Peyton and not some silly-ass girl drooling over you."

He held her gaze. "And you think that's the only women I can draw—silly-ass girls? What about a hot-blooded woman, a luscious, desirable one, with an over-ripe appetite for everything that I want?"

"A woman like Lela Stillwell," she snapped.

He hardened his gaze. "No, Lela would be the last person I'd consider. I was thinking more along the lines of a woman like you."

She was shocked. "A woman like me!"

"Yes, a woman like you. I can feel your heat, and I'm sure you feel mine."

She snatched her hand from his grasp and snapped her finger in front of his face. "Hello…remember me? It's Peyton, the rough-around-the-edges attorney who grew up in Chicago's South Side, the one who has no qualms about taking a brother down a notch if I have to."

He smiled. "I know who you are. Now maybe it's time for you to know who I am."

With that, he dipped his head as his lips connected to hers.

God, how he needed this, Angelo thought as he slid his tongue into Peyton's mouth. He took the risk of her biting it off if she wasn't receptive to his kiss, but some risks were worth taking. Although she resisted at first, that only lasted a few seconds before she began returning his kiss with as much passion as he put into it. He didn't intend to leave one inch of her mouth untouched.

He deepened the kiss as he tried to control the sensations stoking the fire inside of him. She felt soft against him, curvy—all woman. It wouldn't take much to just scoop her up into his arms and carry her into the bedroom. But he knew that was something he couldn't do, at least for now.

Although he was trying to make progress, he wasn't going to rush things or push her into anything she wasn't ready for yet. Then something she'd once said came to mind. *Having a good time doesn't mean I want guys to think I'm ready and willing.* And Angelo didn't want her to think he was just another man who thought that way. He wanted her to know that he felt more than that. The thought that she had that much power was unsettling to him, yet there was nothing he could do to stop it. Not even his sister Sam knew the intensity of his feelings for Peyton. And to be perfectly honest, until this weekend, he hadn't really understood them himself.

And this was the result. A mind-boggling kiss that he felt in every part of his body where the passion he had kept under wraps was now escalating to a need so fierce he had to struggle to contain it. But Angelo's need for control didn't stop him from pulling Peyton closer into his arms as he tilted his head at an angle to deepen the kiss even more.

And when he heard her moan, he nearly lost it.

He pulled back slightly to give her a chance to breathe but kept his lips close to hers, taking his tongue and tracing a line around her top lip, then using his lips to pull hard on the bottom one. Then he angled his mouth to take hers again, pulling her closer into his arms. Angelo pressed his body against hers and wondered if she could feel his arousal pressed against her stomach. She probably could since he left no doubt as to his level of desire for her. But what she didn't know was that he was fighting like hell to control it.

A knock at the door startled them both, and Angelo pulled back and drew in a deep breath. He looked at her as she cast an accusing glance at him. He took a step back, slid his hands into the pockets of his jeans and looked right back at her. There was no way she could pretend that she didn't want him or that she hadn't enjoyed the kiss. He'd heard her moans and groans, the way her tongue had latched onto his, drawing his tongue into her mouth just as hard as he'd been pulling on hers.

He watched as she quickly walked to the door, appreciating the way her jeans hugged her curvy backside.

She snatched the door open. "Yes?"

"A delivery for you, ma'am."

The guy handed her a huge bouquet of flowers. She closed the door behind her and stared at the floral arrangement in a state of total shock. "Someone sent me flowers," she mumbled, carrying the huge vase of flowers over to a table.

"Did they?"

She barely glanced over at him. "Yes." Then she opened the card and looked back at him in surprise. "They're from you."

Yes, they were from him, but he hadn't counted on being here when they were delivered.

"Yes, tomorrow is your birthday."

She nodded slowly as she put the card aside and looked at the flowers again. "They are beautiful. Thank you."

"You're welcome."

She looked back at the flowers a moment and then looked at him. "Why?"

"I told you, tomorrow is your birthday."

She shook her head. "No, I'm not just asking about the flowers, Angelo. I'm talking about you and me. We've kissed twice now. What's going on?"

He drew in a deep breath. "What do you think is going on?"

She lifted her chin. "I thought I was supposed to be helping you with Lela."

"You are," he said.

"But why do I get the feeling there's more to it than that?"

"I don't know, you tell me."

She glared at him. "What I will say is that people don't go around kissing each other for no reason."

He couldn't help but smile. "You're right. There is a reason. I want you and you want me. You can deny it, but your kiss tells me a different story."

"Could be I just needed that kiss."

Angelo chuckled. "Could be." He smiled. "So what's my excuse?"

"You're a man, you don't need one."

"Ouch." He glanced at his watch. "I think I need to let you rest for a while. You seem a little grouchy. I'll be back to take you to dinner around—"

"That's not necessary. I'm not going anywhere with you."

If Peyton thought she could avoid him then she had another thought coming. "Remember our agreement about Lela."

"She's your problem, not mine."

He nodded. "Yes, but we agreed. And I expect you to keep your end of the bargain."

"And if I don't?"

"You will. You say you're not a coward, and I'm taking you at your word. But if you don't think you can handle a little competition from a woman like Lela then I understand."

She stiffened her spine. "I can handle Lela, but I'm warning you, Angelo. Keep your hands to yourself."

He stared across the room at her and the tension between them was palpable. He knew her stubbornness would keep her from backing down and it was the same way with him. "I'll be back at seven."

"You do that, but I might not be here."

When he reached the door he glanced back over his shoulder, met her gaze. "Wherever you are, I will find you."

Chapter 10

The place was perfect, Peyton thought as she glanced around. She'd first seen the lighthouse when she'd arrived and had inquired about it then. The resort concierge had told her it was a place that was popular if you wanted to be alone and a good place to watch the cruise ships.

Although it was located on the grounds of the resort, it was a couple of miles from Dunwoody Cove. She figured Angelo wouldn't look for her here. He would think that she had run scared, but she really didn't care. She was feeling down about her thirtieth birthday and the only thing she wanted was to be left alone.

When Angelo had left her earlier that day, she hadn't bothered taking a nap as planned. Instead, she had packed an overnight bag and rented a car. After making a pit stop at a market, she had driven along the scenic route to the Dunwoody Lighthouse, which stood well over two hundred feet tall. The outside of the lighthouse was built to resemble the black-and-white spiral pattern of the Cape Hatteras Lighthouse. But that's where the similarities ended. Once inside, the entry opened onto a bank of elevators next to a spiral staircase. Each floor had a parlor and at the top was a beautiful circular bedroom just below the lantern room.

She'd told the receptionist at the resort front desk that she was going shopping in case Angelo inquired about her whereabouts. So here she was at the very top of the lighthouse, standing on the balcony overlooking the Atlantic Ocean. She was glad she'd brought along a shawl to ward off the summer breeze from the ocean. She watched the ships passing. Most were cruise ships, all brightly lit. The view from the top of the lighthouse was simply breathtaking.

She rubbed her arms to ward off the chill. Even with the shawl she felt the cool breeze off the waters. She was grateful the lighthouse room she had rented for the night—the only one in the place—was available. It provided the solitude she wanted. She planned to stay overnight and all day the next day as well. She would turn thirty in peace and quiet, and *alone*.

She tried ignoring the loneliness she was feeling. This was the first birthday in years that she wouldn't be celebrating with Mac and Sam. Even when they lived in different cities, they had always gotten together on her birthday, especially since they knew how hard it was for her after her grandmother's death.

Peyton missed her two best friends, but knew that considering everything, this was probably how things would be from here on out. Honestly, there was no way she could expect things to remain the same. She had to be fair to Mac and Sam as well as to herself. She had to move on with her life. They would call her tomorrow—she had no doubt of that. And when they did, she would pretend she was having a wonderful time and even make up names of guys she'd met to satisfy their curiosity. They didn't need to know the truth. No one needed to know that on her thirtieth birthday, she was the loneliest she'd ever been in her life.

She stretched before walking back inside. The studio was a nice size, despite its circular design. She'd never been in a round room before and found the idea rather interesting. In the center of the room was the spiral staircase that led to the lantern room. The king-size bed was covered in beautiful white linens with large fluffy pillows. There was a room divider that separated the bedroom from the small eat-in kitchen, which had a mini-fridge and a microwave that was built into the cabinets. There was a spacious spa bathroom with an enclosed shower and a sitting area with windows that faced the ocean.

Peyton glanced at the table where she'd placed the items she'd purchased from the market—sandwiches, cheese, chips, a magazine and several wine coolers. She smiled, thinking she mustn't forget the Little Debby snack cake. What would a birthday be without a cake? She studied the beautiful flower arrangement Angelo had given her for her birthday. It was a nice gesture. She couldn't remember the last time a man had sent her flowers. A guy she'd dated some time ago had told her that she really wasn't the flowers type. At the time, she hadn't taken offense and thought he was probably right since she'd never really considered it. But for some reason, Angelo's flowers made her appreciate them in a way that surprised her. It was something she definitely wasn't used to. Was it the arrangement or the fact that Angelo was the one who sent them?

Drawing in a deep breath, she crossed the room, grabbed a wine cooler off the table, placed it in an ice bucket and went back outside to the balcony to watch the ships passing by. She had some serious thinking to do. Why after all this time was she attracted to Angelo? Granted she hadn't been with a man in almost a year. But still, was she that hard up? And if so, why him when she knew what he was about?

Moments later she glanced at her watch. In less than four hours she would be turning thirty, which was depressing enough. And now on top of that she had to figure out how to deal with the likes of Angelo Di Meglio.

Angelo climbed the steps of the lighthouse, all the while thinking that if Peyton was here, he was going to wring her neck...but only after kissing her senseless for the hell he'd been through over the past two hours.

When he discovered she wasn't in her room, he had assumed she'd already left to go downstairs for dinner. However, he hadn't been able to find her anywhere and began to panic until someone mentioned they had seen her leaving. Then he really got pissed when the resort personnel wouldn't divulge any information—even to him—citing the privacy policy, something he was damn well aware of since he had implemented it.

Luckily Saul had felt sorry for him and had pulled him aside and told him that the car Peyton had rented was parked in front of the lighthouse. Angelo hadn't wasted any time getting here. And now that he was, he wasn't sure how he would handle the situation after chewing her out...*and* kissing her. He couldn't forget that part.

The main door to the lighthouse was locked but Saul had given him a key. The older man had asked if something was going on between Angelo and Peyton that first night, and Angelo assured him there was. He was glad Saul trusted him.

He quietly closed the door behind him and glanced up and saw how high the spiral stairs went and sighed upon seeing the elevator. He had been to the lighthouse before on a tour but had forgotten just how nice it was. He remembered being told it was used mainly as a honeymoon retreat and to spend a night there cost a pretty penny.

He found out that Peyton had rented the place for two nights, which meant she didn't have a problem paying to be alone on her birthday. Why? Why would she not want to celebrate with others? Sam and Mac had planned to take her on a four-day cruise. But he had talked them out of it and suggested Dunwoody Cove—insisting that they not come along. At first they balked at the suggestion until he talked to them individually, pleading his case.

He stepped in the elevator, and was anxious to see Peyton. He was probably the last person she expected to see tonight. Did she really think she could pull a stunt like this and he wouldn't come after her? Evidently she did.

The elevator came to a stop and the door swooshed open into a tiny parlor encased in glass that provided a stunning view of the ocean. His gaze swept around the room. He remembered the setup. At the time he had thought the studio would be the perfect hideaway. Evidently, that had been Peyton's thought as well.

Suddenly he heard the sound of soft, jazzy music playing, and a song that somehow fit the place. He moved from the parlor into an area that was bathed in soft light from a single bedside lamp. He glanced around and saw the huge bed, the flowers he'd sent her, a big bag of chips and several wine coolers in an ice bucket. From the looks of it, she had started the party without him.

He wondered where she was and was about to call out her name when he heard the sound of soft sobbing. He moved toward the open French doors and that's when he saw her. She was wearing an oversize T-shirt covered with a shawl, curled up on a chaise longue facing the ocean with a wine cooler in her hand—crying. The tough-as-nails attorney was bawling like a baby.

He moved toward her. "Peyton?"

She jerked her head around and accusing eyes bore into him. "What are you doing here, Angelo? How did you find me? Who told you?"

He came to a stop in front of the recliner, deciding to sum up her questions in a single answer. "Doesn't matter, I'm here."

She wiped at her eyes and looked away, as if she was embarrassed he had caught her crying. "It does matter. I don't want you here. I want to be alone. So go away and let me enjoy my birthday in peace."

He lifted a brow, wondering if that was what this was all about. He'd heard some women got pretty damn emotional when it came to their birthdays—especially ones ending in a zero. He never took her for the emotional type. But if she was it didn't matter one iota…except for the fact that she was in tears.

He eased down beside her on the chaise as she tried scooting away from him. "Did you hear anything I said, Angelo? I don't want you here."

"At the moment it doesn't matter what you want," he said, reaching out for her and pulling her toward him while lifting her slightly to place her in his lap. She hadn't resisted, which meant some part of her needed to be held.

The one thing he knew not to ask was whether or not she wanted to talk about it, so he decided to use another approach. "Getting old can be a bitch, can't it?" he asked softly, holding her gently. "But then it's not all bad considering the other alternative, which is death. Then you wouldn't have to worry about it one way or the other."

She pulled back and glared at him. "If that was meant to be funny..."

"No, Peyton, it was meant to be serious. And I think if you take a moment to look back over your life and consider all the things you've accomplished over the past thirty years, then you'll agree that you have lived a very successful and productive life."

He pulled her back closer into his arms. He liked the way she felt pressed against his chest. "Now take my advice and take a moment."

Holding her in his arms and listening to her even breathing, he reflected on the exact moment he realized the depths of what he was feeling for her. It had been at Mac's wedding when a couple of Luke Madaris's rodeo friends had been checking her out, much too overtly to suit him. He'd watched them and brooded over it. He fought back the desire to knock the hell out of a few of them before FDR, who'd evidently seen Angelo's anger, had asked what was wrong. He'd told FDR nothing, but he'd known at that moment it was *something*. It took him another year to finally admit to himself just what that something was.

"It's not the same for men."

Her words cut into his thoughts. He glanced at her as he dabbed the tears from her eyes with a tissue. "What isn't?"

"Turning thirty."

He nodded, deciding not to disagree with her, even though he felt the inclination to do so. "How is it different?" he asked.

"Men think about…just what you said earlier. All their accomplishments and all they've achieved. While women think about what they haven't achieved. For some, but not all, what they think about most is the lack of a ring on the third finger of their left hand or the fact that they don't have children."

He rested his chin on the crown of her head as he felt a glimmer of hope. "Are you saying you want those things? The ring on the finger? Motherhood?"

She shook her head. "No, that's not what I'm saying. But things aren't the same anymore."

He was trying like hell to follow her. "Aren't the same anymore for whom?"

"Sam, Mac and I," she continued. "We're still close and everything. But we used to do practically everything together. Now they have their own lives. They have husbands. They have babies."

Now he understood. Mac and Sam were married and were mothers.

"Don't get me wrong, I'm happy for them. But we don't get to hang out like we used to," she interjected. "They have other priorities, and I understand that. And I don't want to sound like a whiner, but I miss our girls-night outings."

She not only missed them, he concluded, she felt left out in the cold without them. She'd probably had these feelings for a while, but on the eve of her thirtieth birthday, it was hitting home, hitting hard and making her realize that in addition to getting older, her life was changing.

He wondered how he could reason with her, make her see that this particular change was all good. Should he come clean and tell her that Sam and Mac had planned to spend her thirtieth birthday with her and that he had talked them out of it?

He remained silent and held her in his arms. Even two hundred feet high they could hear the sound of the waves washing against the shore, the ruffling of ship sails in the wind and the occasional sound of crickets. There was so much he wished he could say, but knew he would have his chance in due time. And now was not the time. Right now she needed him for another reason. She needed him to be there whether she admitted it or not.

"Angelo?"

He glanced at her. In the darkness he could barely make out her features. "Yes?"

"Why are you here?"

She'd given him an opening to level with her, and God knows he wanted to. But he still wanted more between them, before he bared his soul…and his heart. "You were supposed to meet me for dinner," he reminded her.

"I told you I wasn't coming."

"I guess I didn't believe you."

Neither said anything for a few brief moments. "How did you find me?"

"I called Alex Maxwell."

He heard her soft chuckle. Alex Maxwell was married to one of the Madarises and when it came to solving cases or finding people, he was legendary. Everyone in the Madaris family joked that if anything or anyone was ever missing, just call Alex.

"Seriously, Angelo, how did you find me?"

He wasn't about to throw Saul under the bus. "I have my ways."

She breathed in a deep sigh. "Did it ever occur to you that I didn't want to be found?"

"No, especially not when—" he glanced at his watch "—in less than forty minutes you'll be celebrating your birthday. Do you honestly think I'd let you celebrate it alone?"

She didn't answer. "When I arrived a few nights ago and checked out the place and saw all the good-looking guys here, I initially had another plan to celebrate my birthday."

He really didn't want to know she'd been checking out other guys. "What had you planned?"

He could see the hint of a smile forming on her lips. "I figured when the clock struck twelve on the eve of my birthday that I would be in bed with one of them, in the middle of having the big O. Now isn't that hilarious?"

He didn't see a damn thing funny about it—not a single thing.

"What good is celebrating the big 3-0 without having a big O in the process?" she said, chuckling.

He didn't see a lot of good in it, especially if her bed partner was anyone but him. "Well, I guess that won't be happening. You're going to have to come up with another fantasy."

Her gaze lifted to his face. "Why should I have to when you're here?"

Angelo froze. And when he was able to get his heart back to beating normally again, he said, "Come again?"

"Now that you mention it, it's been more than a year since I've been in bed with a man."

He drew in a deep breath, thinking that was way too much information, especially considering how he felt about her. Like just now, when he inhaled, he got more than a whiff of her cologne. He'd picked up her scent, a luscious aroma that made his erection ease into a hard throb.

"You're not going to say anything?" she asked him.

He reached out and took the wine cooler from her hand. It was practically empty. "Yes, I'm going to say something. You've had too much to drink again tonight."

She shook her head. "No, I haven't."

"Yes, you have, and I hope it doesn't become a habit."

She slowly eased up to face him and wrapped her arms around his neck. "I've decided I want to celebrate, after all. I was going to do it alone, but since you came here uninvited I might as well put you to work."

He stared at her, assessing her honesty, and liking the feel of her arms wrapped around him. He could see her features a little more clearly now with the light streaming in from the bedroom. Her eyes were clear, but he thought he saw a hint of mischief in them and couldn't help wondering what was going on in that pretty little head of hers. "Put me to work doing what?"

She leaned closer to him and whispered against his lips, "Making love to me."

Chapter 11

He wasn't saying anything, Peyton noted. He was just staring at her with those gorgeous dark eyes of his. And why did he have to smell so good, so delicious and so masculine? Her mouth hovered close to his lips. All she had to do was stick out her tongue and quickly lick them. How would he react if she did that? They'd already kissed twice, and he'd initiated it both times. How would he respond if she took things into her hands and...

"You don't understand what you're asking me to do."

His words invaded her thoughts. Did he think it was the wine cooler talking, controlling her thoughts, her desires? Granted she felt warm and relaxed, but it was because he was holding her. She was in his arms. She had wanted to be in his arms before, but hadn't allowed herself to think about it. But she was about to turn thirty—in a matter of minutes—and wasn't her birthday supposed to be about her and what she wanted?

Okay, maybe she had given him too much information, especially about the big O. But she hadn't slept with
a man in over a year. She'd put her desires and needs on
hold, case after case after case. Simply put, she needed
to get laid. But not just with anyone, only with him. He
was someone she knew and trusted. She knew he was
a man who would not hurt her.

"I think it's time for you to go to bed, Peyton."

His words heated her lips, and she knew what he
was saying. "Only if you get into bed with me," she responded boldly.

He shook his head slowly. "I don't think that's a good
idea."

"You think too much." With that, she leaned in and
did what she'd been tempted to do many times, especially when he'd stayed at her place and she'd bumped
into him late one night when she'd gotten up to raid the
refrigerator only to find he'd had the same idea.

She took her tongue and slowly traced it across
his lips. She felt the way his stomach muscles tightened against her torso and heard his sharp intake of
breath. "What do you think you're doing?" he asked
through tightened lips, as if he were too afraid to
open them for fear she might go further. Now, who
was the coward?

She smiled at him as butterflies floated around in her
stomach. But she refused to back down now. "I'm being
naughty. I've been a good girl for a while, at least I've
tried. I don't even use as much profanity as I used to.
I've been working hard. I haven't given Judge Cham-
bers another ulcer with my courtroom theatrics, and I'm
even doling out more compliments than I normally do.
But tonight I don't want to be nice. I want to be naughty.
Got that? And more than anything I need to get laid."

She chuckled softly, thinking that she couldn't be any more blunt than that. She watched his eyes darken, and with the way she was sitting on his lap she could feel the moment his erection came to life, becoming more rigid under her backside. She liked the way it felt pressed against her like steel.

Their mouths were just inches away from each other. "Um, something is starting to grow I see," she said playfully.

"What do you expect? You're a very desirable woman."

Her eyes widened at his words. Did he really find her desirable? He could have any woman he wanted and there were a slew of them back at the resort just itching to get into his pants. There was no doubt in her mind that good old Lela would just love to jump his bones. But he was here with her, and with an enormous hardon. She met his gaze. "You think I'm desirable, huh?" she said softly.

"Hell, yes."

She licked her lips and felt him harden even more. "How desirable?" she asked.

"More than you need to be at this moment and that could be dangerous."

She lifted a brow. "Dangerous for who? You or me?"

He reached out and softly stroked the side of her face and said in a husky tone, "Both of us."

It wasn't what he'd said, but how he'd said it that made her panties wet. Then there was the way he touched her face, the gentle way he'd caressed her body. Such tenderness from him turned her on *big-time*.

She held his gaze as he moved his hand from the side of her face and pushed a few locks of hair behind her ear. "You probably won't remember any of this in the morning," he said in a soft voice.

"Wanna bet?" She knew he thought she'd had too much to drink, but he was wrong. She always drank wine coolers when she wanted to relax and unwind. She could handle them and the effect on her was no more than what a couple of beers would have on him.

He glanced down at his watch. "You don't have much longer now."

He was right. She didn't have much longer. What she'd said earlier was true. She wanted to be naughty. Since he wouldn't make the first move then it was up to her to do so.

Wiggling off his lap, she stood up and tugged at his arm. "Come on, Angelo. Make yourself useful and make love to me. It's my birthday, and I should be able to have what I want. And I want the big O. Either you do it or I'll go find someone else." She was lying of course. She only wanted him.

He eased up off the chaise longue. She could tell from his expression that he hadn't liked what she'd said. His glare said as much. But she hadn't expected him to respond by reaching out, grabbing her and pulling her into his arms. "No other man is going to make love to you—*ever!*"

For a second she thought he sounded possessive, serious, even a wee bit territorial. She pushed the thought from her mind. He probably didn't mean it the way it had sounded, she was sure of that. But now that she had his attention, she might as well go for it. "Well I guess you better do what you need to do then."

She shrugged the shawl off her shoulders and whipped the T-shirt over her head and stood stark naked before him. She gave him one of those what-you-see-is-what-you-get kind of smiles and before she could draw her next breath, he had swept her off her feet and into his arms.

Angelo deposited Peyton in the middle of the bed as his gaze raked over her naked body. Simply put, she was beautiful. He'd seen her in next to nothing before. One day when she, Mac and Sam had been out by his parents' pool, she'd been wearing a skimpy bikini. He'd taken it all in and had imagined those parts of her body the bikini had covered. Now he was seeing everything.

She had pushed him over the limit. This was not how he'd imagined things would go in his quest to make her his. He had wanted to take his time. Was there no justice in the world with a woman like her? The woman was temptation. Had he really thought a relationship with her wouldn't be complicated?

"Are you going to just stand there and stare at me or are you going to take care of business?"

Oh, he planned to take care of business, all right. But first he needed to make sure they understood each other—completely. He ran his gaze over her again, tried not to concentrate on the dark curls at the juncture of her thighs. But damn if that part of her wasn't calling out to him—big-time—and his manhood was throbbing mercilessly in response.

Placing a knee on the bed, he reached out and angled her face in his hands to fully see her in the soft light from the bedside lamp. He wanted her to see him. He wanted to make sure she understood. "Let's get something straight. If I make love to you, I claim you. Do you understand that, Peyton?"

He could tell from the look in her eyes that she really didn't understand. She had no way of knowing the extent of what he really meant. But eventually she would.

Making love to her meant she would become his in a way she never thought possible. Not just now, but even after they parted. No matter where she was—night or day, seven days of the week—once he made her his, that was it. She would be his forever.

She shrugged. "Yes, I guess so."

He shook his head. "There can't be any guessing about it. You either understand or you don't."

She threw her head back and narrowed her gaze at him. "Fine, I understand." She raked her gaze up and down him, noticed his erection had enlarged even more. "Boy, you're big. Come on. Let me test the waters."

Oh, he planned on letting her do more than just test the waters. She was about to take the full plunge. "As long as we understand each other," he said.

"All right already. I said I did, didn't I? Now let's get it on."

If he didn't want her so damn much, if he didn't crave her with every fiber of his being, he would've pulled her into his arms and held her, sang "Happy Birthday" to her and then rocked her to sleep and nothing more. But now the die had been cast. She'd asked, and he intended to give her whatever she wanted. Heaven help him, but at the moment the only thing he could think about doing was burying himself between those luscious thighs of hers.

He stepped back from the bed, kicked off his shoes, removed his socks and began unbuttoning his shirt. She watched every move he made. That was fine with him. He wanted her to see it all because just like he claimed her, he wanted her to claim him as well.

Angelo heard her sharp intake of breath when he eased his jeans and boxers down his legs and stepped out of them and then stood before her, naked and fully erect. Never had any woman aroused him so profoundly. His pulse surged in response to her reaction at seeing him without any clothes. He believed in staying physically fit and regularly worked out at one of the exclusive sports clubs in Manhattan. It seemed his hard work was paying off.

He moved toward the bed and took note of the heated look in Peyton's eyes. She wanted him. That much was pretty damn clear. He wished he could say she wanted him for all the reasons he wanted her, but he couldn't be sure. He had to change his strategy and would have to try a new approach, but it was okay as long as the end result was the same.

He moved toward the bed, trying to maintain control when all he wanted to do was rip the bedsheets off to get to Peyton. Where was patience when you needed it? Once his knee touched the mattress, Peyton leaned forward on her haunches to meet him, making no attempt to hide the fact that she wanted him. He wanted her, too, and was certain the room was so steamy that the gentle breeze off the patio couldn't cool them down. His nostrils flared when he picked up her scent and desire rushed through every part of his body. He reminded himself to take things slow, but doing so proved to be extremely hard.

"Do you have any idea how much I want you?" he murmured, his words a warm breeze across her lips. He watched as her full lips parted in a way that sent a sensuous spike up his leg and straight to the head of his erection.

"No. Show me."

Oh, he could do better that that. He reached out and took her mouth in a long, druggish kiss.

* * *

Be careful what you ask for...

Peyton released a gasp the moment Angelo's tongue invaded her mouth, claiming everything it touched, tasted and devoured. He had kissed her twice before, but never like this—never this boldly, possessively. It was as if he'd found a new frontier, and he intended to conquer it on his own.

She felt the warmth from his hand spread across her waistline, while the other hand moved slowly toward her breasts. How did he know her nipples were aching, throbbing for his touch? At that moment he did something with his tongue to reclaim her attention. Rapid-fire heat swept through her. Where had he learned to kiss like this—using some sort of whirling technique that sent fire to her lower extremities? If he could work his tongue like this in her mouth, she didn't want to think what he could do with it down below. The thought made her womanhood throb in anticipation. Heaven help her.

He released her mouth and before disappointment could overtake her senses, his lips latched onto a nipple and she nearly arched her body off the bed. "Calm down, baby," he whispered from the side of his mouth. "I just want to cop a taste."

How did she know he intended to do more than that? The pressure of his mouth caused her womanhood to tighten with each deep-throated suckle. He used his tongue to graze kisses lightly across the tips of her hardened nipples, making her body shiver.

"Angelo," she groaned in sensual pleasure.

Instead of answering, he moved to the other nipple, closed his mouth over it and tormented it the same way. She knew the moment his free hand began traveling down her body, over her stomach, past her waist. And when he got to the pubic curls below, she felt his hand delve inside, clutching him at the exact moment he inched a finger inside of her.

She moaned when he touched her clit, and then he begin fingering her, pushing her over the edge, bringing her back and then pushing her over the edge again. This was more pleasure than she could have ever imagined. Her muscles clenched his finger, and she panted long, deep breaths. The need he was building inside of her was almost killing her, working her into a sexual frenzy.

He released her nipples and began using his tongue to lap his way down her torso. "What are you doing to me?" she asked in a tortured moan.

He stopped for a second, lifted his head and met her gaze. "Claiming you."

He nibbled around her belly button then traced a ring around the center with his tongue. He pulled back, sat on his knees and lifted her legs up over his shoulders. And then he lowered his mouth to her, going straight for the opening of her womanhood.

He used his tongue in ways she couldn't have imagined, couldn't have begun to anticipate. Unbridled sexual sensations tore through her as she bolted upright in acute pleasure, and murmured his name. When his tongue did that wiggly, figure-eight movement again, she couldn't help but scream.

"Angelo!"

She screamed his name not once, but twice. She couldn't pull back even if she wanted to. His mouth was locked on to her, and he used his tongue as a weapon of mass seduction. She cried out in sexual ecstasy, turning her hips as if to escape his mouth, and then thrusting them forward. This was too much—more than she'd asked for—a lot more than she had expected. His mouth was driving her mad with need and desire.

A shudder passed through her, and she moaned his name just seconds before her body erupted in one incredible explosion. Angelo held onto her hips tightly, keeping his tongue planted deep inside of her, refusing to let her go. He kept lapping up the taste of her as if he were a starving man. It was only when the last shudder had passed through Peyton's body that he pulled his mouth away and lowered her legs from his shoulders.

"Condoms are in my wallet."

The need to be taken by him had Peyton's senses reeling. Desire was burning her skin. "Okay, but I'm on the pill if you prefer going that route. I'm safe," she said, easing on her back, barely having the strength to do so.

"I'll take that route. And I'm safe, too."

She knew from Sam that Angelo always practiced safe sex, so she believed him. She extended her arms to him as he eased into her embrace and wedged himself between her open legs. He leaned down and kissed her, taking her mouth with the same intensity he had earlier. She moaned when she felt him, the hardness of his erection trying to slide into her. The head of his erection was slick and massive and she couldn't help wondering how on earth she was supposed to take it in.

She shifted her hips as he gazed down at her. "You're small."

She shook her head. "No, you're just big, but I can handle it."

He drew in a deep breath. "You sure?"

She wasn't sure but that didn't much matter. She wanted him and somehow her body would adjust. It had to. "Yes, I'm sure."

Taking her at her word, he held her hips and before she could blink he had thrust inside of her. Fire rushed through her veins the moment he did so. She remembered watching him undress and seeing the thatch of dark hair that bedded his groin and knowing that thatch was pressed against her and his entire manhood was embedded deep inside her sent shivers reverberating through her.

He glanced down at her. "You okay?"

She nodded. "Yes."

"Now we're going to make love," he whispered.

He slanted his mouth across hers the exact moment the lower part of his body began thrusting deeply in and out of her. His tongue kept time with the rhythm of his body's thrusts. And each time the hard length of him slid in and out of her, all she could do was moan in pleasure.

He released her mouth just long enough to ask, "You like that?"

Unable to speak, she could only nod. Yes, she liked it. She loved it. Her hands went to his shoulders, clutched him and held on tight as he rode her hard. She was grateful the mattress had a good spring to it, because they were definitely giving it a hell of a workout.

"Come now," he whispered hoarsely against her lips. Her body obeyed his command, and she was caught in the throes of one hell of an orgasm—the magnitude of which she'd never experienced before. It was as if her entire body became fragmented into a million little pieces.

"Angelo!"

"Happy birthday, Peyton," he said as he continued to ride her. She knew at that moment it was midnight and he was giving her just what she wanted on her birthday, the big O. His timing was perfect. It was one hell of a way to celebrate turning thirty. She could feel herself letting go, and she cried out his name when the surge of sensuality toppled her into sweet oblivion.

Still Angelo kept riding her—straight into a second

orgasm. She'd never had two orgasms back-to-back. Now on her birthday, in this bed inside the lighthouse at Dunwoody Cove, he was giving her the orgasm of a lifetime and plunging her body into mindless ecstasy.

When she thought she'd reached her sexual peak, he called out her name as his body jerked and bucked. She felt a stream of hot release shoot off inside of her, coating everywhere inside her, instinctively spewing straight toward her womb. Her pelvis responded as pleasure ripped through her body.

She had turned thirty in the throes of what had to be the biggest, most intense orgasm any woman could ever imagine. Even the aftershocks had her moaning and groaning as her body continued to quake and quiver as every muscle in her body felt electrified—reborn.

"Happy birthday," he whispered again before lifting his body off hers. He pulled her into his arms, cradled her close to his body. Completely exhausted and feeling unadulterated pleasure, Peyton closed her eyes as sleep overtook her.

Chapter 12

Angelo awoke to the scent of a woman and couldn't help the smile that curved his lips when he saw that Peyton was still asleep in his arms. Had they slept like this through the night in this same position with her legs entwined in his? Her buttocks were pressed against his manhood, which was getting more aroused and rigid with every breath he took.

The primal instinct in him wanted to beat his chest after having claimed the woman he wanted. But he had a feeling that one night of lovemaking with Peyton didn't mean any guarantees, and it was way too early to pop the champagne. There was a chance that when she awoke, she wouldn't remember anything about last night. She might even accuse him of taking advantage of her in a weakened state. She probably wouldn't believe him if he told her that *she* had been the sexual aggressor and the first one to strip her clothes off to entice him.

Regardless, if he had to do it all over again he would. And he was looking forward to doing so again. Never in all his thirty-four years had he felt so connected to a woman, so much so that her orgasm had triggered his own. He had felt the explosion that tore into her body as if it had ripped through his own. And moments later, it had.

Everything about last night had been perfect and so damn erotic—from the sound of flesh slapping against flesh, to their moans and screams and the scent of sex that had permeated the air around them. Her birthday had definitely been a night to remember. He knew it was one he would never forget.

"I'm hungry."

He went still. She'd spoken? He could have sworn she was still asleep. "Excuse me?"

She eased onto her side in a way that still kept their legs entwined. "No, I won't excuse you. After last night I'd think you'd want to feed me."

So she had remembered. In fact, she didn't seem at all bothered by waking up having shared a bed with him. "What would you like?"

"Um, hot pancakes with maple syrup and sausage links are probably out of the question, so I'll settle for anything you can get."

"All right. Now can I ask you something?"

She smiled sweetly at him. "As long as it's not too personal."

He had news for her. What he was going to ask was probably as personal as it gets. "Do you remember us making love?"

She gave him a look. "I said I was hungry, Angelo, not brain-dead. Of course I remember. If there was any doubt in my mind, my aching muscles are more than a reminder."

He studied her for a moment, thinking her just-woken-up look was cute, sexy and too much of a turn-on at eight o'clock in the morning. "And you have no regrets?"

"Am I supposed to?"

"I hope not."

"Then don't worry because I don't. What woman would after a night like last night?"

He smiled and felt his chest expand. He was certain his head swelled a few inches. "Yeah?"

"Yeah. Those were the best wine coolers I've ever had."

His smile fell and his chest and head deflated. "Wine coolers?" It was then that he saw the smirk on her lips. "It wasn't the wine coolers and you know it, Peyton."

She deliberately snuggled closer to him and held his gaze. "Then tell me, Attorney Di Meglio, exactly what was it? What on earth would have me screaming my lungs off like a madwoman if it wasn't the wine coolers?"

He shifted positions to ease his body over hers, his legs parting hers. He stared down at her and smiled. "Instead of answering let me give you a demonstration."

Peyton continued to lie in bed long after hearing the door close behind Angelo. Now she knew where the term Italian Stallion came from and it had nothing to do with *Rocky*. How one man could have such staying power, so much stamina, she'd never understand. But what she did know was that Angelo took the prize. If she never walked again it would be entirely his fault. Thanks to him, last night she'd used muscles she hadn't known she had. And how on earth had he come up with that see-saw position. She didn't have to close her eyes to remember how her body had felt like it was almost suspended in mid-air.

Her sore muscles reminded her of everything she'd done last night. She wished she had the leisure of soaking in a hot tub, but unfortunately the room only had a shower. Angelo had left to go get breakfast, and she intended to shower and dress before he returned.

She thought about her conversation with Angelo when she'd awakened. He'd thought she would have regrets or wouldn't have remembered anything about last night. She'd had no regrets, and she remembered everything. Sleeping with her best friend's brother wasn't something she thought would happen, but it had. Besides, it wasn't as if they would continue the affair beyond their time together at the resort. So who was to know and who'd get hurt? Certainly not her. She knew the kind of games that were played when it came to wealthy playboys. Hadn't she fallen hard for Matthew Elton, a guy who was from a wealthy Boston family? It wasn't until her sophomore year of college that she'd learned why Matthew never invited her home with him. She didn't have a clue until she'd overheard him telling another guy that he needed to come up with a reason to avoid inviting her home for the holidays, since she would never be accepted by his family because of her background, and that he could never take their relationship seriously. To this day, Matthew had never found out the truth about why Peyton left Yale. She'd been so hurt by his betrayal that she made up the excuse that she needed to transfer to the University of Illinois to be closer to home.

She had learned a hard lesson, one she would never

forget. There were the Eltons, the Waltons, the DuPonts and…the Di Meglios, and everybody else. Even Mac and Sam had married well, even though Sam's family was already wealthy. Hadn't the Di Meglios tried playing matchmaker for Sam countless times? The rich always married the rich. It was as simple as that. No one—not even Mac and Sam—knew about Matthew Elton and the pain of his rejection.

She heard her cell phone ring and smiled. Evidently Angelo had already forgotten what she said she wanted for breakfast. She picked up the phone off the night-stand. "Okay, what did you forget?"

There was a pause on the other end. "Mac and I should be asking you the same question since you haven't bothered calling to let us know if you're dead or alive, still single or married," said Sam.

Peyton rolled her eyes. "I didn't know I had to check in."

"Don't be a smart-ass, Pey. Happy birthday."

She smiled, hearing Mac in the background. They had her on speakerphone. "Thanks, guys."

"Well, how is it going?"

There was no way she was going to tell Sam about her and Angelo sleeping together. "Everything's going fine," she said. "This is a beautiful place, and I want to thank you both again."

Mac and Sam proceeded to sing "Happy Birthday" to her in their off-key voices. "Thanks, but I don't feel any older." And she meant it. Whoever said age was nothing more than a number knew what they were talking about. In fact, she felt wonderful, full of life and sore as hell.

A few minutes later she hung up the phone, feeling good about herself and the day ahead. She had the light-house until early afternoon and although she enjoyed

Angelo's company, she needed time by herself to think and regroup. Besides, once they left Dunwoody Cove they would go their separate ways. She would swear Angelo to secrecy about their affair. The less anyone knew the better. There would be no questions asked. She eased out of bed, remembering she wanted to take a shower and be dressed by the time Angelo returned. She didn't have to imagine what would happen if he found her still in bed without any clothes on.

Angelo stepped off the elevator and almost laughed out loud. Peyton was belting out a few lines of "R-E-S-P-E-C-T." He shook his head thinking Aretha Franklin she was not. Not even close.

He set the bags on the small kitchen table and glanced around. He followed her voice into the bathroom and entered just in time to see her toweling her body dry. He leaned against the door unobserved. This was the woman he wanted. Regardless of the fact that she couldn't carry a damn note.

When she came to the end of the song, he said, "I hope you're not holding out for a record deal, Peyton."

She spun around, clutched her hand to her chest and took a deep breath. "What are you trying to do, scare me to death?"

He smiled. "No more than your singing that song is scaring me. Aretha ought to sue you."

She tossed her head back and lifted her chin. "Kiss my butt, Angelo."

He moved toward her. "If I remember correctly, I did that very thing plenty of times last night. I bet you have passion marks all over your backside."

Her cheeks blushed, and he couldn't help but shake his head at the comparison of her behavior just hours ago. The woman had been a temptress in bed last night and now she was shy and demure. She held the towel tightly around her body, as if he hadn't seen her naked already. "I wasn't expecting you back for a while."

He shrugged, deciding not to tell her that he had hurried because he didn't want to be away from her any longer than he had to. "The café wasn't crowded."

"Oh."

"I'll set the table while you put on some clothes. Otherwise, we won't be eating."

He knew he didn't have to spell out just what that meant. He wanted her again. She was already in his blood, under his skin and connected to him in a way no woman had ever been before.

He turned to leave. "Mac and Sam called," she said.

He turned back around. "Did they?"

"Yes. They wished me happy birthday."

He put his hands in his pockets. "You knew that they would."

She nodded. She didn't say anything for a minute but continued to look at him as if there was something else on her mind. "Is there anything else you want to tell me?"

"I didn't mention anything about you being here."

He could tell by the way she'd said it that she expected an argument. He didn't intend to give her one. He simply shrugged. "That's your prerogative."

"You don't have a problem with that?"

"Like I said, it's your prerogative. I'll get breakfast ready."

She came out of the bathroom a few minutes later. He took one look at her and knew why he'd fallen for her and fallen hard. Dressed in a pair of black leggings, a print mini dress and with her hair pulled back, he thought she was beautiful.

He exhaled slowly and turned back around to take the food out of the bags. It was either stay busy or cross the room and take her hard—just where she stood.

"I'm starving," she said, interrupting the quiet.

He turned back to her and smiled. "So am I." She didn't need to know he wasn't starving for food but for her. "Come on, let's eat."

Chapter 13

"So what do you have planned for today?"

Peyton glanced up from taking the last bite of her pancakes and met Angelo's gaze. She wondered why he was asking. Of course being in the throes of passion when the clock struck midnight was one hell of a way to ring in her birthday. And she didn't want to think about how those gorgeous, dark eyes staring at her made her pulse race like crazy. But seriously, she knew better than to let good sex go to her head, although she had to admit it had been the best she'd ever had hands down. And she wasn't about to get attached to a man whose family had money. She had learned the hard way. A broken heart took a long time to heal. Hers had healed years ago—despite the emotional scars—and she didn't want a repeat performance.

"Why do you want to know?" she asked, wiping her mouth with a napkin.

"Because I intend to spend it with you."

Wrong answer, she thought. He would not be spending any more time with her. "I haven't planned anything yet, but whatever I do it will be alone."

He tilted his head to the side as if staring her down. "No, it won't. There's no way I'll let you spend your birthday by yourself."

Did he think he had a choice in the matter? Besides, why was he making it a big deal when it wasn't a big deal to her? Hadn't he done what she'd expected? The fact that it didn't bother him that she hadn't told Mac and Sam that they had been together pretty much meant that last night had only been about sex to him. It had been nothing more than a one-night fling.

She met his stare. "There's no way I won't be spending the rest of my birthday solo," she said in her most determined voice.

Peyton had to give it to Angelo. He had a way of looking at her that made her think twice about refusing to give in to whatever he wanted. She wondered if it was the same look he gave jurors in the courtroom to win a verdict. If so, then that was just tough. Little did he know, but *stubborn* was her middle name and she rarely backed down from a fight.

She stood when he didn't respond and felt the heat of his gaze on her back when she carried her plate over to the sink.

She was standing at the small sink when she felt the heat from his body as he stood directly behind her. He reached out and snagged her around the waist, pulling her body snug against him. She felt his erection, hard and firm on her backside. If she measured his desire by the size of his erection, then it probably wouldn't have taken much to push him over the edge.

She turned to face him. "Okay, Angelo, I feel you, loud and clear. We'll have another roll between the sheets before you go."

If his expression was anything to go by, he didn't seem pleased with her response. "Do you think that's all I want, Peyton?"

Maybe it was her, but she really thought it was a stupid question. "Yes, that's all I think you want."

"Then you're wrong."

If it wasn't all he wanted, then what else was there? The last guy she was involved with thought her charge card also had his name on it, but Angelo certainly wasn't after her money. More than once her last "boyfriend" of two weeks had tried getting her to pay for dinner, even though he had been the one to invite her out on a date.

She crossed her arms over her chest. "Then tell me, if that isn't it, what do you want?"

"I want you to get to know me better."

Now she was really confused. He wanted her to get to know him better and not those sensuous lips of his? Or that humongous erection he was packing?

She reached out and felt his forehead with the back of her hand. He was slightly warm. She wondered if he was running a fever or maybe the tropical heat was affecting him. He definitely wasn't thinking straight. "Okay, Angelo, what's this about?"

"Don't you remember last night?"

Of course she remembered last night. "Yes, what about it?"

"Our agreement."

She frowned wondering what agreement he was talking about. "Refresh my memory about the agreement."

"You're mine."

She stiffened. "Excuse me?"

"I said you're mine. Last night before I made love to you I warned you that I would claim you."

Peyton stared at him, remembering the conversation she'd dismissed as nonsense. She had agreed because she'd wanted him so much that she would have agreed to just about anything. At the time she'd thought it was just his ego foolishly talking about claiming her. Angelo certainly wasn't the type to *claim* a woman.

"Fine. Well, now I'm backing out of the agreement," she said with finality.

"Sorry, I can't let you do that."

She glared. "And why not?"

Now he was the one who crossed his arms over his chest. "Because I told you what I want."

"You can't be serious."

"Trust me, baby, I am."

"Well, too bad. No one claims me."

"I do, and I did." He reached out and hauled her into his arms.

Angelo muttered a low groan the moment his tongue touched Peyton's. If she thought for one minute he intended to allow her to weasel her way out of their agreement then she had another thought coming.

And speaking of coming…

He was convinced he could do that very thing with just this kiss. Fire was quickly spreading to his loins. She was laying it on thick with her tongue, which greedily mated with his, as she sucked on it with a fervor he felt throughout his body. He was the one who initiated the kiss, but she took it to the next level with her lip-lock, exerting so much pressure that it forced him to deepen the kiss even more. Angelo obliged her, going tit for tat, devouring her mouth with a desperation that astonished even him.

Already his erection was throbbing so insistently that it wouldn't have taken much to haul Peyton over to the bed and lose himself between those luscious thighs of hers. But doing so would defeat the purpose. He wanted her to know that there was more between them than just sex.

But when he felt her hand slip between them to toy with his zipper before slowly easing it down, his mind began debating whether making love some more wasn't such a bad idea. Lovemaking was a form of communication, and if he couldn't get her to go along with his plan, then he wasn't above using whatever means necessary to win her over.

When she inserted her fingers through the opening of his jeans, between the slit in his boxers, to palm his shaft, his mind went blank. Her touch had sparks of electricity shooting through him. She broke off the kiss and started licking the side of his face, using the tip of her tongue in a way that only made him moan her name. He reached out and cradled her face in his hand as she moved lower to his neck. What seemed like firing pistons scorched his abs.

"You're bigger than you were last night," she said, pausing long enough to prolong the torment. "I want to see if that's the case or if it's just my overactive imagination."

Yes, he wanted her to see his emotions. He also wanted her to feel them, too. When she released him and began unbuttoning his shirt, he knew she intended to kiss and lick him all over. The thought of that nearly brought him to his knees.

He drew in a deep breath and decided if he didn't

put a stop to this, that's just where she intended to go—down on her knees, taking him into her mouth. The very thought of that upended what little control he had left. He was certain if she did so, he would be addicted to her mouth. He was a healthy, hot-blooded male, and she was bringing him to heel.

The horn blast from a cruise ship close to shore had the effect of dousing water on a blazing fire. Angelo stopped Peyton moments before she was about to drop to her knees. Taking her by the arm, he eased her back up.

A luscious smile curved her lips. "You sure you want me to stop?"

Although he desperately wanted her to continue, he knew it was best that she didn't. "No, I don't want you to stop, but today should be all about me treating you and not the other way around. And since you don't have any plans for your birthday, I'll make some for us."

"Us?"

"Yes, us, so get used to it. I plan to stick to you like glue today and make love to you again tonight."

She raked her gaze over him. "Get used to what? You sticking to me like glue or you making love to me?"

He lifted her chin. "Both."

"And what if I don't agree?"

He reached out and slid his palm up and down the back of her neck. "Then I'll just have to convince you that it's in your best interest. And I intend to start doing that later, right over there in that bed."

She pulled back and placed her hands on her hips. "Sorry to disappoint you, but I'm supposed to check out of here by four."

He shook his head. "Not anymore. When I got breakfast at the resort this morning I had someone check the reservations, and this place is still available for the next couple of days."

She narrowed her eyes. "That doesn't mean I can afford it."

"I wouldn't expect you to. I reserved it."

He saw her reaction, and it wasn't good. "You had no right to do that, Angelo. I don't need you to pay for me like I'm destitute."

"I wasn't. Will it make you feel better to say I had ulterior motives since I plan to get something out of this anyway?" He could just imagine what she thought he had in mind, but for the moment he'd let her think whatever she liked. In the end, she would discover just how wrong she was about his motives.

"So come on, Peyton, put your shoes on so we can go. The day is flying by."

"And just where do you think we're going?"

A mischievous smile touched his lips. "Parasailing."

Angelo and Peyton returned to the lighthouse late that afternoon. Parasailing had been just the beginning. It had been a full day of activities that included looking for buried treasure in the dunes, snorkeling in the Atlantic, bird watching and nature hiking on several outer islands. They even rented bicycles to ride around the island.

Peyton dropped down on the loveseat in the suite, too tired to go any farther. Through the glass windows she could see the ocean and could tell a thunderstorm would be rolling in later. Angelo had suggested they stop by the resort to grab more clothes. She had been prepared to run into Lela, but they hadn't. She watched Angelo put the bags on the bed before rejoining her in the parlor.

He kicked off his shoes and dropped down to the floor beside the sofa, lying flat on his back. He was exhausted and understandably so. They had crammed a lot of activities in that day. He had made her birthday special and she'd done things she'd always wanted to do but had never found the time for.

The highlight of her day was when they stopped to eat at a restaurant on one of the piers and the staff came out and sang "Happy Birthday" to her and presented her with a cake with candles. There was no way the restaurant would have done that unless it had been arranged beforehand. The thought that Angelo had gone to all the trouble to make her birthday special touched her.

"Thanks, Angelo."

He glanced up at her. "For what?"

"For today. You made my birthday special, and I appreciate that."

He pulled up into a sitting position as a smile curved his lips. "It's not over yet. Look over there."

She glanced past him and saw that someone had lined the spiral staircase that led up to the lantern room with colorful balloons. At the top of the landing was a candlelit table set for two. Her hand flew to her mouth in total surprise. It was the most romantic thing she'd ever seen.

She glanced back at him, amazed. "How? When?"

He chuckled. "I made arrangements with the resort staff to come in while we were out."

She just stared at the brightly colored balloons and the huge one with the words "Happy Birthday." "You did this for me?"

"It's your birthday. I wanted to make it special for you."

As far as she was concerned, he'd done so, starting with the lovemaking at midnight. She was deeply touched by the gesture. "Thanks, Angelo," she whispered, fighting back tears.

Peyton doubted Angelo knew how much everything he'd done meant to her. She'd been determined to spend her birthday alone. Not only had he stopped her from doing so, but he'd made sure it was a birthday she would never forget.

"Come on, let's get ready for dinner. The chef will be sending his staff over to feed us soon."

Chef? Staff? It all sounded pretty formal, and she was wearing a mini-dress and leggings. He must have read her mind. "You look fine."

"But I want to look even better. Give me a few minutes to freshen up." She quickly jumped up from the sofa and rushed over to her suitcase on the bed with their clothes. When they returned to the resort, he had suggested they toss a couple of items of clothing into one bag for the sake of convenience. She had agreed, but now as she opened the luggage it seemed too personal finding his change of clothes mixed in with hers. She pulled out what she needed and raced off to the bathroom, closing the door behind her.

After a quick shower, she began to get dressed. She blushed at her reflection in the full-length mirror on the back of the bathroom door that plainly showed the passion marks on her body. She closed her eyes momentarily, remembering the exact moment each one was made. She knew the memories would remain etched in her memory, and there was no need to pretend otherwise. Although she was good at bluffing, if the truth be told, her sexual experience was limited. She'd preferred it that way. But last night Angelo had taken her beyond anything she had thought possible.

And she knew tonight he planned on a repeat performance. Although she didn't want to admit it, she wanted a repeat performance, too. She shook her head smiling. Her good friend Sam had helped send her here because she thought Peyton needed to get laid. But little did Sam know her own brother was doing the honors.

A firm rap on the bathroom door interrupted Peyton's musings. "Yes?"

"The chef and his staff were here and are gone now. I don't want your food to get cold," he said.

"I'll be right out."

She quickly finished dressing and added a light application of makeup. She took a second to study her reflection in the mirror. Tonight, on her thirtieth birthday, she looked just as she did on her twenty-ninth. She couldn't help but giggle at the thought, even though she felt different now. The difference wasn't obvious to the naked eye. But today was the first time she'd been with a man with whom she'd felt relaxed and completely herself— there was no pretense on her part. She actually enjoyed herself and had fun. And the man who made her feel that way was Angelo.

"Okay, girl, come back down to earth," she chided herself. "Before you get any crazy ideas, remember Matthew." She drew in a deep breath, knowing there was no way she would ever forget that painful lesson. Still there was no reason she couldn't enjoy the moment. And since Angelo had gotten it into his head that he had every right to claim her, she wanted to see just how far he would take it. She was smart enough to know that even though he'd said he claimed her, it would only be while they were in the Bahamas. They had a little more than a week left on the island, and she was convinced that by the time they left he would be back to his old self again.

In the meantime, she would enjoy the "I Claim You" game they were playing. If claiming her meant more days like today, she didn't have a problem with that.

Chapter 14

Angelo turned around the moment he heard the bathroom door open. His fingers tightened on the wineglass he was holding. He was about to take a sip, but paused and lowered the glass from his lips. He had given himself a pep talk earlier, reminding himself not to pounce on Peyton again anytime soon…at least not until after dinner. But now he wasn't so sure. She had to be the most beautiful, desirable woman he'd ever seen.

"I thought you stopped doing that, Angelo."

He lifted the glass back to his lips to take a sip. He needed something to take his mind off of his arousal. "Stopped doing what?"

"Staring."

He shrugged. Okay, so he had been staring. Some things just couldn't be helped. Like a man's reaction to a beautiful woman. "It bothers you when I stare?"

She smiled. "Honestly, I think it would probably

bother just about anybody, especially if the person doing the staring had your eyes."

"My eyes?"

"Yes, you have the most penetrating stare of anyone I know."

Funny, he'd been thinking about penetration of another kind. He decided to put that thought to the back of his mind. "Ready for dinner?"

"Yes, I'm starving." She crossed the room. "What about you?"

"I'm hungry as well." *Good thing she didn't ask me what for.*

"Then by all means, let's eat," she said.

They climbed the stairs, and when they reached the top, she glanced around the room. The lantern room was open and spacious and surrounded by glass windows. A huge decorative lantern was in the center of the room. The table was set for two and had vanilla-scented tapers in the candleholders. Angelo had placed the flowers he had sent yesterday in the middle of the table.

"The flowers are still beautiful," she said, taking the chair he pulled out for her.

He had to agree. The flowers were still beautiful. But nothing, he thought, was as beautiful as she was at that very moment. The candlelight danced off the profile of her face, making her appear even more beautiful.

"You're staring again, Angelo."

"Sorry."

"No problem. What do we have to eat?"

He chuckled, appreciating her appetite. Instead of answering the question he uncovered each dish. "So what do you think?" he asked.

A smile touched the corners of her mouth. "I think

if claiming me means I get to eat like this, then you can claim me anytime you want."

If only it were that easy, he thought. She said that now, but he knew when the time came she wouldn't be singing the same tune.

"So how are you handling your newfound fame?" she asked.

He chuckled. "Not very well."

"Which is why you came here."

He wondered how she would react if she knew she was the real reason he was here. "I guess you could say that."

She nodded. "I thought I would probably never say this, but I'm glad it worked out this way."

He lifted a brow. "What way?"

"That we ended up here together, at the same time. That's some coincidence."

Not really, he thought. *Just planning,* he mused, taking another sip of wine.

"I'm surprised we didn't run into Lela when we went back to the resort earlier," Peyton said.

He shrugged. Of course he wasn't going to mention that yesterday, when he'd been frantically trying to find out where Peyton had escaped to, Lela had made a nuisance of herself one too many times. She'd tried cornering him in an elevator and started taking off her clothes. She had gone too far. And because her actions had violated the resort's harassment policies, she had been forced to leave. The only thing he had to say was good riddance.

"Everything is delicious."

He smiled and glanced over at her just as she bit into a dinner roll. There was something about the way she took it into her mouth that had his stomach clench-

ing. And when she used her tongue to lick some but-
ter from her bottom lip, he shifted in his seat to tamp
down his arousal.

He needed to touch her, so he reached out and captured her hand in his. "I'm glad you're enjoying it. Like
I said, I wanted this day to be special for you."

Their gazes held, and at that moment he realized not
only was he firmly holding her hand, but his thumb was
stroking it. Her skin felt soft to the touch. He released
her hand, knowing that if he didn't, they wouldn't make
it through dinner. The room was charged with electricity, and he felt it. He was actually inhaling it and decided then to make the first move.

"So tell me, what was the most memorable part of
your birthday?"

He saw the blush that quickly tinted her features and
figured out what she was probably thinking about—the
orgasm at midnight.

"Doing something I'd never done before."

"And what was that?" he asked, playing along.

He watched her draw in a deep breath before she
leaned forward. As if they were in a room filled with
people and she didn't want anyone else to overhear what
she was about to say, she whispered, "Falling asleep with
a man still firmly embedded inside of me."

Peyton saw Angelo's reaction to her words in the
darkening of his eyes, the flaring of his nostrils and the
heated curve of his lips. He was replaying the image of
what she'd said in his mind, thinking about it and remembering. And what she'd told him was true. That
had never happened to her before because she wouldn't
have let it happen. But with him, she hadn't wanted to
separate from his body.

"And why is that most memorable, Peyton?"

She looked at him. His voice was deep by nature, but it sounded even lower, throatier and sexier. It seemed he wanted her to spell it out in detail. She could do that, but would Angelo be able to handle it. Would she? She'd never thought *talking* about sex was a turn-on. But if that's what he wanted, then she didn't have a problem with it. No telling where it would lead…

She leaned back in her chair, crossed her legs and felt the temperature between them rise a few degrees. "Knowing that you'd already come, but you were still hard was a first. Talk about staying power. I felt every inch of you deep inside of me. You kept me aroused and fulfilled in a way I've never been before."

She paused. "It was a tight fit—tight yet satisfying. It felt like the perfect fit. It was as if that's where it belonged."

She chuckled. "At least my body thought so at the time. Even though I was drained, I didn't want you to pull out. There's just something about that connection—skin to skin, just lying there with you. I know it sounds crazy, but at that moment it had felt so right."

There, she'd said it. And now that she thought about it, she'd probably said too much. Some things she should keep to herself. But she was finding that talking to Angelo came easily, even when it shouldn't have—at least not for her. She wasn't one to prattle on, and she'd definitely never had this kind of conversation with a man. Yet she'd spent the past few minutes telling a man how good it felt to have him snug inside of her, even though they weren't making love. She wondered if he thought she had gone off the deep end or something.

He wasn't saying anything, just sitting there staring at her with those penetrating eyes of his. But she could hear his breathing becoming labored. She couldn't help wondering what he was thinking.

Then suddenly, everything that surrounded them ceased to exist when he slowly stood and moved to where she sat. Without saying a single word, he reached out his hand to her, and she took it. He was going to make love to her again. His intent was reflected in the depths of his eyes, in his stance and definitely in the huge erection pressed against his zipper.

She was not immune to his silent seduction. In fact, the fire stirring within her—most notably at the juncture of her legs—made her ease out of her chair and stand so close that her body was pressed smack against his.

"Now let me tell you how I feel being inside of you," he said huskily, as he leaned close and whispered into her ear. Her heart rate increased at the thought, and then she practically held her breath, anxious to hear him describe their lovemaking.

"You and I are a perfect fit," he said. "And the moment I was skin-to-skin inside of you, I felt your heat. You were so damn hot, all I wanted to do was drown in your inferno. You clutched me, your inner muscles held me tight. I was a willing hostage, and I never wanted to escape. You were wet, and I wanted to make you wetter. And when you exploded, shuddered in my arms, I've never felt such intense pleasure all the way to my bones. All I wanted was to hear you cry out and call my name."

And she had, several times during the night. And each time she'd done so, he had clutched her body closer, thrust into her deeper. There was no doubt in her mind that he had made love to her the same way he handled all of his business—thoroughly and completely.

She drew in a deep breath. His words had stirred up a thick cream that was flowing through her. His words were more erotic than anything she'd heard before, and the feeling of lust and need was building deep inside of her. A part of her wondered if he actually meant everything he'd said, or was he just saying what he thought would be a fitting response to her sensual confession.

He didn't give her much time to dwell on the sincerity of his words. The next thing she knew he had backed her up against the wall.

Angelo wasn't sure which pulse point was pounding more—the one in his neck, wrist or his manhood. Probably the one in his groin, which would be the reason for the aching throb lodged there.

First things first, he thought, going straight for her lips, and uttering a guttural moan. The feel of her body pressed between him and the wall sent bolts of carnal pleasure shooting through him. And when he slid his tongue inside her mouth, her taste sent everything inside of him rocking. Never had he experienced such eroticism from kissing a woman. But Peyton wasn't just any woman. She was his.

When she began kissing him back, drawing his tongue into her own mouth and doing wild and crazy things with it, he nearly buckled at the knees. With the strength he had, he slid her up steadily against the wall while lifting her dress and spreading her legs as she wrapped them around him.

He didn't remember unzipping his pants or releasing himself. But he was well aware of the exact moment he eased between her wet womanly folds, entered her and began thrusting deep and hard at a mind-boggling pace. An urgent, primal groan rumbled deep in his chest with each thrust.

And then she screamed, loud enough to burst his eardrums. The sound snapped his control, and he began shuddering from the force of the climax that ripped through them both. Never had he experienced a climax so powerful, so earth-shatteringly explosive.

She wrapped her legs around him, locking their bodies tighter while he continued to thrust and rock into her—taking all she had and giving her all he could give. More than he'd ever given any woman.

He broke off the kiss and closed his eyes as sensations continued to ram through him as her body clenched him, demanding even more. And he gave it. For once, he didn't hold anything back. And then, unable to help himself, he said her name, and when she tilted her face upward, he leaned forward and kissed her again, taking her mouth in desperation that bordered on starvation.

Passion mingled with a fierce need suffused his entire body. And when she broke off the kiss to catch her breath, he began nibbling around the corners of her mouth. It was as if no matter what, he couldn't get enough of her. Deep inside he knew the truth of the matter was that he never would.

Chapter 15

Peyton lay in bed as desire raced through her body the moment Angelo walked into the room. He had awakened early to go jogging on the beach, shirtless in a pair of running shorts. It should be outlawed for any man to have a body that looked like his. Just watching him had her breasts tingling and heat simmering through her.

He had a rock-solid chest that was brushed with dark hair that led a trail down toward the waistband of his shorts. Then there were his shoulders, which she had clung to as her fingernails dug into them. And the firm thighs that would hold her steady, almost immobile, with each and every hard thrust. Last, but not least, were his legs. Most men didn't know that women admired their legs just the way they liked women's legs. His were long, muscular and hairy, just the way she liked them. She was turned on just remembering his legs entwined with hers after they'd made love and he'd held her in his arms. He also used his muscular legs to spread hers, right before…

"Ready for breakfast?"

Her eyes gazed back up at his face. He was looking at her in a way that made her wonder if he could read her mind. If so, then he knew breakfast was the last thing on her mind. "Yes, but I have to get dressed. It won't take long to throw something on."

"No rush. You can flash me anytime you like."

He was leaning against the door, and the look he gave her sent more heat flooding through her body. Peyton sat up in bed and looked at his hands that were resting at his sides. She remembered everything his hands were capable of doing, and how they could make her feel. How those hands touched her all over, especially between her legs, and made her scream.

The sound of Angelo clearing his throat made her glance back up at his face. "Did you say something?" she asked, swallowing deeply. Peyton was almost certain that he had said something, but her mind was on other things—like tasting and licking him all over, the same way he'd done to her last night.

"Yes, I asked if you were hungry."

Um, it depended on just what he had in mind for her to put in her mouth. "Why do you ask?"

"I thought we would spend some more time—"

"We can't do that," she interrupted. She had a good idea what he had in mind. "We agreed that we were returning to the resort today."

He shrugged. "Only because you insisted."

Yes, she had. Even though he had wanted to foot the bill for the entire stay at the lighthouse, she had refused to let him. So they had compromised by splitting the bill for the three days they'd stayed. They planned to return to the resort, even though she knew Angelo would have preferred staying at the lighthouse. He liked the privacy and seclusion the lighthouse provided. She did, too, but all good things came to an end. Just like the affair she was having with Angelo. And when it did, she tried to reassure herself that she would be able to handle it, since she had no expectations of anything more.

She grabbed her bathrobe and quickly slid it over her naked body, tying it around her waist. "How was your run on the beach?"

"Fun. You should have come with me."

She threw her head back and laughed. "Thanks to you, I didn't have any energy."

He chuckled. "You want to blame me for that?"

She did blame him. "Yes."

He had definitely started it before they'd finished eating dinner last night. That had been the beginning of their lovemaking. Afterward, he carried her downstairs and they stripped each other's clothes off before continuing things in bed. Later that night, he called the resort to have dessert delivered. And for the finale, he had poured wine all over her and lapped it up.

"If you're not starving and can hold off eating breakfast for a minute, I want to take you someplace with me."

She arched her eyebrows. "Where?"

"It's a surprise, and I think you'll like it."

Now he had her curious. "All right." She quickly moved toward the bathroom to get dressed.

Angelo could tell by the look on Peyton's face that she liked this place. He had discovered it while out jogging, and from several conversations with her, he knew that a secluded spot like this would become her favorite.

The area was on a remote part of the island with a private lagoon hidden behind marshland that extended out from one of the pristine white sandy beaches. He had been jogging along the beach, not paying much attention to what was beyond the six feet or so of coastal grasses on the other side. When he'd heard the sound of rushing water, he stopped and pushed aside the Typha reeds to reveal what was the most beautiful lagoon he'd ever seen, surrounded by palm trees, natural vegetation and a coral reef. He asked one of the resort groundskeepers about the property and was told that it was privately owned by a family living on the island. Although the resort had tried negotiating with the family for years to buy it, they had refused all offers to sell.

He watched as Peyton dropped down in the sand and looked around, amazed by the sheer beauty of the spot. He knew how she felt since he'd been bowled over upon first seeing it as well. It was small but simply breathtaking.

"It's so calm here. So peaceful," she said moments later.

He had to agree. This was like having a little piece of heaven. He told her that it was owned by a family who refused to sell it to the resort.

"I can't blame them," she said, letting the sand filter through her hands. "It's beautiful here. I could have used a place like this a few weeks ago, after the stressfulness of my last case."

"I can imagine," he said. Angelo knew the man-hours that went into preparing for trial, not to mention the time spent in the courtroom. He knew that in addition to Peyton's beauty, she was smart as a whip and invested time and energy in every case no matter who the client was. According to Sam, Peyton had gotten a scholarship to go to Yale, but had left in her sophomore year to be closer to home and her grandmother. After law school, she had turned down a six-figure job at a well-known law firm in D.C. Instead, she had taken a job in Chicago that paid less than half of what she could have been making.

She took on cases Mac and Sam had concerns about and put her all into every case, winning many of them. She didn't know it, but he'd followed most of her cases. And it always amazed him how she pulled it off even when victory appeared doubtful. In his mind, she was the kind of lawyer the media should be focusing on, not him. But she fought for the underdog, and took on those cases that didn't matter to the media. But to her, they did matter.

He sat on the ground beside her, feeling tired. They had stayed up making love last night and when they did grab a few hours of shut-eye, they'd awakened with the urge to mate again. The desire had been mutual and each coupling had been even more explosive than the last.

The only reason he had left their bed to go jogging was to give her body a rest. She was like an addiction he couldn't kick. And when she'd told him how she felt when they made love, their passion seemed like the most natural thing. He'd never gone to sleep still embedded in a woman, and it was as if that's where he was supposed to be.

"Would you like to come back here for a picnic before we leave?" he asked, glancing over at her as he leaned back, cradling his head in his hands.

A huge smile lit her lips—lips he'd tried devouring last night.

"Do you think we can?"

"Yes." No need to tell her he already had a plan in the works to make it happen.

"Then, yes, I'd love to. Thanks for sharing this place with me," she said, glancing up into the sky. "It's rare when I can just go somewhere and sit and enjoy nature's beauty."

She chuckled. "I thought of buying some land in Oklahoma, on the outskirts not far from Luke and Mac's, and building a place. But the first time I heard one of Luke's men mention something about a mountain lion being spotted in the area, I changed my mind. That's all I need is to have to tangle with a mountain lion or some other wild animal."

Angelo smiled, thinking that if it came to that, he'd put his money on Peyton. There was no doubt in his mind that she could handle herself.

"But first things first," she said. "We have to go back to the resort and tackle Lela. I'm sure she's fit to be tied that we've been missing in action for the past few days."

He shook his head. "No need. Lela's gone now."

She raised a brow. "Gone?"

"Yes. I had management ask her to leave."

"Why?"

His jaw tightened. "That day that I was looking for you, she cornered me in an elevator and began taking off her clothes."

"Wow! Evidently she didn't learn her lesson with that NFL player."

"Evidently."

"So with Lela out of the picture there's no reason for us to pretend to be in a relationship, is there?"

"I think you need to understand something, Peyton," he said calmly, glancing over at her.

"What?"

"All pretenses between us stopped when we made love."

She pushed a lock of hair from her face. "You're really hung up on that 'claim me' thing, aren't you?"

"Yes, I guess I am." He had news for her. He was more than just hung up on it.

She gave him a long-suffering look. "Okay, for how long?"

"How long?"

"Yes, for how long? How long do you intend to be in this possessive mode?"

Angelo suddenly saw his future flash right before his eyes. He saw her in a long white wedding dress, and with a baby in her arms, and then…

She snapped her fingers in front of his face, making him blink. "What on earth are you thinking about that has you smiling all over the place?" she asked him.

He decided to be honest with her, at least somewhat. "I saw my future flash before my eyes."

"Really?" she said, evidently intrigued. "What was it? An upcoming case or something?"

He shook his head. "No—something a bit more personal…my wedding day."

She threw her hands over her mouth to keep from laughing out loud. "Your wedding day? I didn't know there would ever be such a day. I hope I'm around to see it."

"Actually, Peyton, you will be around to see it."

She tilted her head to look at him. "How can you be sure of that?"

He stood and smiled down at her. "Because in my premonition, you were the bride."

Chapter 16

Peyton suddenly got a funny feeling in her stomach as she studied Angelo's face. She couldn't tell whether he was serious or just pulling her leg. Moments later, when his lips eased into a smile, she figured he had to be kidding. "The bride? Yeah, right."

He held his hand out to help her up. "I take it you don't believe me."

She rolled her eyes as she came to her feet to stand in front of him. "Angelo, you don't believe yourself. Why would I be the bride at *your* wedding?"

He chuckled, and she tried to ignore how the sound sent shivers all through her. "I guess that means we're getting married one day."

She began walking beside him as they strolled back toward the lighthouse. "No kidding. I guess that also means the tooth fairy is real."

He stopped walking and turned to her. "Anything is possible."

Yes, anything was possible. However, she wouldn't hold out for his crazy premonition, because it wasn't going to happen. She hadn't decided if she would ever marry, although the thought briefly crossed her mind whenever she would see Mac and Sam with their husbands, and how happy the two men had made them. But she just didn't see herself as a candidate for the wedded-bliss thing.

First of all, she worked crazy hours, too crazy for a husband who probably wouldn't understand or accept the amount of time she spent at the office. Second, the thought of a man crowding her space was a major turn-off. Granted, she and Angelo had spent the last few days at the lighthouse together, but she liked her space.

They began walking again, and he asked, "So what are your plans for today?"

She glanced over at him. He was changing the subject, which meant that bride stuff had been total nonsense, after all. In a way she was glad. Yet another part of her was disappointed. *Why?* "I haven't thought much about it. I'm going to have to get used to having people around again."

"We can always find another place to escape to."

She stopped walking and placed her hands on her hips. "Excuse me, Mr. Di Meglio, but *we* didn't escape anywhere. I was looking to spend some alone time, and you…"

"Found you, and we spent some wonderful time together," he interrupted. "Right?"

She couldn't deny it and wouldn't. She nodded. A slight smile replaced her frown. "Yes. They were nice." They began walking together again.

"You never said what you planned to do today."

No, she hadn't because she didn't have any plans.

"Not sure, although I'm sure there're a lot of activities going on at the resort that I'll check out."

"That *we* will check out."

This *we* stuff was beginning to hit a nerve. "I hope we aren't getting clingy, Angelo."

"Um, clingy like this?" he said, reaching out and grabbing her around the waist and pulling her body against his. He was solid and being pressed against him felt right. She could remember how solid and hard this same body felt against hers while naked.

"Peyton."

He whispered her name, and the sound seemed to caress her skin, clear her head and revitalize her. She was wearing a tank top and a pair of shorts, and they were standing so close, her legs were brushing against his.

She opened her mouth to answer him and evidently that's what he'd been waiting for, an opening to slide his tongue inside. He slanted his mouth against hers and began devouring it with a hunger that astounded her, yet begged her to reciprocate. And when he cupped her backside to bring her closer to him, she felt the hardness of his erection. Instinctively, her body reacted as she placed her arms around his strong shoulders and kissed him back with all the pent-up passion he was stirring inside her.

A part of her brain was saying this must be madness. But another part responded to this most intense kind of pleasure. At first she wanted to think the reason she was responding to Angelo with such intensity was because she'd put her social life on hold for a while, and now she was dealing with years of sexual denial. But deep down she was having doubts. Could any man other than Angelo make her feel this way? Make her do things she'd never done before without thinking twice about it? Make her share her innermost thoughts and feelings?

For the past few days she had been introduced to a hunger the likes of which she'd never known before. Was it her or was it him? Did he have this sort of effect on all women or just the sexually deprived ones? And Lord knows she'd been deprived *and* sexually unfulfilled. She'd never known an orgasm could make her feel this way. She'd been simply amazed at the way her body became so wet and lubricated at the slightest provocation from Angelo. She'd heard about it happening to some women, but never imagined it could happen to her. But all it had taken was Angelo's should-be-outlawed fingers stroking her G-spot at the right time and in the right way.

When Angelo broke off the kiss she pulled in a deep breath. He kept his mouth close to hers. "I love the way you taste, but not just here," he said in a whisper, taking his tongue and trailing it from one end of her lips to the other. "I like tasting you all over, licking you all over. Remember when I poured the wine over you last night?"

How on earth could she forget? He had licked it off of her body, but deliberately poured more of it between her legs, letting his tongue linger between her thighs as he licked it off. But that hadn't been all he'd done. Even now the memories sent shivers running through her body.

"Do you know what I suggest?"

She shook her head, momentarily unable to speak. She swallowed. "No. What?"

"I suggest we go back to the lighthouse and eat. While we were away I arranged for the chef to prepare breakfast. It should be ready now. I think we should go back and eat and then go to bed and enjoy each other. I promise we'll be out of the lighthouse by noon."

God, the man was a master of seduction. The sound

of his voice alone could make her do anything he said. The thought that he had already planned everything should have ticked her off. But what could she say when it was precisely what she wanted to do anyway?

She stared at him and saw the smile that tugged at his lips. They were lips she'd gotten to know over the past few days. Lips that had gotten to know hers as well. There wasn't a part of her those lips hadn't touched, tasted and devoured. And his lips had certainly left their mark on places that made her blush just to think about.

"What's going on in that pretty little head of yours, Peyton?"

She couldn't help but return his smile. He had a way of bringing out the naughtiness in her. "I'm thinking about your lips."

"What about them?"

"How much pleasure they give," she said, easing her lips closer to his.

"Do they?"

"Mmm-hmm. Especially when they touch me in certain places. Your lips and tongue should be outlawed."

His soft chuckle sent blood rushing through her veins. She suddenly stuck her tongue out and snaked it around his lips to cop a taste of him. "I want to learn how to do all the things you do with your tongue."

"Do you?"

She nodded. "I think that maybe tonight I'm the one who should have the wine bottle."

The smile on his lips widened from corner to corner. "Baby, you're on."

Too late she'd realized what she had done. She'd made plans for them to continue what they'd started. With Lela out of the picture there really wasn't a reason. She met his gaze and almost drowned in the dark, sexy eyes staring back at her. She knew at that moment, that yes, there was a need, and it was growing inside of her by leaps and bounds.

"Come on, baby." He took her hand in his, and they silently started walking back toward the lighthouse.

Angelo returned to his room back at the resort with a huge grin on his face. To say he had enjoyed breakfast with Peyton was an understatement. Once he'd gotten her in bed, he had made her forget all about leaving the lighthouse. Even though he made sure they checked out on time, they still had time to indulge in more sexual play.

He was definitely looking forward to tonight, especially after Peyton outlined what she had in store for him. He glanced at his watch. They would meet for dinner around seven and then afterward he planned to bring her to his bedroom since it was larger. After dropping Peyton off in her room so that she could take a nap, he still had time to rest after a game of tennis. He needed to be well-rested for tonight.

He was about to head toward the bedroom when his phone rang. He hoped it wasn't Sam calling again. He pulled the phone out of his pocket and was relieved to see it wasn't Sam, but Lee Madaris.

Since his sister Sam had married into the Madaris family, he'd grown close to the Madarises, especially his brother-in-law Blade's cousin, Lee. They had hit it off right away and since they both enjoyed skiing, they had taken a number of ski trips together. "Lee? What's going on?"

"Just checking to make sure you got my text about the contracts. They will be ready for our signatures in a couple of weeks."

Angelo smiled. "Yes, and I'm ready to sign." Lee and Angelo were partners in a resort hotel development in Dubai.

Lee chuckled. "So am I. I'm looking forward to getting away for a while. I need the change in scenery."

Angelo nodded. Lee was anxious for the resort to be built, and the contract had already been awarded to Madaris Construction, the company owned by Angelo's brother-in-law Blade. Others in the Madaris family were involved, including Jake, the youngest uncle in the first generation of seven brothers, along with Mitch Ferrell and Sheikh Rasheed Valdemon, both of whom were close friends of the Madaris family.

Angelo and Lee talked for another ten minutes or so before ending their conversation. Angelo was just as excited about the Dubai deal as Lee was. The building Slade Madaris had designed was simply elegant and would be one of the most expensive resort hotels the Madaris Construction Company had ever undertaken.

After the phone call, Angelo's thoughts returned to Peyton, and he was definitely looking forward to tonight.

Chapter 17

"And you're sure you don't want any dessert, Angelo? How about more wine?" Peyton couldn't help the smile that touched her lips when she mentioned *wine* and saw the way his eyes gleamed.

"I'm positive. Thanks for asking."

They had been playing a game of cat-and-mouse most of the night, with her dropping hints and sexual innuendos to get him aroused. It made her more daring just knowing she had the ability to stimulate his sexual ego in ways she didn't think possible.

"Then I guess we should call it a night. Dinner was great, by the way," she said, rising to her feet.

Tonight she was wearing a dress she'd bought in one of her shopping trips with Mac and Sam. She could tell by the way Angelo had looked at her when he'd seen her that he liked her in it. She licked her bottom lip, deciding that she was going to make sure he liked her out of it as well.

He walked beside her, and the feel of his hand on her back sent shivers up and down her spine. He must have felt them as he glanced over at her, smiled but said nothing. When they reached the elevator she saw he was annoyed that others had gotten on behind them. Evidently he had hoped that they would be alone.

To torment him further, she intentionally stood in front of him, eased back a little and drew in a deep breath when her bottom came in contact with his hard erection. He reached out and placed his arms around her waist, leaned closer and whispered, "Behave now or pay later."

She didn't have a problem telling him she wouldn't mind paying later when she glanced over at the two other women in the elevator who were trying to keep their eyes off Angelo. She understood their dilemma. The man was eye candy of the sweetest kind.

The elevator arrived at the other guests' floor first. Peyton moved to step out of the way, revealing Angelo's full-frontal arousal, making one of the women's eyes nearly pop out of their sockets. Peyton wanted to laugh out loud. There was nothing like seeing an aroused man.

"You did that on purpose," Angelo growled, grabbing her around the waist and bringing her next to him as they walked down the long corridor to his room.

"Of course not," she said, unable to keep the smile from curving her lips or hide the glint in her eyes. "Why would I do something like that?"

Instead of answering, he stopped in front of the door to his suite and pulled out the passkey. He kept his eyes on her while he opened the door, and when he pushed it opened, she breezed inside.

She stood in the middle of the room and glanced around, and chuckled when she saw the bottle of wine and two glasses. *Lord, the man was prepared.* "Nice room, Angelo."

"Thanks."

"It's a lot bigger than mine, but then I'm finding out you have a knack for doing things in a *big* way. But then I shouldn't be surprised."

Angelo was leaning against the doorway doing what he usually did when they were alone—staring at Peyton. His eyes raked over her face and body and she felt the heat of his scrutiny of her in the most intimate places— her lips, the nipples of her breasts and the juncture between her thighs, especially there.

She stared back, taking him in as well, appreciating his muscular physique, his dark and sexy eyes, and especially his lips. She decided it was time to make her move. She crossed the room to be closer to him.

"You are one fine specimen of a man, Angelo." She tiptoed and leaned into his body and then pressed her lips to his.

Angelo kissed her with all the desire, need and longing that he felt. His passion went deep, all the way to his groin. He reached out and slid his hands over her bottom and down her hips, feeling possessive in ways he'd never felt before. He knew she didn't understand, didn't have a clue about what he felt for her.

He began walking her backward while cupping her bottom until they were in the middle of the suite. He slowly pulled his mouth from hers and studied her face for a minute. Her lips looked swollen, and he liked the look. Hell, he liked every single thing about her—even the little mole just above her lip.

"Tell me what you want." He leaned down and whispered against those same moist lips.

She smiled saucily. "It's not about what I want. Tonight is about you." She reached out and cupped his arousal in her hands as she felt him grow larger at her touch. "Tonight, this is mine."

He bit back the impulse to tell her that what she was cupping was always hers, anytime. Instead he whispered, "What are you going to do with it?"

She lifted a brow and took a step back. And then she reached up to begin undressing him, beginning with his shirt. His heart began beating loudly in his chest when her fingertips brushed against him. He drew in a deep breath when she removed the shirt from his shoulders and then licked his collarbone. Feeling bold, her mouth traced a path down his chest. She glanced up at him and smiled. "Mmm, nice."

She took a step back. "Take off your shoes and socks for me, please."

He wasted no time doing as she requested, placing his socks in his shoes and kicking them aside. She moved closer to him and slowly removed the belt from his slacks and tossed it aside as well. Unable to resist his lips, she stood on her tiptoes again and glided her tongue over them.

"Anticipation is killing me," he growled when he reached to slide his hands under her dress. It was shorter than she usually wore, but Sam had pushed her into being daring.

"You mean patience is not one of your virtues?" she asked, moving back to unzip his pants. Because of the size of his erection, it wasn't an easy task.

"Not when it comes to this, and to you."

"Do you tell all your ladies that?" she asked, tugging his pants down his legs.

"No, just you. You're the only one who has ever mattered."

She jerked her head up to look at him. It wasn't what he'd said, but how he'd said it that had given her pause.

"Anything wrong, Peyton?"

She drew in a slow breath, not really sure why her heart had begun beating so crazily in her chest and why every nerve ending in her body was in a frenzy. "No, nothing's wrong." She knew there was, but she didn't want to dwell on it. The only thing she wanted to do was finish taking off his clothes.

She eased down to her knees and slowly pushed down his pant legs and smiled when his shaft all but popped out at her. She laughed. "Down, boy."

"Trust me, he can't go down."

She glanced up at him as she brought her mouth closer to his arousal and used her tongue to lick the massive head of it. "You sure about that?"

"Trust me, I would know."

Peyton leaned back on her haunches as he stepped out of his pants. She couldn't resist reaching out and touching him. His manhood was standing, fully erect, like a real work of art. And she had a thing for the thatch of dark hair surrounding it. A hunger, the likes of which she'd never experienced before, consumed her just from looking at it.

Rising to her feet, she took a few steps back. "Now your turn."

Before she could get the words out of her mouth, he had reached out to pull the dress over her head. He then proceeded to unsnap her bra and her breasts tumbled free. And when he leaned down and captured a nipple in his mouth, between his teeth, and began licking it with his tongue, the sensations that began swirling around in her stomach almost made her forget that tonight was his night of pleasure and not hers.

She reached down and pulled his head away from her body. "Behave, Angelo. You need to finish what you started."

He smiled. "My pleasure."

It was his pleasure, he thought, easing the last stitch of clothing from her body. He stood back and looked at her, and let his gaze take in every inch of her. He liked the smoothness of her skin and the silkiness of the curls covering her womanhood. He felt his tongue thicken in his throat just looking at that part of her.

"You're ready for a glass of wine, Angelo?"

His eyes slowly moved up to her face. He saw the smile that curved her lips and couldn't help but return it. "Yes, I'm ready." If he got any readier it would kill him.

He watched as she sashayed across the room, naked. She had the best-looking backside of any woman he knew—plump yet firm cheeks and a gorgeous pair of legs. He stood there and watched as she poured two glasses of wine. His arousal grew just watching her.

She looked over at him. "Would you like a cherry in your wine?"

He smiled. "I've never had one in my wine before but tonight anything is possible. Right?"

"Tonight, everything is possible." She offered him a glass of wine.

Crossing the room he took it from her hand. "Thanks. You looked great in that dress tonight," he whispered. "And you look pretty good out of it, too."

"Glad you approve." She took a sip of wine. Leaning closer to him, she whispered against his lips, "Mmm, good. Now I want to see how it tastes on your skin. She tipped her glass, and wine spilled onto his skin, trickling its way down his chest to settle in the curls around his groin. "Oops. Don't worry. My tongue will take care of it."

He sucked in a deep breath when the tip of her tongue swirled around the nipples of his chest. Would he be able to survive her brand of torture? He wasn't sure. The only thing he was sure about was that the degree of desire he had for her was infinite.

He began concentrating on what she was doing as she nipped, licked and tasted her way down his chest, lowering her body and grabbing hold of his waist to devour the area around his naval. He glanced down to watch as the tip of her tongue swirled around his belly button. The feel of her hot, wet tongue gliding across his skin sent sensations escalating through his entire body. And when she moved her hand toward his middle and cupped his shaft, he felt every cell in his body become consumed with a need that he felt in every pore.

He groaned her name on a tortured breath the moment she dipped her head and, with her tongue, captured some of the wine that had landed on the head of his manhood. She took him into his mouth in a way that started a throbbing at the base of his testicles and coursed its way upward to the head of his arousal. She went at him, working her mouth and tongue in a way that had him jerking his head back as if he were having a seizure from the intensity of the pleasure she was giving him. Unable to stop, he grabbed hold of her head and his fingers tightened around her hair. The wet, sucking sounds she was making were enough to send him over the edge…and it did.

His thighs tightened, and he parted his lips, emitting a desperate groan that started every nerve ending—especially at the base of his shaft—firing its way up his shaft into an uncontrollable explosion. He tried to pull back, but she wouldn't let him. So he stayed firmly locked between her lips in the warmth of her mouth.

There was no way he could suppress the sigh of satisfaction that flowed from his lips or the shudders of erotic pleasure that continued to make him quake even when she released him from her mouth. He watched as she leaned back and stared up at him as the corners of her lips curved into a smile of unbridled pleasure. It was the look of a woman who had satisfied her man and damn well knew it.

Her man.

More than anything he wanted to be that to her. The man she thought of upon waking every morning and the man she thought about when she went to sleep at night. He intended that he, and he alone, would be the one who'd invade her dreams. When she thought of pleasure, he wanted her to think of him. Whenever she was filled with a sensuous need, he wanted her to think of him.

With a heart filled with need and a devotion she didn't even know existed, he pulled her naked body up into his arms. Instinctively, she wrapped her legs around him as he moved toward the bedroom. By the time her stay on Dunwoody Cove ended, she would know that he was a man on a mission.

Operation Peyton.

Chapter 18

Peyton's next week at the resort seemed to fly by. There were times when she wished that she could capture each and every minute in a bottle and keep it with her always. Although she didn't want to dissect what was going on between her and Angelo, she knew it was safe to say they were fully involved in a relationship. Since returning from the lighthouse, there hadn't been a single night or day that they had spent apart.

He had planned a picnic at the lagoon for them one day, and on another they had rented a car and left the resort to go into town to shop at some of the boutiques. Every day she would tell herself not to get caught up in the time they were spending together, especially since it would be coming to an end soon. But she couldn't help it. Angelo was always so attentive that at times she had to pinch herself to remember this was only temporary. What was happening between them didn't mean anything.

The more they were together the harder it became for Peyton to convince herself that that was true. She was beginning to fall for Angelo, and that wasn't good. She'd always been a loner for a reason. Heartbreak was a bitch. She'd found out the hard way not to put too much stock in relationships, especially when the man had more money than he knew what to do with. Okay, she knew that was a big hang-up of hers, but it was still a problem nonetheless. There were the haves and the have-nots, and she was comfortable in the world where she belonged and not in the one she didn't.

"Ready for breakfast?"

She glanced across the room where Angelo stood holding a breakfast tray. She hadn't heard him return. She sat up in bed and smiled. "Yes, I'm ready."

She knew when it came to him she would always be ready. She had made that pretty darn clear when she thought of the places they'd made love over the past week. Her favorite place had been at the lagoon. It had been absolutely perfect.

Angelo crossed the room and placed the tray across her lap. It was loaded with everything she liked. In the short time they'd been together, he had gotten to know her well. He knew her likes and dislikes…and he knew her tastes. Yes, he definitely knew her tastes.

She glanced up at him. She'd also gotten to know him well enough to figure out when something was on his mind. This was one of those times. He stood leaning against the dresser, watching her eat, and said nothing.

"You aren't going to join me, Angelo?"

He shook his head and smiled. "No, you're the one who needs it for now."

She couldn't help but grin. During the night she had definitely worked up an appetite, but then so had he. But she knew his appetite wasn't always as healthy as hers. At least when it came to food it wasn't.

"We'll be leaving here soon."

She took a sip of coffee. Why did he have to remind her? A part of her had tried to ignore the fact that tomorrow was their last day. At least it was hers. He could come and go whenever he pleased, but her two weeks were officially up. "Yes, I loved it here."

"Would you come back, Peyton?"

She stopped in the middle of biting into a croissant when the answer to his question struck her and struck her hard. No, she wouldn't come back. There were too many memories. There was no way she could come back here and spend time with another man after all the things the two of them had shared here. She knew it was ridiculous, but she thought of this as "their" place. It was the place she had become sexually liberated in his arms. The place she had been able to relax, unwind and enjoy life. *And him.*

Things hadn't just been sexual. Every morning they would take a walk on the beach together, where they would talk. She knew he didn't have any desire to practice law after his fortieth birthday and was working hard to make that happen, independent of his family's law firm. She knew all about the hotel he and Lee Madaris were building in Dubai, and the other business ventures he had invested in.

"I enjoyed myself these past two weeks, Peyton."

His words reclaimed her attention, and she smiled over at him before taking another sip of her coffee. "So did I, Angelo."

"I don't want our time together to end."

She chuckled. "Well, unfortunately some of us have to return to work eventually and—"

"That's not what I mean."

She held his gaze. "Then what do you mean?"

He moved away from the dresser to come to sit on the edge of the bed. "We started something pretty darn good here. You. Me. And I think it's too special to let go of. I claimed you, remember?"

She rolled her eyes. He would remind her of that on occasion, and she would ignore him. "In your mind, what does claiming me mean to you?" she asked.

"Do you really want to know?"

"Yes."

"Honestly?"

She didn't say anything for a minute and then, "Yes, I really do."

There were times when they'd made love that he'd made her feel as if she was the only woman in the world, the only woman that mattered. The only woman he wanted. The only woman that he...

She drew in a sharp breath, refusing to let her mind go there. He didn't love her. He lusted after her and that was the only *L*-word involved in their relationship. But what woman didn't want to feel that way at times, especially with a man like Angelo.

"So what's the real deal, Counselor?" she asked when he didn't say anything.

He gave her a look that at that moment almost took her breath away. She put her coffee cup down when her hands became shaky. It was then that he grabbed her hand and entwined his fingers with hers.

"The real deal, Counselor, is that I intend to marry you."

Peyton narrowed her gaze at Angelo, wondering where that had come from. She remembered that he'd told her that day down at the lagoon about his premonition. She pulled her hand from his. "Be serious, Angelo. Don't play games."

He leaned back on his arms and smiled at her. "I'm not playing games."

She rolled her eyes and picked up a muffin and took a bite. She decided to play along with the game. "Fine! We'll get married, have a bunch of kids, a cute dog, his and hers Snuggies and start our own law practice."

He grinned. "Sounds like a plan to me. Glad you're in agreement." He reached out and snagged his own muffin off the table and took a bite. "I'll talk to the folks when I get back home and you can decide what kind of wedding you want and—"

"Hey," Peyton said, reaching out and touching his arm. "I was teasing, and I hope you were, too."

He leaned in closer and brushed a kiss across her lips. "I wasn't teasing. I'm serious."

Peyton didn't say anything for a moment, just sat there and stared at him. Without saying a word, she removed the tray from her lap and sat it in the middle of the bed. She eased from the bed and crossed the room to grab her pajama bottoms off the floor and put them on. Then she gave him her undivided attention. "Would you like to tell me what this is about, Angelo? You know as well as I do that these two weeks were about having a good time. We did that, and after tomorrow things will go back to being normal for us."

"And did you have a good time?" he asked her in a low, husky voice. He was staring at her with the intensity she had gotten used to over the past two weeks.

"Yes, I had a good time." She decided not to tell him it was really incredible. Even if their lovemaking weren't part of it, she would have still had a wonderful time with him. She'd enjoyed being with him, sharing breakfast, lunch and dinner, taking walks and sharing intimate thoughts—especially once she began to see a side of him she hadn't known.

"And what about me, Peyton? What about our relationship now? Is it different than it was before?"

His question jarred her back to reality. Yes, their relationship was different. How could it not be? Before, he was Sam's handsome-as-sin, fun-loving brother who women drooled over. He'd always been nice to her and spent time with her whenever she'd been around. But he had done the same with Mac. Now things were quite a bit more personal. He knew her physically in ways no other man did. But what was scarier was that he understood her emotionally.

He had made love to her more than any other man had. He had touched her. He had kissed her and tasted her in ways that made her blush just thinking about them. He had penetrated her, and even stayed embedded inside of her, seemingly making her womb a permanent home for a certain body part of his. Over the past two weeks she had begun to feel close to him, to cherish him, want him, need him and lo—

She shook her head, wondering why that one word… *love*…kept creeping into her mind. Why that one word wanted to settle into a place where it didn't belong. Angelo didn't love her, and she knew that. And she simply refused to even consider the possibility. She refused to be the kind of woman who saw an act of kindness, signs of lust and attention, as being more meaningful than they were.

"Peyton?"

He moved the tray out of the way and was now stretched out on the bed, with his head resting against the pillows. It might have been a relaxing position for him, but it wasn't for her. He looked especially appealing stretched out in a lazy, relaxed pose—even with his clothes on. Mainly because she knew firsthand how he looked with his clothes off. And boy did she know.

She drew in a deep breath as she contemplated his question about their relationship. Was it different now than before? "Yes, Angelo, it's different. How can it not be?" she finally answered. "We'd never slept together before. Now we've made love so much, it's practically like we're mating rabbits. Our relationship is more intimate."

She paused. "But all that will end soon, after tomorrow in fact," she said. "When we leave here, things will go back to being like they were."

"Do you honestly think that, Peyton?"

She didn't see why not. She glanced away from him to look out the window. She was a realist and understood reality versus fantasy just as much as she understood the underlying problems that would make a relationship difficult for them. It was all a part of life. She had been taught that lesson early, thanks to Matthew.

With Matthew, she had thought they would marry after finishing college and together they would live a perfect life. He would accept her as she was. But he hadn't been willing to do that. And if Matthew, the first man she'd ever loved, the man who'd taken her virginity, the man who'd carved a place in her heart, had thought her unworthy, then why would she assume anyone else whose family was wealthy would feel any differently?

She glanced back at him. "Yes, I can honestly say that, Angelo. But why are you asking? What's going on here? Why are you making what happened between us over the past two weeks a big deal?"

He shifted his body to sit up in the middle of the bed.

"Because it is a big deal. The reason I came here in the first place was because of you."

She stared back at him, drew her brows together, thinking surely she'd misunderstood what he had just said. "Excuse me? Can you repeat that?"

Angelo would gladly repeat it as many times as she thought she needed to hear it. But the big question was whether or not she was listening. Was she taking it all in? Would she be able to grasp what he was about to tell her *and* believe it as well?

"Yes, I'll repeat it," he finally said, fully aware the next few minutes would be the most important ones in his life. He knew now, at that very second, that he loved her. He hadn't thought it was possible to love a woman as much as he did her. Over the past two weeks he had gotten to know firsthand why he had chosen her in the first place out of all the others. Now he had to convince her of that reason.

"I said the reason I'm even here is because of you. I knew you would be here, and I came to spend time with you."

He watched her brows knit into a frown. Then he saw how anger spread from her eyes to other parts of her face. And when she placed her hands on her hips and her spine stiffened, he knew she was fit to be tied. "Wait a minute. I get it now. Sam mentioned to you that I was coming here and joked about me needing to get laid and you decided to take it upon yourself to be the one to do it."

Now it was his time to frown. He hadn't been aware that Sam thought she needed to get laid. But knowing how his sister's mind worked, he wouldn't doubt she'd said it or thought it.

"No, that's not how it was. I knew you were coming here. In fact, I'm the one who suggested this place to Mac and Sam," he said.

He saw confusion settle in her face. "Why?"

"Because I wanted to be alone with you."

She shifted her hands from her hips to settle them across her chest. "So I was your primary target?"

He nodded. "Yes, if you want to say that. You were my primary target mainly because for the past two years I've been thinking about you a lot."

He rubbed his hand through his hair and said in a frustrated tone, "Hell, it's been more than a lot, Peyton. I'm surprised I was able to win any cases for thinking of you so much. So I decided it was time to spend time with you to figure out why. And now I know."

Peyton narrowed her eyes at him. "Well, I don't. So tell me what you know. Just why have I been on your mind lately?"

He could see the curiosity in her eyes; also the confusion. Little did she know that what he was about to tell her would probably confuse her even more. "I've fallen in love with you."

Chapter 19

Peyton hadn't been aware she'd been holding her breath. She exhaled deeply, but her heart was still beating fast in her chest and a huge knot had settled in her throat. She backed up a little, needing space. More than that, she needed a stiff drink. She needed—

"Peyton?"

She blinked. Angelo was now standing on his feet by the bed. She backed up some more, trying to make sense of what he'd said. It was like she was in another world and crazy things were happening. She swallowed and asked in a quiet tone. "How can you say something like that?"

He shoved his hands in his pockets. "Easy, since I know it's true. I love you."

She turned her face to the side as if she'd been slapped. In a way, she had. The only other man who had professed his love for her had said it just that way, like he'd meant it. But then that same man hadn't thought she measured up to his family's standards. He had been ashamed of her. And if Angelo Antonio Di Meglio thought he would put her through that kind of situation again he was crazy.

She turned back to him, filled with fear more than anger. She didn't believe in love at first sight, nor did she believe you could simply wake up one morning and decide you were in love with someone. She believed feelings had to grow, and that took time. She had watched Mac fall in love with Luke and knew that Sam had fallen in love with Blade even before Sam probably knew it herself. Her two best friends shared loving relationships with their husbands. She both envied them and was happy for them.

Maybe there was a man out there who would love and cherish her one day. But there was no way on earth she would even consider the possibility that that man was Angelo. First of all, she didn't love him. She enjoyed his company, his lovemaking skills were off the charts and he'd always been the most handsome man she'd ever met…but she didn't love him.

She quickly turned away to look out the window, wondering why she'd had to reassure herself that she wasn't in love with Angelo twice now. Okay, maybe a part of her had *some* feelings for him. She'd had a crush on him for a while, and she knew it was still buried somewhere in her heart. And maybe on occasion, she had looked at him and felt some sort of tug at her heartstrings. She would even admit that he had found his way—and quite easily—into a few of her fantasies. And over the past two weeks, he had done things that had rekindled those feelings so deeply embedded within her. But she was convinced that none of that meant anything. The bottom line was that he was who he was and she was who she was. And the two didn't mix.

"It won't work, Angelo. The feelings aren't mutual," she heard herself say. There, he had needed to hear that and she had needed to say it. There was no need for both of them to act foolishly, especially about something as complicated as love.

"Then I'm going to make it work, and I feel confident in the end the feelings *will* be mutual," he stated quietly.

She shook her head. "You can't."

"I will."

A feeling of dread coursed through her body. The fear she felt began tightening in her lungs and old anxieties began eating away at her as memories came flooding back. She would never forget how she felt when she'd heard Matthew's words, how painful they had been and how she had to endure all the heartache of leaving Yale, the friends she had made, the teachers she had come to know and respect. She assumed she was well on her way, that with the scholarship she'd gotten she'd be set for life. All it had taken was a broken heart to make her run in another direction—home.

When she returned to Chicago, if it hadn't been for her grandmother's love, Ms. Lora's kind words of wisdom and the hardworking people of the Third Ward and their acts of kindness and encouragement, she might not have been able to finish her last two years at the University of Illinois and go on to law school. Once at law school, she'd met two women who were destined to be her best friends for life. Now, Angelo's words threatened to break her and could end her relationship with his sister, her best friend. What on earth could he be thinking?

Peyton gazed back at him and studied his features. The same determination and stubbornness she'd seen in Sam so many times was there in his face. She wasn't sure just what kind of breakdown he was experiencing to make him think he had fallen in love with her. But he needed to get a grip on things and not drag her into it. Had winning the case done such a number on him that he was trying to escape his newfound celebrity status by mistakenly believing things that just weren't true—like he had fallen in love? It was time for Angelo to come to his senses. When it came to juries, she was good at that. Hopefully, she could be just as persuasive with him.

"When did you realize you had these feelings for me, Angelo? When did you, uh…fall in love with me?"

Angelo stared at Peyton knowing full well what she was trying to do. She was cross-examining him like he was a witness on the stand. That was fine, if that's what she felt comfortable doing to get some answers. Being a lawyer, he was obviously prepared to respond to every one of her questions.

"I think I've always had this thing for you," Angelo said. "I thought you were pretty damn hot, but it really hit me about two years ago."

Disbelief contorted her face. "Two years ago?"

He nodded. "Yes, right after I spent time at your place when Sam was out of town."

"And you think you fell in love with me then?"

"I'm not sure exactly when it happened, Peyton. All I know is that I was drawn to you in a way that I've never been drawn to another woman. You had an effect on me, and I wanted to explore what that feeling was about."

"So it was sexual?"

He didn't intend to let her lead him down that road. "No, if you remember, we didn't sleep together. In fact, there was nothing sexual between us. It was just two friends getting to know each other better. That was the first time I'd ever really spent time alone with you without Sam being around. I got to know you. You shared a lot of yourself with me. We talked. We laughed. I didn't have to worry about you coming on to me, and you didn't have to worry about me coming on to you. It felt good. It felt right."

He paused, probably a moment too long for her taste. "And?" she asked.

"And I returned to New York thinking I had a great time being around you. After that, you were on my mind constantly. I would think of you at some of the oddest times. And I would remember certain things, like the way your eyes would light up when you smiled. The nervous way you would lick your lips with your tongue when you were thinking really hard about something. And your playful side that you don't often show others. I remembered those things, although I tried not to."

"Sounds like infatuation to me," she said as if diagnosing his symptoms.

"Yes, it was that, but it became even more. First, there was Luke and Mac's wedding and all those guys who tried coming on to you. I got angry. I was pissed to the point where I wanted to hit somebody. Then after that, at all the family gatherings, I found myself seeking you out, having jealous fits if a man got too close to you. I tried coming up with excuses to come to Oklahoma just to see you."

He paused briefly. "It was pretty bad at Sam's wedding, but at Reese and LaKenna's wedding it was even worse. I wanted to punch one of Reese's friends from college when he made a comment about how beautiful you looked and that he planned to check you out."

Angelo felt his jaw clench in anger remembering that day. "There was a group of us standing around, including six of the Madaris cousins and Reese's friend from college. The moment the guy made the comment, all eyes turned to me."

He paused a second then said, "The Madarises weren't surprised by my anger, and it was then that I realized that I hadn't done a good job of keeping my feelings for you in check. The cousins took me aside and let me know I needed to take action regarding you or move out of the damn way. It was then that I decided to find out just what my feelings for you were and whether they were for real. Spending time with you these past two weeks verified that they are."

She didn't say anything. She just stood there, staring at him as if she was trying to digest what he'd said. But he knew what she was getting ready to say wasn't what he wanted to hear.

"I should be flattered, Angelo, and I am—really. But I think you're getting lust confused with love."

She was still fighting it, making excuses. But he intended to make her see the truth. "I love you, Peyton, whether you want to believe it or not."

"I don't want to believe it." She drew in a deep breath and added, "I can't believe it, Angelo."

And then in a tortured voice, she said, "And please don't try and make me. You don't know what you're asking of me."

"Then tell me. Why is it so hard for you to believe that I love you? Why are you so hell-bent on rejecting me?"

She didn't say anything for the longest time, and then he saw the single tear fall from her eye and flow down her cheek. "Okay, I'll tell you," she said softly. "The reason is because I can't handle another heartbreak."

Pain. He heard it in the very depths of her voice. But

he never knew she'd been seriously involved with any-one, let alone suffered heartache. If so, why hadn't Sam ever mentioned it?

"I think you need to tell me about it...so I can un-derstand."

Peyton moved past him and sat on the edge of the bed. "Yes, maybe I should," she said, glancing over at him. "Then you'll know why I can never get seriously involved with you, Angelo."

Peyton watched Angelo walk to the wingback chair and sit in it, his penetrating dark eyes keeping her in constant focus. "All right, Peyton, tell me."

She mulled over his request. What she was about to tell him was something she hadn't shared with any-one—not her grandmother, not the lady back in Chicago whom she considered her godmother or the two women who were her best friends.

It was something she had tried to forget about. Some-thing she'd sworn she would never reveal. She knew An-gelo was waiting for her to speak. "Have you ever heard of the Elton family from Boston?"

He nodded slowly. "Yes."

She wasn't surprised since most people had. "In my freshman year at Yale, I met Matthew Elton. He was in one of my classes. We had to do a project together and spent a lot of time at one of the coffee shops around campus. He was nice, and I liked him. I didn't know who he was until one of my roommates told me. But that didn't matter to me."

She paused a moment. "After the class project, Matt and I continued to spend more and more time together, and everyone knew we were dating. I loved him. He was my first boyfriend and, as far as I was concerned, my only boyfriend. He would tell me things about his family, and I had looked forward to meeting them. It never dawned on me until later that in all his trips home, he never once invited me to go with him."

She drew in a slow breath. "My close friends on campus began hinting that maybe he was afraid to take me home to meet his parents because I didn't have the background his parents would expect of someone their son was serious about."

She paused again. "They were right. I overheard him asking one of his college friends to help come up with an excuse to tell me about why he couldn't take me home to meet his parents, because in their eyes I was unacceptable. I also heard him say that although he did care for me, he felt I wouldn't ever be accepted."

She ignored the muffled expletive that came from Angelo's lips. "I couldn't believe he'd actually said that. I didn't even bother confronting him about it. I waited for him to come to me with his 'excuse' as to why he couldn't take me home for the holidays to meet his family. That's when I told him that was fine because I wouldn't be returning to Yale after the holidays anyway. I lied and said my grandmother needed me closer to home and that I would be transferring to the University of Illinois."

"He didn't try to talk you into staying?"

Peyton shook her head. "No, I think he was relieved that he wouldn't have to come up with any more excuses. A part of me wanted to believe that Matt did love me, but just couldn't get beyond the fact that I was a nobody— someone without a social pedigree."

"And you think that's important, Peyton?"

"Wealthy families evidently think so."

"Not all of them."

She narrowed her gaze. "I won't risk another heartbreak finding out if that's true or not."

Angelo didn't say anything for a while, but he was quietly fuming with anger. He had never met the Eltons, but knew his family had. In fact, his parents and the Eltons ran in some of the same social circles. And he'd heard the Eltons were big on preserving their family's impressive legacy in Boston with ties that went back to Crispus Attucks. Did Peyton really think everyone with money was a snob?

"Okay, the guy who broke your heart happens to be an asshole from a wealthy family. So what does that have to do with me?"

She lifted her chin. "I won't let myself get serious about a guy whose family has as much money as yours."

He shook his head, not believing what she'd said. "That's the craziest thing I've ever heard, Peyton. You're letting that relationship cloud your judgment. First of all, you're best friends with my sister. Even with all of Sam's hang-ups, she's still your best friend. Right or wrong?"

"Right."

"And you've met my family. We can be a rambunctious bunch when we all get together, but I think you'll agree there's not a snooty bone in our bodies, and it would deeply offend me if you thought so."

And he meant it. Granted the Di Meglios had more money than they knew what to do with, but it was money someone in their family tree had busted their ass to earn. His grandparents had worked from sunup to sundown to get to where they were in life. And the Di Meglios contributed more than their fair share when it came to charity.

"I don't mean to offend you, Angelo, I'm just telling you how I feel."

He shrugged. "Then rest assured I won't ever break your heart."

"You say that now."

"And I'll be saying it later, Peyton. What happened with you and that guy was unfortunate. In all honesty, I can think of a lot of expletives to describe him and none would do him justice. If he really loved you, regardless of what your background was, he should not have been ashamed to take you home and introduce you to his family. I wouldn't have been ashamed."

He watched as she stared at him for several minutes, not saying anything. Hopefully, she was thinking about what he'd said. He knew he loved her, and he knew he would never hurt her. She knew his family, and in a way they had already adopted her as one of their own. His mother had begun thinking of Peyton and Mac as her "other" daughters years ago. Her background wasn't a big deal to the Di Meglios. Hell, his own mother was a prime example of how accepting the family was. Kayla Blake, the strong, beautiful African-American attorney from Atlanta, had infiltrated the tightly knit Italian clan of the Di Meglios when she'd captured Antonio's heart. Oh, he'd heard his grandparents hadn't been too happy about it at first. They preferred that their youngest son marry a nice Italian girl. But in the end they had accepted the woman Antonio had fallen in love with and welcomed her into the family with open arms.

Now, close to forty years later, his parents' marriage was still going strong despite their knack for getting into their children's business at times. The best thing to ever happen to them was becoming grandparents. Because they doted on their granddaughter Blair, it kept them out of his affairs. And that was definitely a nice change of pace.

"I'd like to offer a suggestion, if I may," he said, his voice breaking the quietness of the room.

He saw the wariness that appeared in her gaze. "What sort of suggestion?"

"Since you say you don't love me, you don't have to worry about heartbreak on your end. Right now, I'm the only one at risk."

He slowly eased out of the chair and crossed the room to sit beside her on the bed. "First, I'm going to have my hands full convincing you that I've fallen in love with you. Then, I need to convince you that your heart is safe with me. Will you let me do both, Peyton? Starting now?"

Peyton was mesmerized by his gaze. She wanted to believe him, but a part of her held back. "You live in another city, Angelo. Building a relationship is tough enough. A long-distance romance only increases the problems."

"That means we're both going to work harder at it then. It has to be something you want, too, Peyton. You don't love me now, but I believe given time, you'll fall in love with me."

He was probably right, she thought. What woman wouldn't fall in love with him if given the chance? And truthfully, deep down, she'd been keeping her feelings for him at bay, in hopes that they'd go away. "I need time to think about it," she said softly.

He reached out and touched her cheek. "Take a chance on me, Peyton. Go ahead and take a chance, baby."

And then he lowered his mouth to hers.

She knew she was a goner the moment her tongue touched his, then took hold of it and began sucking on it with a hunger she felt all the way in the pit of her quivering stomach. He tasted like peppermint and all the good things she'd gotten to know. He pulled her body toward him and held her tightly as he deepened the kiss. Pleasure began tingling through every bone in her body, and she wrapped her arms around him to hold on.

She was very much aware of him slowly easing her back on the bed and his body straddling hers. Instinctively, her body shifted, her legs widened and she felt him, every hard inch of him, pressed against her pelvis.

He slowly lifted his head and held her gaze. And the intensity in the dark eyes sent heat flowing through her. "I won't ever hurt you. I promise," he whispered huskily.

A part of her wanted to believe him, but for some reason she couldn't. Her heart just wouldn't let her. "I want to believe you, but I can't. I'm going to need time, Angelo. My heart just isn't there yet."

He reached out and gently caressed the side of her face. "That's fine. But rest assured that one day it will be." His voice was low, determined. And he said it with such finality.

She didn't want to burst his bubble. Instead she stared into his eyes as intensely as he was staring into hers. It was if he was willing her to feel what he was feeling and take it and accept it. But still a part of her remembered the pain, the agony of lost love, and held back.

"We leave tomorrow, and I want to make love to you until then. I want to leave my imprint all over you, Peyton, so even when I'm not *here*," he said, reaching down to cup her womanhood through her pajama bottoms, "you will remember the times that I was." He breathed the words against her lips.

His voice actually made her shudder inside. She remembered all the times he had been inside of her, all the times they'd connected intimately, every position. And all the times she had lain in his arms with him still buried deep inside her.

And then he kissed her again, taking her mouth with a hunger that had her moaning. How could he do that when no other man had? Over the past two weeks he had unleashed a sexual passion in her that she hadn't known existed. She had felt things, experienced things she had only read about. Beginning with that night at the lighthouse, he had brought her sexual fantasies to life.

"I've fed you in one way, now I need to feed you in another," he whispered against her moistened lips, pulling his mouth back from hers.

He eased away from her to stand, and she watched as he removed his clothes. She started to scoot to the center of the bed but his next words stopped her. "No, stay right there."

She did as he said and watched as he removed every stitch of his clothing, giving her a strip show like no other. Her heart rate increased when he stood in front of her in his naked, glorious, male splendor. He knelt on the mattress to remove her pajama top and bottoms.

When he had her totally naked, he leaned closer to her ear and nibbled around it. "I need you on all fours, facing the headboard, baby," he whispered. "By the time you leave here tomorrow, there's no way you won't know the depths of my feelings for you."

She studied his features and saw the intensity in his eyes as she did what he asked. She glanced over her shoulder and met his gaze when he came to stand directly behind her with his feet spread apart.

He leaned closer and placed his hands on her hips

and her body shivered at his touch. "I want you to close your eyes and feel me. Feel me everywhere inside of you," he whispered.

She closed her eyes and seconds later she felt his desire when he tilted her hips upward and eased the head of his shaft inside of her. Drawing in a deep breath as it inched deeper and deeper, she moaned at the snug fit when he finally delved inside of her to the hilt. And then he began moving, thrusting hard and maneuvering her hips at an angle that ensured he hit her G-spot every time he drove in and out of her.

She threw her head back as sensation overtook her body, producing pangs of pleasure. His penis felt rock-hard, and it definitely made its presence known inside of her. Then suddenly her body seemed to fragment into a thousand pieces, and she couldn't hold back her scream.

It was then that he bore down on her, went deeper, and she felt his release shoot to every part of her, all the while his skilled hands continuing to stroke her all over. He began whispering words to her, words she knew were Italian. But there was something about the tone of his voice, the sexual texture of the words that flowed from his lips that had her shuddering inside.

"What were you saying?" she asked, wanting to know. He eased her body down onto the bed, inched her to the middle of the bed to lay beside her. Their breathing was labored as if they'd run a marathon while the aftershocks of shared pleasure echoed between them.

He smiled and instead of answering her right away, he leaned over and took her mouth in a long, passionate kiss. She felt her body fire up for him.

When he finally released her mouth, he said, "I was cherishing you in words, saying how beautiful you are, how much I want you not just for physical release but for emotional release as well. Not just for today or to-morrow but for all the years to come."

His words touched her. She wished she could believe everything he said, but at the moment she could not. She no longer loved Matt, far from it. However, she needed to protect herself.

Whatever thoughts she had vanished when he lifted her atop his body so that she straddled him. She immediately felt his hard erection pressed at the juncture of her thighs. And already he'd gotten big again.

Spreading her legs, she positioned herself above his manhood and eased down, taking him in. Her body tingled in renewed anticipation, eager to have him inside of her again. Maybe it was knowing that tomorrow they would leave the resort and return to their separate homes that made Peyton feel needy. Or perhaps it was the way he stroked his hands down the sides of her thighs and legs that made her want him all over again. Whatever it was, she could feel him pushing through her inner muscles, determined to plunge all the way to the hilt, filling her body with white-hot lust.

He cupped her backside as he lifted his body off the bed to continue to push his way inside of her, stretching her all the way. "You feel me, baby?" he asked in a throaty whisper.

She drew in a deep breath. "How could I not?"

Whether he was satisfied with her answer or not, he didn't say. What he did do was begin moving again, this time thrusting upward into her. She closed her eyes as their bodies began a frenzied mating. Suddenly she felt his hips jerk, and she opened her eyes and met his dark gaze.

Her name rushed from his mouth in an orgasmic gasp. He thrust upward deeply and uttered her name at the same time she felt him spill inside of her, the heated essence triggering her own body's response. She screamed his name as shockwaves passed through her, beginning at the center where their bodies were connected.

"Angelo!"

They came together, their juices combining in a maelstrom of sensations that flooded her entire being. He ran his fingers through her locks as he continued to stroke her hair and look into her eyes.

"I love you, Peyton."

She wished she could whisper the words back to him, but she couldn't. When the lingering effects from the orgasm had passed through her body, he shifted so she could lie beside him, their bodies still connected.

She glanced at the clock. In less than twenty-four hours she would be leaving. And she knew he would make good on what he'd said. This would definitely be a night she would remember forever.

Chapter 20

"You sure you have everything, Peyton?"

She turned around and Angelo watched as her gaze swept around the room, a room they'd spent the past thirty hours in, behind closed doors, locked in each other's arms. It was as if a craving, some sort of an addiction, had been unleashed inside of him, and he had needed her in a way he hadn't ever needed another woman.

It was as if he'd tried convincing her with his body just how much she meant to him, just how dedicated he was to her. He had come here to find out why she'd gotten to him, why he was so attracted to her and why he was jealous of any man who got close to her.

Now he knew. He loved her. He had fallen in love with a woman who was the complete opposite of the kind of woman he'd always thought he would share his life with. She had not only wiped his slate clean, she had engraved her name right smack in the middle of it.

For years, he always thought he knew the type of woman he wanted in his life, the type of woman he would one day settle down with. He wanted to marry and have plenty of children to carry on the family name. After all, it was the Di Meglio way. No telling how many babies his mother might have had if a doctor hadn't cautioned her about getting pregnant again for medical reasons after his sister Samari was born.

He figured the woman he married would be beautiful, intelligent, quiet, easily controlled and devoted to him, his career, his wants and needs. Although he admired his mother and her successful career, he'd wanted his wife to be a stay-at-home mom and take care of all the babies he planned to have and be at his beck and call. His home would be his castle.

His uncles had married women like that. His father had not. Everyone knew there was nothing docile or domestic about his mother. If Antonio Di Meglio had been looking for a wife like that then he'd definitely missed the boat. But then Angelo believed his father wouldn't have it any other way, which was why they had a good marriage. They were equal partners, at work as well as at home. And like his father, Angelo had fallen in love with a strong woman. His home would still be his castle, but Peyton would be his queen.

"Yes, I got everything," she said, breaking into his thoughts. "And you don't have to take me to the airport. I can catch a cab."

He shook his head. "No, I want to take you." He wanted to spend every single second that he could with her.

"What time will Lee get here?" she asked.

"Around noon. Then we'll fly out to Dubai together in a few days," he said, getting up from the wingback chair in the bedroom to walk over to where she stood at the window. Peyton had pulled her hair back and the effect was astounding. The rays of sunlight streaming through the window highlighted her features, accentuating her beautiful bone structure and giving her face an ethereal glow. "I'm sure the two of you will enjoy yourselves before leaving for Dubai."

He lifted a brow. Was that a hint of jealousy in her tone? "I'm sure we will, but not the way you think. I can't speak for Lee, but there's not a single woman here I want. My heart is already taken."

He saw it—that look of uncertainty in her eyes, the disbelief that made her lift her chin. "You think you feel that way now…"

"And I'll feel the same way an hour from now, tomorrow, next week and next month. This isn't a phase that'll pass a year from now, Peyton. You're the one who had the birthday, not me. But it doesn't matter. I know what I feel."

"Do you?" she asked, letting her gaze roam over his face.

"Yes." He stepped closer to her and reached out and cupped her face in both hands. "I know. It's you who doesn't know, and I'm going to make it my job to see that you do. I'm going to make sure you know how things are when a man loves a woman."

He leaned down and kissed her in a long, passionate and sensuous kiss, letting her feel just how much he desired her, wanted her and loved her. One day there would be no doubt in her mind, and it was only then that they could move forward and make plans for their future.

He released her mouth and whispered against her wet lips. "I need to get you out of here or you'll miss your plane." He chuckled. "But if you did miss the plane, it wouldn't bother me at all."

He was telling the truth about that. The past two weeks had been the best. He had enjoyed being with her…making love to her. He didn't say anything for a minute and then reached out and caressed her cheek. "When I get back from Dubai I'm coming to Oklahoma to see you."

When she parted her lips to say something, he placed a finger on her lips. "Shh. Don't tell me not to, Peyton."

She released a sigh before saying, "It's your time you'll be wasting."

He took her hand and brought it to his lips. "You've been friends with Sam long enough to know that when a Di Meglio sets their mind to doing something, nothing stands in their way. So get ready, baby. I'm coming."

He pulled her into his arms and kissed her again.

Chapter 21

"Well, you certainly look well-rested, Peyton."

Peyton looked up from her desk at the two women standing in her doorway. She leaned back in her chair and narrowed her gaze. Of course it was Sam who'd given her assessment of Peyton's well-being. "I haven't decided if I'm still speaking to the two of you."

"And why not?" Mackenzie asked, an innocent smile curving her lips.

Before she could answer, Sam said, "The way I see it, you owe us. You can't convince me that you didn't enjoy yourself and have fun."

Sam was right. She did have a good time. But still...

"The two of you set me up."

"We did not," Sam said, dismissing Peyton's objections as she braved the lion's den by stepping into her office. Mac decided to hang back and stand in the doorway.

"What we did was make sure you went somewhere to

relieve all that stress. There's nothing like a good round of lovemaking to take the edge off."

Peyton narrowed her gaze. "And what makes you think Angelo and I made love?"

Sam rolled her eyes. "Because I know my brother," she said. "He's had the hots for you for a while now, and it's been driving everyone crazy. It was high time for him to find out exactly what all that meant."

She dropped down in the chair across from Peyton's desk. "And I know you. You might think you were fooling Mac, but you weren't fooling me. You have a thing for Angelo, too."

Peyton opened her mouth to rebut Sam's assertion, but decided to keep quiet as Mac entered the room and took the other chair beside Sam. "Actually, she hasn't been fooling me," Mac said. "That's the only reason I went along with Angelo's plan to send her to Dunwoody Cove. Even though Angelo might have had the hots for Peyton, she's always had the hots for him."

"Excuse me," Peyton said with an edge in her voice. "Why are the two of you discussing me like I'm not here?"

"Because until you own up to it, that's how we're going to deal with it. We are your two closest friends. Don't you know we pick up on stuff?"

Peyton tensed as she arched her brow. "Stuff like what?"

"Like how your eyes would light up whenever Sam mentioned Angelo's name, and how you liked talking about the time he stayed at your place when Sam was out of town," Mac reminded her. "You kept telling me how hot he was."

Peyton rolled her eyes. "He is hot."

"Yes, but I thought there was more," Mac said. "Only

because in all the years we've been friends, you've never carried on about any other man like you did Angelo."

Peyton didn't say anything for a moment. She abruptly rose to her feet and leaned forward, placing her hands palms down on her desk, making sure she had Mac and Sam's attention. "I want you two to listen to me and listen to me good," she said in a steely tone. "I am *not* in love with Angelo."

Neither Mac nor Sam were perturbed by her words. "I remember a time when I wasn't in love with Blade either," Sam said, grinning. "In fact, I seriously didn't like him at first."

"And I didn't care one way or the other with Luke," Mac added. "I thought he was eye candy in a pair of jeans, but that was about it."

Peyton knew the history of how Mac and Sam first met their husbands. "So what are you two trying to say?" Peyton asked in a snappy voice, clearly annoyed.

Sam glanced over to Mac to let her do the honors. "All we're saying, Peyton, is that Angelo has this thing for you. We knew it. Hell, everyone knew it but you. And Sam and I detected that you had this thing for him as well, although you've managed to hide your attraction better than he hid his. We never said you loved him or that he loved you. All we're saying is that we thought there was enough there to explore and felt the two weeks at Dunwoody would do both of you some good."

Peyton glared. "Who the hell died and made you two matchmakers?"

Mac and Sam exchanged glances, and then Sam looked over at Peyton. "We see you're in one of those moods. Evidently Angelo failed to take care of business like we thought he would since you're in the same mood that you were in before you left."

Sam stood. "Good thing you're only in the office one day before leaving for Chicago or else Mac and I would be tempted to take you somewhere and work you over. Knocking some sense into you isn't such a bad idea."

Peyton's glare deepened. "You just try."

"And we would succeed," Sam threw back. "Come on, Mac, let's leave Peyton to stew about what could have happened between her and Angelo, but didn't."

Mac stood, and she and Sam headed for the door when Peyton's next words stopped them. "It did happen!"

Both Sam and Mac stopped and turned around slowly and stared at Peyton, who sat back down in her chair. It was Sam who asked, "So, what's your problem if you got laid?"

Peyton rolled her eyes. Leave it to Sam to think a good roll in the hay was the cure for just about anything. "My problem is that your brother thinks he loves me," she said in a frustrated voice.

Mac's expression changed to complete surprise. "Angelo actually said that?"

"Yes."

"And you have a problem with that—with a man loving you?" Sam asked, as if it was such a crazy idea.

"Yes, I have a problem with it," Peyton replied.

Neither Sam nor Mac said anything as they returned to their respective chairs. "I knew Angelo had this thing for you, but I hadn't expected him to confess anything about love so soon. Usually it takes men a long time to come to grips with their feelings for a woman," Mac said. "You've scored big-time, so what kind of problem do you have with it?"

Peyton shook her head. "That's just it. I don't want

to score. I don't want Angelo to think he loves me, and I don't want to start loving him."

Mac and Sam exchanged glances again. "Is there a reason why you wouldn't want such a fine-looking man, who's also pretty damn successful, to love you?" Mac asked.

Peyton nodded slowly. "Yes, there's a reason. And his name is Matthew Elton."

Mac raised a brow. "Who's Matthew Elton?"

Peyton knew it was time to tell her two best friends everything, including the part of her life she hadn't shared with anyone…except Angelo. She'd told Angelo to get him to understand why she could never have a serious relationship with him. But even now, she wasn't sure she'd gotten through to him.

Drawing in a deep breath she began talking, sharing with Mac and Sam the period of time in her life that had caused her such heartbreak.

"I can't believe you've been here for two weeks," Lee Madaris said, glancing around and smiling back at the women who were openly flirting with him. "I bet you've been having a hell of a lot of fun."

Angelo took another sip of his drink. He remembered how he felt the first time he'd come to Dunwoody Cove over five years ago as a guest. Upon seeing all the beautiful women, he'd thought he had died and gone to heaven. Evidently Lee was now feeling the same way.

"Yes, I had a lot of fun, all right, but not in the way you think. Peyton was here celebrating her thirtieth birthday," he said.

Lee rubbed his chin thoughtfully as he gazed over at Angelo. "Oh, I see."

There was no need to ask Lee what he meant by

that. Angelo was well aware that Lee knew how he felt about Peyton, since Lee had been one of those who'd picked up on it at some of the family functions they'd attended together.

"So you finally decided to make your move?" Lee asked.

Angelo stared down into his drink. He had, for all the good it had done. "Yes, I finally decided to make my move." There was no need to go into detail or explain that the woman he'd fallen in love with wasn't receptive.

He didn't say anything as he continued to sip his drink and watched as Lee checked out the ladies. Despite Lee's interest, Angelo detected an edginess in the man he'd gotten to know pretty well over the past few years. At thirty-two, and a college graduate of Harvard, Lee had headed the Madaris Foundation up until a year ago, when he decided to step down to pursue his lifelong dream of owning a chain of international resort hotels.

"So what's going on with you, Lee?"

Lee glanced over at him. "Nothing much. Nolan and I are working together to restore a 1985 'Vette and it's a beauty."

Angelo nodded. "And how are the other cousins?" By "other cousins" Lee knew who he was referring to. The Madaris family was close, and the matriarch of the family, Felicia Laverne Madaris, and her husband, Milton, had given birth to seven sons. All were alive except for Robert Madaris, who had been killed in the Vietnam War.

Those seven sons had sons and grandsons and their grandsons were extremely close—especially Lee, Corbin, Nolan and Reese, who were close in age as well. Reese had gotten married last year to LaKenna, even though they'd been best friends for years. No one had been surprised when the relationship between the two had turned serious, just as Angelo knew no one would really be surprised if he and Peyton's affair was out in the open.

"Everyone is doing fine. I can't wait to tell them about this place. If we didn't have to catch that plane to Dubai, I would extend my stay here."

Angelo chuckled, watching the eye contact between Lee and the woman sitting at a table across the room. "Yes, I'm sure you would."

An hour later, Angelo returned to his room and, as soon as he shut the door behind him, felt a surge of loneliness. He missed Peyton already. She had definitely left her mark, and already Dunwoody Cove provided memories that he couldn't let go of. He knew he had his work cut out for him because even as he was driving her to the airport, she was trying her best to convince him that any affair between them wouldn't work. He was determined to show her that it would.

He was about to strip down for a shower when his cell phone rang. His heart kicked up a beat, hoping it was Peyton, and he tried to downplay his disappointment when he checked caller ID and saw it was his father. "Yes, Dad?"

"When will you be back in the office?"

Angelo raised a brow, surprised by the question. His father was aware that he was on a well-deserved extended leave from the firm and hadn't planned on returning to the office for another month or so. "Not for a while, Dad. Why?"

"A case has come up. It's a new client who asked for you—specifically."

"Who are they?"

"Gallant Mercantile."

Angelo released a low whistle. No wonder his father was calling. Gallant Mercantile was a billion-dollar company, and it was the kind of account any legal firm would love to represent. He was well aware that his father and uncles had been courting them for years. It was also rumored that Gallant hadn't been satisfied with how their current law firm had botched their last big deal with some manufacturing giant in China and was discreetly looking around for another firm to represent them.

Angelo rubbed his hand down his face. The last thing he was interested in was going back to work. Maybe it was something they could handle outside the courtroom. "What's this about?"

"It's regarding their plant in Chicago. Some of the residents in a nearby community are claiming their water is being contaminated by the company's factory there."

Angelo nodded. "Is it true?"

"Gallant spent money on several environmental studies and installed stringent safeguards a few years ago."

Angelo rolled his eyes. That didn't mean a thing to him. If he was going to take the case he had to be certain they were dealing with the facts. "I want to see those reports and would prefer having current tests done. That means they are going to need to do updates."

He heard his father's low whistle. "That's going to cost money."

"And it's money I'm sure they have. If I take the case, I don't want to go into it blindly."

"So you will take the case?"

"Do I have a choice?" He knew his father knew the answer. Angelo was in a position to snag the one account the firm had been trying to nail for years. Turning down the case was not an option.

"I'm on my way to Dubai for a week, and when I return to the States I'm heading to Oklahoma for a few days. I should be back in New York in two weeks."

"That long?"

Yes, that long. He had business that was more important to him than jumping through hoops for the people at Gallant. He'd heard about them and understood they were pushy. So it was better that they started out knowing he was nobody's yes-man, and he didn't jump through hoops very well.

"Yes, Dad—two weeks at the minimum. If they really want me to take on the case, they'll sit tight. In the meantime, tell them I won't touch it without updates on their contamination test results."

Moments later he hung up the phone, satisfied that he was not changing his plans. He would go to Dubai and then take a trip to Oklahoma. There was a certain woman there that he couldn't wait to see again.

Chapter 22

Peyton stared into her refrigerator. There were times that she wished Rachael Ray was her neighbor. There was never anything in her fridge that she could whip up in thirty minutes. She'd been back from Dunwoody for four days and in another two would be leaving for Chicago, where she would spend the next two weeks. So it didn't make sense to go grocery shopping for food now.

She'd closed her refrigerator and decided she would do Chinese takeout when she heard the doorbell ring. It was Friday afternoon, and she was flying out first thing Monday morning. She looked forward to visiting with Ms. Lora, the woman who'd been her grandmother's best friend for years.

She glanced out of the peephole of her door. Peyton's heart nearly stopped when she saw it was Angelo. She knew he had planned to come to Oklahoma, but a part of her had hoped it would be after she'd left town and their paths wouldn't cross. She wasn't sure she was up to seeing him now. Especially since she'd been thinking about him so much over the past few days and couldn't get their Bahamas affair out of her mind. And why did thoughts of those times make her smile even when she didn't want to? Even when she tried to remember it had only been a brief affair?

"Pretending I'm not here is not going to make me go away, Peyton," he said softly through the door.

She blinked, wondering how he'd known for certain she was home and how she could hear him when she was certain she hadn't made a sound. As if he'd read her thoughts, he said, "I can pick up your scent even through the door."

Her eyes widened. Could he really? Drawing in a deep breath she took the security chain off the door, opened it slightly and stepped back. He pushed the door open all the way and walked into her condo, seemingly bigger than life, and when his gaze latched onto her, heat immediately spread through her body.

He looked as handsome as ever, and for some reason even more so. In jeans and a pullover shirt that showed what a great body he had, it wouldn't take much for her to start drooling. And she couldn't help noticing his hair was longer. It hung way past the collar of his shirt.

He didn't say anything. After closing the door behind him, he just stood there in the middle of her condo doing the one thing he liked doing, which was staring at her. She felt the intensity of his gaze touch her everywhere—her face, the tips of her breasts, the juncture of her legs and the soles of her feet.

Then he simply said, "Come here."

And like a magnet, her body was drawn to him. He grabbed her when she came within arm's length and slanted his mouth over hers. Her lips parted automatically and their tongues began mating in a desperate attempt to get reacquainted.

Electrified charges sizzled through her body, while pleasure, as ripe as the peach she'd eaten at lunch, had her moaning. Why? Why now and why him? She'd been absorbed in her work for years, and if she missed a date, so what? Male companionship was something she'd never *had* to have. It wasn't at the top of her list. But all it had taken was two weeks spent with Angelo, and her body now seemed to have a mind of its own.

He released her mouth as quickly as he'd attacked it, and she saw desire spark in the depths of his eyes. She reached out and tugged his hair and whispered, "You need a haircut."

"No, what I need is you," he muttered huskily against her lips, and then he quickly moved toward the sofa.

At that moment, Angelo knew he wanted Peyton with an urgency that he'd never felt before…at least not since he'd been with her last. He felt the need, the craving and the want all the way to his bones. He placed her on the sofa and pulled back slowly, looking down at her with a yearning that was like a slow burn in his stomach. He had to make love to her, entwine her body with his and become one with her. Claim her.

He leaned down and kissed her with a greed that had his loins throbbing. But first he needed to make her understand that his desire wasn't just physical. He pulled back from the kiss and took her hand and placed it over his heart and whispered, "Yours."

He knew his heart would be crushed if she said she didn't want it. He stared into her eyes, waiting.

Then she finally asked, as if she still wasn't completely certain, "Mine?"

Holding her gaze, he nodded slowly and said, "Yes, yours. Nobody else's." If only she knew just how much he meant that. Just how much what he'd said was true. She had spoiled him for any other woman.

"You're beautiful," he said, caressing her cheek.

She chuckled softly. "You don't lie very well."

He fought to keep the frown out of his eyes. She didn't believe him about that either. That Elton guy had done more than broken her heart. Whether she knew it or not, he'd also undermined her confidence. At the moment, if Elton had been here, Angelo would love to have planted his fist in the man's face.

Deciding not to argue the point with her he slowly pulled her up so he could join her on the sofa and placed her in his lap. He then cradled her in his arms.

She cleared her throat, and he glanced down at her. "You have something on your mind, Peyton?"

"Yes, I thought we were about to..."

He smiled. "We are. I need to hold you just as much. I missed you."

She leaned back and grinned. "It's only been four days."

"That's four days too long," he said, meaning it. He wondered how he would handle things when he had to return to New York and didn't see her for weeks on end.

"Well, if you must know," she said, wrapping her arms around his neck, "I missed you, too."

He actually felt a glimmer of hope that made his heart flutter. Her admission was a start. For the moment, he couldn't say anything, and then he repeated what she had said to him. "It's only been four days."

Following his lead, she smiled up at him and said, "That's four days too long."

Pleased, he leaned down and kissed her.

"I'm hungry," Peyton said, stretching out in bed beside Angelo. They'd made love a number of times since he'd arrived and she was exhausted and hungry.

"I take it you didn't eat dinner," he said, turning her toward him to cuddle.

"I was checking out the fridge when you showed up and figured the best I could do was order takeout. You in the mood for Chinese?"

He chuckled. "Actually, we've been invited out."

She lifted up and stared at him. "By whom?"

"Sam. I stopped by the office thinking you were there and was told you left early. I got to see everyone, and Sam invited us over. Luke and Mac will be there as well."

Sam and Blade, who lived in Houston seventy percent of the time, had purchased a home in Oklahoma after they'd married since Sam was still associated with the law firm and spent time in Oklahoma at least three months out of the year. Blade was involved with several construction projects here as well.

Peyton didn't say anything as she thought about the implications of Sam's invitation. If Peyton and Angelo arrived at Sam's together, then they would be seen as a couple when that was the last thing she wanted. She had tried making it clear to her two best friends that she did not want a serious involvement with Angelo.

His leg that was entwined in hers moved, reminding her that whether she admitted it or not she was involved with him. She wasn't one who had sex for the fun of it, so there had to be something serious going on between them. But she would be the last to claim it had anything to do with love.

Angelo said he was returning to New York in two days, the same day she would be headed to Chicago for two weeks. Distance is what she needed from Angelo. Hopefully that would give her space to clear her thoughts. She'd discovered that too much lovemaking had a tendency to muddy the waters. Angelo mentioned that when he returned to New York he would be working on some case that was guaranteed to keep him busy. She didn't plan to do anything in Chicago other than rest, relax and visit with old friends.

"So what do you say?" he asked, using his finger to tilt her chin toward him.

She figured that he knew she was thinking about the implications of going with him over to Sam's, being seen together as a couple. She'd talked to Mac and Sam and had even gone into detail about Matt and what he'd done. They thought it was time for her to move on and not look back. Both women had been hurt by men they assumed had loved them, only to be proven wrong. She understood what they'd said. But still, heartbreak was a personal thing, and Peyton just wasn't ready to make a move just yet.

She met his gaze. "What do you want me to say?"

He chuckled softly. "Plenty. None of which I'm sure you're ready to say, so I'll wait patiently until you are."

She let out a deep sigh. "Will you, Angelo? Will you wait patiently, knowing it might be a long wait?"

He moved his finger to stroke the side of her face. "Yes, because, baby, you're worth the wait."

"I know you don't want to hear this," Mac said, glancing over at Peyton as she helped her set Sam's table for dinner.

"What?" Peyton asked looking up from arranging a place setting.

"You and Angelo look really good together."

Mac was right. She didn't want to hear it only because she thought the same thing. She had caught a glimpse of their reflections in the full-length mirror in her bedroom right before they left her place. Granted, Angelo would look good with any woman he was with, but it had been something about him standing close beside her while she'd checked her appearance one final time before leaving that had almost made her go still.

Knowing Mac was waiting on a response from her, she said, "I told you and Sam my history. Not that I felt you needed to know, but because I felt in knowing my past the two of you would understand."

Mac rolled her eyes. "Understand what? That Matthew Elton was a jerk? Trust me, he joins the ranks of many others. Remember Lawrence Dixon?"

Peyton drew in a deep breath. Yes, she remembered Lawrence Dixon and what his betrayal had done to Mac. "Yes, I remember him," she said softly.

"After him I thought I could never love another man," Mac said. She chuckled. "It sure didn't make things easy for Luke, and I think you're making the same mistake with Angelo."

Peyton placed silverware beside a plate and then turned to Mac. "It's not the same."

Mac smiled softly. "Heartbreak is heartbreak." She didn't say anything for a moment. "Do you know what I think?"

Honestly, Peyton thought she was afraid to ask but decided to do so anyway. Mac's thinking usually wasn't as off-the-charts as Sam's. "What?"

"I think it's not that you don't think Angelo is really

in love with you, it's that you're afraid to believe that he truly is."

Peyton rolled her eyes. "And why is that?"

"Because then you have no reason to carry that chip on your shoulder." And without saying anything else, Mac walked off.

Peyton frowned. Although Sam had accused Peyton of having a chip on her shoulder many times, this was the first time Mac had ever said so. Did she really have hang-ups about people with money, or was it that she was looking at things more realistically than others?

She turned to head back into the kitchen to see what Sam needed her to do next when she glanced toward the living room. Luke, Blade and Angelo were standing around, drinking beers and talking about the upcoming football season and how they were looking forward to it.

All three were extremely handsome men, but the one that kicked up her pulse a notch was Angelo. She had to congratulate everyone. When she and Angelo had arrived, no one acted as if it was out of the ordinary to see them together. In a way that bothered her, although she wasn't sure just what she'd expected. Maybe a look of disbelief on their faces would have sufficed.

She wasn't sure just what caused Angelo to choose that moment to look her way, but he did. His gaze locked with hers and immediately she felt an intense stirring in the pit of her stomach and a rush of desire that nearly consumed her. It was as if some sort of sexual stimulation was transmitting from him to her.

And for a quick minute, she felt something else, something she hadn't felt in a long time and never with this intensity. It transcended all levels of sexual attraction, instinctively drawing her to him. It gave her pause, made everything inside of her go still, as a flicker of recognition of an emotion she thought she would never feel again burst to life.

"If you would take a moment to stop staring at my brother like you're going to stalk across the room and rip off his clothes any minute, I'd appreciate your help in placing a few of the platters on the dining room table, Pey."

She turned and glared at Sam's smarmy grin. Peyton felt there was really nothing she could say because in all honesty, she had been tempted to cross the room and tear off Angelo's clothes. Sam didn't need to know that she'd done that very thing earlier that day.

"Don't mess with me, Sam," she warned, moving past Sam to head toward the kitchen. As far as she was concerned, she couldn't get to Chicago fast enough.

Chapter 23

"Angelo, are you listening?"

Angelo glanced up at his father. He really hadn't been and that was unfortunate, especially when the old man was giving him a briefing on the Gallant case. "Sorry, my thoughts drifted for a moment," he said.

Antonio Di Meglio leaned back in his chair and stared at his son. "I take it you had a good time in the Bahamas."

Angelo grinned. His father had no idea, and he didn't intend to enlighten him as to what that good time had entailed. "Yes, I enjoyed myself."

"That's good, you definitely deserved the time off and I hated calling you back into the office, but if Gallant is considering hiring us as their law firm, we need to be ready to step in if their current attorneys are released."

Angelo nodded. He'd only been back a full day but

already he'd done his research. The people over at Gallant still weren't happy with their law firm's failure to put together a Chinese deal. "I went over all the reports and the community group in question really hasn't made any move. They don't even have an attorney, just the backing of some local advocacy group."

"Yes, but it's coming. You know the media. They will be on it like white on rice. Gallant wants to avoid a situation like BP in the Gulf a few years ago. But then they don't want to be taken advantage of either."

"I can certainly understand that. The city council has set up a hearing to air the community's concerns," Angelo said.

His father nodded. "Yes, and Gallant wants us there since they've officially made a decision to hire us if any trouble arises. And of course, you know they want you to handle things if there's a need."

Angelo hoped there wouldn't be a need since he had planned to head back to Oklahoma the first chance he got. He might be imagining things, but a part of him could feel Peyton softening. She wasn't as hard-nosed as she had been regarding them continuing their affair. And when they'd parted at the airport and he'd kissed her and told her he loved her, she had held his gaze with a strange look in her eyes. He wasn't sure what that meant, but he did know that he had Mac and Sam in his corner. He'd had a long talk with them the day he'd stopped by their law firm. They knew his feelings for Peyton were genuine, and he refused to give up hope that one day those feelings would be reciprocated.

"You're daydreaming again, Angelo."

Angelo simply nodded. "Yes, I was."

His father didn't say anything for a minute. "I guess

you've got that business with Peyton pretty much settled?"

Angelo lifted a brow, wondering how his father had figured out that Peyton played a part in his wayward thoughts. "What business are you talking about, Dad?"

"You finally realized just what she means to you."

To say he was surprised by his father's comment was an understatement. Deciding there was no need to deny a thing, he said, "I think I realized it some time ago but just recently decided to act on it."

His father grinned. "I'm glad. Does that mean your mother and I need to plan another wedding?"

How he wished Peyton could have been there to hear his father's question. Just like that, he'd admitted to having feelings for Peyton, and already his father was welcoming her to the family. There had been no question or concern about her background.

He decided to test the waters a little more. "So you think it will be a good match?"

His father laughed. "Hell, it will be a perfect match. Peyton's a bright and intelligent girl. She's beautiful, energetic and has a heart of gold. That's evident from all of those hours of pro bono work she donates to community organizations, helping others every year."

Angelo felt it was as well.

"And then there's the way she holds Mac and Sam's babies in her arms. It's like she longs to have one of her own."

Angelo had seen her hold his niece and Mac and Luke's baby several times, but hadn't ever picked up on anything.

"I'm more observant than you are," his father said, smiling. "Comes with the age."

Angelo chuckled and then became serious. "I'm in love with her, but she's not there yet with me."

"Is that what she said?"

"Basically."

His father's smile widened. "Your mother told me that same thing, in a lot of different ways—some not so nice. But I hung in there. I take it that you're going to do the same thing."

Angelo leaned back in his chair. "Definitely."

Peyton settled on the bed and glanced around the room, remembering how many times she'd spent the night there when her grandmother had to pull a night shift at the rubber plant. Those were the times when she and Serena would lie in bed as kids and plan their futures. Back then, neither of them knew that she would grow up to live out her dream of becoming an attorney and that Serena's life would be cut short, just days before her seventeenth birthday. Losing her best friend had been hard, but with her grandmother and Ms. Lora's help Peyton had gotten through it.

That was one of the reasons she loved Lora Lattimore so much. Besides being Serena's mother, she had been like a daughter to Peyton's grandmother, since Ms. Lora and Peyton's mom had been childhood friends. What little Peyton did know about her mother had been what her grandmother and Ms. Lora had shared with her.

Peyton knew she could have easily stayed at a hotel since there were several in the area. But she knew Ms. Lora wouldn't hear of it and would probably get offended if she chose to stay anywhere else.

The first thing Peyton had done after picking up a rental car at the airport had been to drive through places she used to frequent as a child. A lot of the old section had been torn down to make way for city revitalization projects. She was pleased with the progress that had been made and that longtime residents hadn't been displaced in the process. She was glad most of them had moved to Pembrook Pines, a development on the outskirts of the old neighborhood that was fast becoming its own little city. Most of the people living there were first-time home-owners and some even owned businesses in the area.

Mr. Griffin, a man who used to be her grandmother's neighbor, had opened a meat shop, and Mrs. Florence, who used to attend her church back in the day, had opened a flower shop. And Seymour Conyers, a high-school classmate of hers, had opened a printing shop.

She thought of her own roots back in the community where she'd grown up. You know you've arrived when they put a Starbucks on the corner. Yes, the old neighborhood didn't look like it used to, and she thought that was a good thing. The people of the South Side of Chicago were hardworking folks who wanted the best… and some of the best had come from this side of town. You couldn't get a better role model than the First Lady.

When a car drove by blasting loud music, Peyton couldn't help but smile, thinking some things never changed…or did they?

She eased off the bed and went to the window, not to see anything in particular but just to think. It seemed she'd been doing that a lot lately and most of the time—a good ninety-five percent of it—Angelo had dominated her thoughts.

She threw her head back and closed her eyes. What was he doing to her that she couldn't go to bed without thinking of him at night? His face was the first thing that flashed in her mind upon waking up each morning. Whenever she took a shower, she vividly remembered taking one with him, and how he would run his hands all over her body, stroke her, get down on his knees and taste her before thrusting inside of her. And his thrusts were as good as it got. She'd never before screamed so loud and so often. Never before had any man possessed the ability to make her nipples harden and tingle just with the sound of his voice. And no man had ever made her secrete spontaneously without foreplay. She was totally, absolutely convinced such a thing wasn't possible…until Angelo had proven her wrong in so many ways.

She drew in a deep breath. Okay, she understood all the physical stuff, that strong sexual chemistry that had her moaning in her sleep when she dreamed of him. But what was going on with her wanting to pick up the cell phone and call him just to say hello and to tell him she was thinking about him? Why, yesterday, when she'd sat beside a woman holding a little boy, did she imagine a little boy with hers and Angelo's features?

She moved away from the window, hoping and praying that what she thought was happening to her really wasn't. There was no way she could be falling for Angelo. *No way.* She needed to get her mind together, and her being here in Chicago and him back in New York was the perfect thing. He told her he would be returning to Oklahoma a week after she got back from Chicago and that was fine with her. By then she should have her priorities back in order and be more focused on what could and could not be.

There was a knock at the bedroom door just seconds before Ms. Lora stuck her head in. "You ready for lunch? I made your favorite sandwich and iced tea."

Peyton didn't need a mirror to know her face lit up.

Ms. Lora knew her special chicken salad sandwich and a huge cold glass of iced tea would do it every time. Besides, it was time she brought Ms. Lora up to speed on everything that had been going on since she last visited more than a year ago. Of course, she wouldn't tell her everything. There was no way she would let her know she had the hots for Sam's brother. And definitely not about all the time they'd spent together at that resort in the Bahamas.

"Yes, I'm starving." Peyton laughed. "You didn't have to go to all that trouble, but my stomach is so glad you did."

"Well, I'm glad you won that case. I'm so proud of you."

Peyton smiled. "Thanks, Ms. Lora, and I'm proud of you as well."

The woman waved away her words. "What on earth for?"

Peyton knew Ms. Lora had always been very modest and never patted herself on the back for anything, especially for everything she'd done in the community. And all it had taken was a few conversations with some of her old neighbors to learn that Ms. Lora had achieved a lot of progress lately.

When the school district's budget was cut, Ms. Lora had started an after-school program to help working mothers. And she had been instrumental in getting a number of well-known entertainers from Chicago to put together a benefit concert to help raise money to repair and replace playground equipment. She had worked closely with the mayor to turn one of the high schools into a place for people in the community to take vocational and educational classes at night. Thanks to her, three high school graduating seniors had received full scholarships to attend the Florida Memorial University's Aviation program.

And she was not just concerned with the way of life in the South Side. Peyton knew Ms. Lora was involved in several advocacy groups, and other community groups routinely went to her for advice when problems arose in their neighborhoods.

There was talk of nominating her for one of CNN's "Heroes," and Peyton couldn't think of a more deserving person. She knew if Serena had lived, she would be so proud of her mother. It would have been so easy for Ms. Lora to give up after losing her daughter and then her husband a couple of years later to cancer. But she hadn't. Instead she had used her love for people to make life better for others by setting up programs for families of victims of violent crimes, support services and crisis intervention for those in need. She did it all.

"Everything is well," Ms. Lora said as she took a sip of tea. "Now if we can just get those people at Gallant to take us seriously things would be better."

Peyton lifted a brow. "Take you seriously about what?"

Taking another sip of coffee, Ms. Lora said, "Around Christmastime last year, a couple of people living in this particular community on the outskirts of Chicago, not far from a chemical plant, became ill from the drinking water. When they reported it to the water company, they got the brush-off—until someone in that community brought the problem to my attention. Of course, I made such a fuss that the chemical company had no choice but to check things out, especially when I showed up at the plant one day unannounced with the media."

Ms. Lora took another sip. "They were nice, but I

knew they weren't happy I just dropped by like that with those reporters and all. A few days later I got a letter from their company attorney, who told me in so many words to mind my own business, and that if I kept it up they would sue me for slandering their company's reputation."

Peyton frowned. "Has the water been tested by the Department of Environmental Protection?"

"They claim they have and nothing was found. That was two years ago. Another test isn't required for another two more years."

Peyton pushed her cup of coffee aside. "Do you have a copy of the letter you received from Gallant's attorney?"

"Sure do."

Moments later, when Ms. Lora returned with the document, she handed it to Peyton. Peyton's gaze first went to the letterhead. Brody and Brody, LLC. She'd heard of them and knew they were a well-established law firm in Philadelphia.

She read the contents of the letter and frowned. The letter claimed the company had done a chemical analysis of the drinking water a year ago, and concluded that there were no contaminants. The letter stated that no further tests would be done for another two years.

Peyton put the letter down. "Some of the homeowners are still getting sick?"

"Yes, more so now than ever. Unfortunately, none of the people living in the community of Pembrook Pines can afford an attorney to fight their battles since they're living on fixed incomes. That's why we've called this special hearing before a judge on Thursday to try and persuade Gallant to do another test. Judge Carter will be there to hear both sides, and we hope that we can con-

vince him that another test is warranted. We all figure
Gallant will haul one of those big-time attorneys from
that law firm there," she said, pointing to the letter. "Our
group can't afford an attorney, but we're going to stick
to our guns and make sure Gallant's attorney doesn't
try to snow us."

Peyton took a sip of her coffee when an idea came to
her. She glanced over at Ms. Lora. "I think I'm going to
make sure I'm there just in case they do."

Ms. Lora lifted a brow. "What are you saying?"

Peyton smiled. "I don't have any plans for Thursday, so I'm going to be at that meeting to represent the
home-owners group. So now you can rest assured that
you won't get snowed."

Later that night, after sliding into bed, Peyton's cell
phone went off, and she smiled when she saw it was
Angelo on her caller ID. "Hello."

"Hello, yourself. How are you doing?"

"Fine. There's nothing like coming home," she said.
For years it had been hard for her with her grandmother
gone, but Ms. Lora always tried making things special.

"I'll bet. Look, I'm going to be in your area Thursday and Friday and I want to see you."

She knew there was no reason for him to just be in the
area and couldn't help wondering if he was deliberately
seeking her out. Why was she feeling a bit giddy about
it rather than annoyed? Probably because she wanted to
see him, too. She missed him.

Instead of pretending that she didn't, she said, "That
can be arranged."

"Great. I have an appointment Thursday afternoon,
so what about dinner later?"

So, he really was in town on business. "I'd like that."

"Good. I'll stop by your hotel after my appointment and—"

"I'm not staying at a hotel. I'm staying with Ms. Lora, the mother of my best friend growing up. But if you give me the name of your hotel I can stop by later Thursday evening."

"Okay." He gave her the name of the hotel and his room number. She wasn't surprised it was one of Chicago's finest.

"I should be back at the hotel by five, but just in case my appointment runs longer, I'm leaving a key for you at the front desk. Just go to my room and make yourself comfortable."

Peyton couldn't help but grin. "Thanks. And I intend to do that."

He didn't say anything for a minute. "I miss you, Peyton. At night I miss sleeping with your body next to mine, miss inhaling your scent, miss being inside of you, miss waking up beside you, miss—"

"Angelo," she interrupted, taking a deep breath and closing her eyes. His words were stirring emotions inside of her that she'd thought were long dead.

"Yes?"

"I miss you, too." There, she'd said it. She'd been completely honest with him. She had missed him.

"I miss you more," was his comeback.

She gave him a soft seductive chuckle. "I intend to prove just how wrong you are about that Thursday night, Mr. Di Meglio. Good night."

She was about to click off the phone. "Wait!" he said, and then paused. "I love you."

She parted her lips, about to say the same back to him but caught herself. It was true because she did love him. She knew that now. But he shouldn't have to hear something so profound as a declaration of love over the phone. She wanted to be staring into those dark, intense eyes of his when she said it to him. She needed to see and feel the impact her admission had on him.

"Good night, Angelo."

"Good night, Peyton. And I'm looking forward to Thursday."

Chapter 24

Angelo paused at the door to the courtroom to glance at his watch. He hoped the hearing wouldn't last more than a few minutes. That would be all the time it'd take to hear what the opposing side—the community group—had to say. Then he would provide them with the new report absolving Gallant of any responsibility for water contamination. And if there was a problem, it wasn't caused by Gallant.

The last test results that were conducted were good for another two years. So no one could force Gallant to perform additional tests any sooner, unless it could be proven that there was a direct link between those getting sick and Gallant. So far no one had done that.

He had reviewed the documentation on every single test that had recently been conducted, and the hearing today was to reiterate the findings and Gallant's position on the matter and to advise the group that their only legal recourse was to sue. He doubted they would want to pursue that option. Hell, they didn't even have an attorney, only some spokesperson for the group.

Deciding he had a few minutes to kill before the meeting actually started, he moved to a quiet area to call Peyton. He had tried calling her twice today, but hadn't been able to reach her.

He was looking forward to tonight and that was the main reason he hoped the meeting wouldn't last more than an hour. He had instructed the hotel concierge to make sure Peyton got a key to his room, and he'd hoped she would be there waiting for him when he got there.

Just thinking about seeing her again sent chills down his body. He couldn't wait and hoped like hell he'd be able to concentrate on the proceedings, especially when he'd rather be someplace else.

His family had celebrated when Gallant had decided to leave Brody and Brody, hiring the Di Meglio law firm, so he knew he had to deliver, which shouldn't be hard to do. He had to get in there and make sure that a representative from the mayor's office found no reason for the water to be retested. It would be a waste of both Gallant's and taxpayers' time.

He turned off his cell phone when he still couldn't reach Peyton, and moved toward the door to enter the hearing room where the meeting was about to start.

"You don't know how much it means not only to me but to those home-owners to have you stand up for us, Peyton. Especially since you're here in Chicago to rest and relax, not to take up one of my causes."

Peyton smiled at the older woman. "No problem. I'm licensed to practice law in this state."

"I'm glad, too."

Peyton could tell Ms. Lora was nervous about the upcoming proceedings and gave her a breakdown of how things would probably go. They had agreed to let her do the talking, to plead their case and request updated tests from Gallant.

"Now isn't he a handsome devil?" Ms. Lora said, smiling.

"Who?" Peyton asked.

"The man who just walked in the door. He's with that man who works for Gallant, so I wonder if he's a new attorney at Brody and Brody. He definitely isn't the same one that represented them the last time." Ms. Lora chuckled. "If he is an attorney, he probably could win the case just on his looks alone."

Peyton chuckled, tempted to look but decided she didn't need to do so since she had a handsome devil of her own, one she planned on spending the night with. She had dropped by the hotel before arriving to leave her overnight bag. Just the thought that she would be with Angelo later sent shivers through her body.

"I can see the women in here beginning to drool over that guy. At this moment, I wish I was about thirty years younger."

Curiosity made Peyton glance over her shoulder to see who all the fuss was about. She sucked in a quick breath when she looked directly into Angelo's eyes at the exact moment he looked into hers. *What was he doing here?*

"Excuse me, Ms. Lora, I need to speak with him."

Ms. Lora looked at her in surprise. "You know him?"

She nodded. "Yes, that's Sam's brother." And without saying anything else she moved in Angelo's direction.

Excusing himself from the man he was talking to, Angelo automatically moved in her direction as well.

What was Peyton doing here? Had she found out he was here and decided to come to the hearing room instead of going straight to the hotel?

He watched her stride purposefully toward him as he walked toward her. He was so glad to see her that he knew he would have to compose himself and not pull her into his arms and give her the kiss he wanted to. She looked good, was dressed nicely and walked with an air of confidence that some women lacked. But she had it, and something inside of him felt proud she was his. And she *was* his. He had to continue to court her, let her know she was the woman he wanted. Not just in his bed, but in his life.

"Angelo," she said, coming to a stop in front of him.

Before she could say anything else, he reached for her hand, tugged on it gently and said softly, "Let's step outside."

As soon as they were out of the courtroom doors and standing in the corridor, he smiled down at her. "How did you know where to find me?"

She looked up at him. "I didn't. I'm surprised to see you."

Confusion settled in his features and he raised a brow. "I don't understand. Then why are you here?"

"I'm here with Ms. Lora. Why are you here?"

"I'm here representing Gallant."

Now it was confusion that settled in her features. "But why? They're represented by Brody and Brody."

He shook his head. "Not anymore. Brody and Brody was replaced by Di Meglio."

She sucked in a deep breath when the impact of what he'd said became clear to her, but she could tell it wasn't quite clear to him yet, so she said. "That's unfortunate."

He frowned. "Why?"

"Because I'm the opposing counsel." And without saying anything else, she turned and went back inside.

Opposing counsel? Angelo felt as if he'd been sucker punched in the gut. What was she doing representing anyone when she was supposed to be in Chicago on vacation? And why had she walked off from him with an attitude? So what if they were on opposing sides? That had nothing to do with them personally. They were professionals and could handle being on opposite sides. Besides, it wasn't as if they were involved in some ugly feud. It was a matter of the judge listening to both sides and then deciding whether her client had grounds to force his to do more tests on the drinking water for the residents of Pembrook Pines.

He checked his watch, knowing it was time to go back in since the judge would be arriving in less than a couple of minutes. Reentering the courtroom, he moved toward the front to take a seat beside Rodney Gallant, one of the owners of the company.

The man raised a concerned brow and leaned closer to ask, "Is everything okay?"

"Everything is fine" was Angelo's response. He was lying through his teeth. All it took was the sideward glance Peyton had just given him to know things weren't okay.

He would be the first to admit that he'd never imagined in a million years them working against each other in the courtroom. Trying to take his mind off Peyton, he noticed just how full the courtroom was, and it was filling up even more. The place was noisy, and it was evident those there anticipated what was to come. He rolled his eyes and wanted to scream: *People, it's not that kind of party. This is just a hearing, not a retrial of OJ Simpson.*

A part of him was glad that so many people had shown up to support something they felt was important to them, even if they wrongly believed Gallant was to blame.

"All rise," the bailiff said, grabbing Angelo's attention. Like everyone else, he stood. "The Honorable Effie Carter, presiding." Everyone watched as the middle-aged woman took the bench.

Angelo shifted his gaze over to Peyton at the same time she shifted her gaze over to him. He felt it and knew she did to, a connection that wasn't just sexual, it was as emotional as anything he'd ever felt before.

"You may all be seated," the bailiff said.

There was something in the look she'd given him that gave him pause, and for a quick second he thought that maybe he was wrong and it would be *that* kind of party.

"I'd like to remind everyone before we get started," the judge said. "This is not a court trial. This is a hearing where I will give both sides the opportunity to present their arguments. After which, I will decide whether or not I feel enough information has been presented to warrant that more tests be done by Gallant Chemicals..."

Peyton sat there listening to the judge, and at the same time unable to believe that Angelo was the attorney for the company that didn't give a damn about the people of Pembrook Pines. She knew that everyone was entitled to representation, but still. Gallant? Did Angelo actually believe the company had nothing to do with people getting sick? Those tests were done over a year ago and plenty of things could have changed since then. Workers could have gotten careless or developed an I-don't-give-a-damn attitude at the expense of the good people of Pembrook Pines.

"Ms. Mahoney, are you ready to present your argument?"

Peyton stood. "Yes, Your Honor, I am."

Peyton then approached the bench. She could feel Angelo's eyes on her with every step she took. "Your Honor, I want to present documentation in the form of medical records that will verify treatment was provided to ten residents of Pembrook Pines over a six-month period after consuming drinking water. This is where one of the main water lines crosses with those from Gallant Chemicals." She handed the papers to the bailiff to present to the judge.

"I am representing the residents, who are not accusing Gallant of intentional wrongdoing. But what they are accusing them of is negligence and of adopting a careless attitude and blameless approach by assuming there is no way Gallant can be held responsible for the failing health of Pembrook Pines's residents. All we're asking is for Gallant Chemicals to conduct another series of tests. And if they are found negligent, whether intentionally or not, to compensate the good people living in Pembrook Pines accordingly."

Peyton had delivered her summation as cleanly and clearly as possible, only because Ms. Lora wanted it that way. Peyton much preferred going for the jugular. However, Ms. Lora had taken into consideration that over the years, Gallant had done some good deeds for the people of Pembrook Pines, and a huge playground was one of them. However, it was Peyton's opinion that one good deed didn't excuse the outright negligence of not making sure chemicals used in their plant didn't leak into the nearby water supply. It was a responsibility they should not have taken lightly.

The judge studied the papers she'd been given, and then she glanced over to where Angelo sat. Peyton was tempted to turn and look at him as well, but decided it would be best for her if she continued to face the bench.

"Mr. Di Meglio," the judge said. "You've heard Ms. Mahoney and the people of Pembrook Pines's request. Will Gallant agree to have those tests performed?"

"No, my client will not, Your Honor."

"Well then, do you have anything to say?" the judge asked.

It was then that Peyton turned around to stare at the table where Angelo was sitting. Angelo stood to address the bench. "Yes, Your Honor. I have a lot to say—the first being that my client and I don't agree with Ms. Mahoney's assessment of things."

Angelo approached the bench. The last thing he wanted was a courtroom soap opera, but he had a client to defend and he disagreed with the picture Peyton had just painted. He'd been surprised she hadn't used the legal strategy of a community being taken advantage of by Corporate America. By not going for the jugular and accusing Gallant of ignoring the health concerns of the residents of Pembrook Pines, she was painting the home-owners as a group of sympathetic victims who only wanted the company to do the right thing, and nothing more. Fat chance! He could smell a pending lawsuit totaling millions a mile away.

He could also smell Peyton, and her scent was the last thing he remembered from that morning when they'd parted at the airport. They had made love more times than he could count…although he doubted he would ever forget.

"Mr. Di Meglio?"

He glanced over at the judge. "Yes?"

"We're waiting."

It was then that he realized for a moment his mind had drifted in the courtroom and in front of the judge. That wasn't good. Peyton's presence was messing with his mind, and he couldn't let that happen. "Yes, Your Honor. Sorry."

He paused. "First of all, those medical records do not include a clear diagnosis indicating that contaminated drinking water is the cause of the residents' illnesses. Although the symptoms might be similar, in the absence of a concrete diagnosis verifying such, the cause of their health problems is pure speculation on anyone's part."

He didn't have to look over at Peyton to know she was fuming. He could feel her heat, but then he was used to feeling her heat. In the past it worked for him, but this time he had a feeling it was working against him. "And then," he continued, "although they aren't required to do so but every two years, my client routinely checks its water supply every quarter and the last few analyses performed indicated the water supply was not polluted. I have sufficient documentation that will show the last test was done just weeks before the illnesses began and it showed Gallant's water supply was free of contaminants."

He then handed his documentation to the bailiff to present to the judge. The judge studied the papers for a moment, and then glanced first at Peyton and then at Angelo, after which she held them both in her intense stare. "I read the documentation presented, and if Gallant had not been diligent in taking the initiative itself to conduct routine water analysis, I would have no problem requesting that they do more testing. I'm not naive enough not to consider the possibility that chemicals could have leaked into the water supply outside of the required testing time. However, since these tests were done and the results are legit, I see no reason to have Gallant bear the expense of doing more tests."

She paused and looked over at Peyton. "However, Ms. Mahoney, your group is free to request another hearing if additional information can be presented. Otherwise, what you've presented isn't conclusive enough to find Gallant responsible for any wrongdoing, so I'm denying the residents of Pembrook Pines's petition that Gallant do additional tests."

The judge banged her gavel. "The hearing is over."

Chapter 25

Peyton paced Angelo's hotel room, furious. How dare he? He had the judge and every other woman in the courtroom eating right out of his hand. Whether it was his handsome good looks or his smooth talk, she hadn't stood a chance, especially when Ms. Lora had set those parameters regarding not going after Gallant Chemicals the way she'd wanted to do.

She rolled her eyes when she recalled what the judge had said about Gallant not having to bear the expense of additional tests. It wasn't as if the company couldn't afford them. They had plenty of money. They were a *Fortune 100* company, after all.

She glanced at her watch, wondering where Angelo was anyway. They hadn't much to say to each other after the hearing. In fact she made sure she avoided him as she spoke with some of the residents she knew. She had apologized for not being able to get them what they'd wanted.

She felt even worse when they had told her an apology was not needed and that they felt she'd done a good job. It was just a matter of the big guy prevailing over the little guy once again. It happens all the time. Don't lose sleep over it. Their solution would be to boil their drinking water before drinking it.

That made her even madder, that they would meekly accept what the judge had handed down. They shouldn't have to boil their drinking water. They should be able to feel safe about drinking tap water like any other community.

She heard a key card being inserted in the door and glanced across the room at the exact moment Angelo walked in carrying a bouquet of flowers and a bottle of wine in his hand. Her temperature went to boiling when he smiled over at her. What the hell was he smiling for?

"Sorry to keep you waiting," he said, closing the door behind him. "But I wanted to make a pit stop and get you these," he said, crossing the room and handing her the vase of flowers. "And a bottle of wine."

"Why? To compensate for what you did in that courtroom?" she snapped.

He placed the bottle of wine on a nearby table. "Not that I want to discuss what happened this afternoon, but evidently it has you slightly agitated, so let's talk about it and get it over with."

Peyton just stared at him for a moment, not believing what he'd said. Did he honestly think they could talk about it, kiss and move on? That it was back to business as usual between them? Did the man simply not get it?

She shook her head and glanced over at him. "Contrary to what you evidently believe, Angelo, there won't be any getting over it. There was a group of people who were counting on me righting a wrong for them today.

They are people you wouldn't really know about. People who know how hard it is to earn a dollar and go to work whether they're healthy or not. These are the same people that company you're representing evidently does not care about."

"That's not true, Peyton. I checked out everything, especially Gallant's reputation. It's stellar, and they are involved in a number of worthwhile charities in the area."

She placed her hands on her hips. "And that makes them above the law?"

"No, but they should be given a fair shake like anyone else. You failed to prove they did anything wrong. If you had, the judge would not have hesitated to rule in your favor. As it stands—"

"As it stands, Angelo, what we had is another case of the little guy getting taken advantage of by a greedy corporation that puts profits ahead of someone's health—another case of the haves and those who have not."

Angelo's jaw clenched and he felt anger consume him. Would she ever be able to see beyond that? That was the way of the world. He was tired of being made to feel guilty because his family was blessed. Hell, his great-grandparents and grandparents had worked hard to pass a legacy down to their heirs.

"Do you know what your problem is, Peyton?"

"No, because I don't have one. But evidently you think I do."

"Yes, I know you do. And it goes back to that damn chip on your shoulder."

She glared at him. "There's no chip on my shoulder."

He glared right back. "You think not? Then take another look. Even before I took the case, I did my research, Peyton. And I've spent the last three days going

over everything, even as much as taking a tour of the
plant myself."

He took a moment to draw in air, getting angrier by
the minute. She wasn't just attacking his wealth, whether
she realized it or not, she was also questioning his character. "I was not just giving lip service in that courtroom today, Peyton. I honestly don't believe Gallant is
responsible for whatever is making those people sick."

"Well, have you given much thought to the possibility that you might be wrong, Angelo?"

He held her gaze. "Have you?" he asked slowly.

And then knowing at that moment he needed distance
from her before he said things he might later regret. "I
need to take a walk," he said. "I'll be back later." He
then turned and left.

Angelo really wasn't surprised when he returned
from his walk twenty minutes later to find Peyton was
gone. In less than an hour, their relationship had taken a
drastic turn, and a part of him wasn't sure it would ever
get back on track, especially not when Peyton could believe the worst about him, if she thought he would defend a person or corporation that truly didn't care about
others, that didn't give a damn about the environment.
Hell, he'd read those medical reports. More than just
adults had gotten sick. Did she think he was callous
enough not to care about the welfare of a child for the
sake of greed?

Angelo rubbed the top of his head, realizing that apparently she did. Feeling frustrated, he moved into the
room and saw she'd left the flowers with a note scribbled
beneath it that said, *"Today was your victory, not mine.
And since it seems we don't see eye-to-eye on important*

*things, this is where we should end whatever we started
while we can still be friends."*

Friends? Is that all their relationship was now? Back
to friendship and nothing more? Was she so full of anger
that she didn't see that the flowers had nothing to do
with the judge's decision in the courtroom today, but
everything to do with him being so glad to see her?

He walked over to the window and looked out at the
view of Lake Michigan below. If he didn't love her as
much as he did he would throw in the towel and say the
hell with it, and give her what she wanted. Her belief
in the gap between the haves and have-nots was so in-
delibly etched in her mind that he doubted she would
ever see things differently. He realized that in order for
them to forge any kind of relationship, she would have
to trust and have faith in him above all else. He couldn't
share a life with a woman who didn't believe in his sincerity and integrity.

He chuckled, thinking he needed to face the truth.
The bottom line was that she didn't want to share a life
with him anyway. She didn't love him and had said so
more than once. Why was he so determined to make her
love him, make her see that they belonged together—for
better or worse, richer or poorer?

He moved away from the window and rubbed a frustrated hand down his face. Peyton Mahoney had to be
the most stubborn woman alive. And the look on her
face when he'd suggested that she was wrong about Gallant had made her madder. And yes, he had considered
the fact that he, himself, might be wrong, too. What if
Gallant had falsified the documentation they'd given
him? What if they were responsible for everything Peyton had accused them of? There was no certainty about
anything anymore. And she should've known that in

their profession, he had to depend on the facts in evidence unless he had proof otherwise.

He drew in a deep breath and knew he didn't need to prove whether he was right or she was wrong. The bottom line was that something was causing those people to become sick, and if it wasn't chemicals from the Gallant plant, then what was it?

He pulled his cell phone out of his back pocket and punched in a number he'd gotten to know by heart. It was the private number to investigator Alex Maxwell. When he heard Alex's voice, he said, "Alex, this is Angelo Di Meglio. First, I want to congratulate you on the birth of your son. And secondly, I need your help."

Peyton snuggled under the sheets, feeling cold and alone. She was glad Ms. Lora hadn't asked her why she'd returned tonight when she'd told her earlier that morning she would be spending the night with a friend. She had a feeling the older woman had put two and two together and figured out that that "friend" had been Angelo. It probably wasn't hard to tell that she had gotten upset with him in the courtroom.

She shifted and rose up in the bed when she heard a knock on her bedroom door. "Come in."

Ms. Lora opened the door and came into the room with two cups in her hands. "I couldn't sleep either and heard you moving about. I remembered those times when you and Serena would be nervous the night before a big test at school and I would bring you both hot chocolate to help you sleep."

Peyton remembered those nights and the hot chocolate had worked. It was times like this, being here with Ms. Lora and sleeping in what once had been Serena's room, that would make her miss her childhood friend even more.

She glanced over at Ms. Lora, who'd come to sit on the edge of the bed. "I miss her."

Ms. Lora nodded, smiled and pushed back a wayward lock of hair from Peyton's face. "I know you do. And so do I. No matter how many years go by there's not a single day that I don't think about her, miss her. The two of you were so close, just as close as me and your mama."

That was something Peyton often wondered about. How Ms. Lora and her mother could have been such good friends when the two women weren't anything alike. Peyton had heard enough about her mother's wild and reckless ways from her grandmother as well as the people who lived in the neighborhood. To this day, Ms. Lora had never said an unkind word about Tangie Mahoney.

"I hope you aren't mad or anything with your young man, Peyton," Ms. Lora said softly. "He had a job to do and did it."

Peyton lifted a defiant chin. "It doesn't matter, he doesn't understand."

Ms. Lora chuckled. "Yes, I think he does. While he was talking, at no time did he look down his nose at us like that other attorney who worked for Gallant did. And afterward, when the hearing was over, he spoke to a few of us, even then he talked to us and not down to us."

Ms. Lora paused. "And I don't want you to think that you failed us, because you didn't. We're all appreciative that you would go into that hearing and speak up on our behalf. You didn't have much time to prepare and all, but then I heard what the judge said and she's right. We have no proof that whatever is in the drinking water was put there by Gallant."

Peyton shook her head. Angelo had been effective in casting doubt in a lot of people's mind. But she didn't want Ms. Lora to be taken in by his smooth talk as well, no matter how convincing it sounded.

"Ms. Lora, don't fall for anything Angelo said. I plan on filing a motion for another hearing and by then I'll have done my research and—"

"No, you'll do no such thing, Peyton. You're here on vacation. I feel bad for getting you involved in the first place. Besides, Mr. Gallant came over and assured us that he would get to the bottom of this as well."

She rolled her eyes. "Sure he will. His company will use the time to cover their tracks."

The room got quiet. "Sam's family has money, a lot of it. I know that. And I have a feeling that you're holding that against Di Meglio for what that guy at Yale did to you," Ms. Lora said.

Peyton almost choked on her hot chocolate as she stared at Ms. Lora. "How did you know about that?"

Ms. Lora gave her a small smile after taking a sip of her hot chocolate. "Your grandmother.... She found out from Audrey Duncan."

Peyton's eyes widened. "Audrey Duncan?"

"Yes."

Audrey Duncan had been a friend of her grandmother's from church. "How on earth did she know?"

"If you recall, Audrey had a cousin whose daughter attended Yale at the same time you did, and she happened to mention you leaving school after the holidays with some excuse about you needing to be near your grandmother. Well, since your grandmother was doing fine health-wise, Audrey's cousin's daughter assumed you were either pregnant or dumped by some well-to-do guy you were serious about on campus. Since you weren't pregnant, we figured the latter was true."

Peyton nodded. "Yes, the latter was true, but he didn't dump me. I decided to cut out before he did, after over-hearing a conversation between him and a friend as to why he never invited me home to meet his family."

Ms. Lora snorted. "It was his loss and not yours. And I hope you're not holding what happened to you at Yale against that Di Meglio guy. Not all rich people are snobs. Like I don't believe that all big corporations would take advantage of the little guy."

She reached out and took Peyton's hand in hers. "Do me a favor."

Peyton lifted a brow. "What?"

"Keep an open mind where Angelo Di Meglio is con-cerned. At some point you're going to have to give your heart to some man for safekeeping. Don't close your heart to him just because he's wealthy and successful. Unless his family got their money illegally, someone worked hard for it. Besides that, you're not a pauper yourself, you know."

Peyton couldn't help grinning because Ms. Lora was right on that account. Over the years she had put together a nice nest egg. She had worked hard for her money and invested wisely. "Okay, I'll try and keep an open mind where Angelo is concerned."

An hour later, after she was alone in the room once more, Peyton stared up at the ceiling and thought about what Ms. Lora had asked of her. Keeping an open mind about Angelo didn't mean she would open herself up to heartache. Now, since she knew without a shadow of a doubt that she had fallen in love with him, she would have to protect her heart more than ever.

Chapter 26

"Okay, Angelo. What's going on with you and Peyton?"

Angelo tensed as he leaned back in the chair behind his desk. Leave it to Sam to ask the one question he'd rather not answer. He shifted his cell phone to his other ear. "I don't know. How about you tell me?"

"Look, stop being a smart-ass and answer my question. Since Peyton returned from Chicago she's been pretty tight-lipped. She comes into the office early and stays late. It's been almost two weeks. I'm back in Houston now, but I talked to Mac and nothing has changed. What did you do to her?"

Angelo rolled his eyes. Of course he would be the guilty one. "I didn't do anything to her." *Other than give her my heart,* he thought, but refrained from saying. He'd called Peyton a number of times but she refused to return his calls. "And why are you calling me? She's your best friend. Why don't you ask her?"

"I tried but she clammed up on me and said she'd rather I didn't inquire about the relationship between the two of you. But I'm inquiring, at least to you. I love you both, and I hate seeing the two of you miserable."

He shrugged. "Who says I'm miserable?"

She chuckled softly. "A better question might be who says you're not miserable? I hear you're just as bad as Peyton, working long hours and keeping to yourself."

He couldn't deny the truth. Since returning from Chicago, instead of taking time off as planned, he'd decided to return to work at full speed. He arrived early and worked until he was bone-tired at night. That was the only way he could go home and not stay awake most of the night thinking about Peyton. She had made her decision, and he would have to live with it.

He decided to tell his sister what had gone down in Chicago. As he talked he replayed every single moment in his mind.

"And you're sure about Gallant? What if someone has falsified the reports and they are guilty? That many people getting sick is no joke, Angelo."

"I know, and trust me, you don't hear me laughing. I ordered additional tests be done before agreeing to represent Gallant, and the judge accepted those results without ordering new ones as Peyton requested. She wanted the water samples analyzed by an impartial party designated by the courts. Based on the test results I saw, Gallant isn't guilty of anything."

"But someone is," Sam said quietly.

"Yes, someone is. And that's why I hired Alex. If anyone can uncover the truth, it's him. If I'm mistaken and Gallant is responsible, I will no longer represent them. In fact I will work with Peyton to nail them."

"Did you tell Dad that?"

"Yes, and he supports my position." Angelo hadn't been surprised. As much as his family had wanted the Gallant account, they wouldn't hesitate to let it go if they discovered the company had been untruthful. The Di Meglio law firm didn't operate that way.

His phone beeped. He checked the caller ID and saw it was Alex. "Okay, Sam, I need to get this call. It's Alex."

"All right, Angelo. Let me know if he's found anything."

Angelo clicked on the other line. "Alex?"

"Yes. You got a minute?"

"Sure. Is it about the Pembrook Pines investigation?" Angelo asked, hopefully. He needed to know something—good or bad.

"Yes, and I think it's time for someone to go to jail."

"Do you want to do lunch today?"

Peyton looked up from the documents spread across her desk and glanced over at Mac, who was standing in her doorway. She hadn't heard the door open. "No, thanks, I'm not hungry."

Mac shook her head as she came into the office and dropped down in the chair opposite Peyton's desk. "You're still not in a talkative mood about what's going on with you and Angelo?"

Peyton shrugged. "There's really nothing to talk about, Mac. For the second time in my life, I fell in love and then got hurt."

Mac couldn't keep the surprise off of her face. "So you admit to loving Angelo?"

"Didn't have much of a choice once I realized what those feelings were that I had been experiencing. And the sad thing was that I was going to tell him how I felt that night before the hearing happened."

Mac lifted a brow. "What hearing?"

Peyton drew in a deep breath and began telling Mac about what happened while she was in Chicago. Mac didn't say anything but listened to everything she said. It was only when she'd finished and told Mac how she hadn't taken any of Angelo's calls over the past two weeks that Mac offered Peyton some advice.

"First of all, I can't believe this is the first I'm hearing about you and Angelo in a courtroom. And I assume Sam doesn't know as well."

Peyton shook her head. "If she knows it wasn't because I told her. She and Angelo are close so he might have said something to her about it."

Now it was Mac who shook her head. "I doubt it. Mainly because Sam and I have been talking, trying to figure out what's going on with you and Angelo. That night you two were at Sam's for dinner anyone could see how great you were together, and I could see you softening toward him."

Peyton didn't say anything as she remembered that night. It had been a wonderful weekend. *The best.* Her attraction to him was at an all-time high, but her feelings for him had run even deeper. Before the night was over, she admitted to herself that she had found in Angelo something she thought she would never experience again with any man. *Love.*

"I hate to play devil's advocate, but what did you expect him to do once he realized you were the opposing counsel? Tell the people at Gallant he couldn't represent them because the two of you were lovers and he couldn't be impartial? Would you have done the same for Ms. Lora? Or did you expect him not to be on top of his game just because it was you?"

"Of course not!"

"Then what, Peyton? Angelo is an attorney, and like you, he's a darn good one. It's our job to defend people, even people we'd rather not defend. Remember last year when I had to defend that child molester who was out on parole and felt the community he'd moved into was discriminating against him?"

Mac shifted in her seat to a more comfortable position. "I was pregnant at the time and as an expectant mother, a part of me wanted to tell him he was getting just what he deserved for his horrendous crimes. But I remembered the oath I took as an attorney. We have to put our personal feelings aside and do the right thing, and I'm sure you would agree that the right thing was for Angelo to protect his client's interest, just as you were doing."

Peyton slowly got up from her seat and went to the window and looked out. It would be nice if when she went to bed at night she didn't think about Angelo, or didn't think about him in the mornings and during the day. But the bottom line was that she thought about him all the time.

She slowly turned around. "Why does life have to be complicated?"

Mac chuckled. "Good question, and I have another one. Why do women fall in love with men who we initially assume are all wrong for us? You know my history with Luke and Sam's with Blade. But look at us now."

Mac stood and stretched. "And to answer your question, life is complicated when we make it that way. You're upset and hurt over what Angelo was doing, and all he was doing was his job. Maybe that's something that you need to think about."

The next day, Peyton was still thinking. In fact, she hadn't thought much about anything else. She had talked to Ms. Lora, and there hadn't been any reports of any others living in Pembrook Pines getting sick, and that was good. Maybe Gallant had decided not to risk exposure and was cleaning up their act, literally. If that was the case, then maybe something good had come out of the hearing, after all.

But that good news hadn't flowed over to her relationship with Angelo. Had her expectations of him been unrealistic? Had she used the hearing as an excuse to back away because she'd felt herself falling hard and needed some way out?

"Ms. Mahoney?"

Her secretary's voice over the intercom interrupted her thoughts. "Yes, Priscilla?"

"Alexander Maxwell is here to see you."

She frowned. Why was Alex here to see her? "Please send him in." She stood and moved around her desk and was standing and waiting when Priscilla escorted him into her office.

She smiled upon seeing him. "Alex, you're a long way from home, aren't you?"

He chuckled. "Not too far, but I miss Christy and the kids anyway."

As she stared at him she couldn't help but think that Alexander Maxwell was a good-looking man who made no secret about the fact that he adored his family. He was married to Blade and Slade's cousin, Christy. They had a three-year-old daughter named Alexandria Christina, and two months ago Christy had given him a son,

Christian Alexander. "And congratulations on the birth of your son."

She watched his face light up in a huge, proud grin. "Thanks. Christy, AC and I are happy about Christian. Now if we can only get him to sleep through the night," he said, taking the chair Peyton offered.

"Yes, I bet. So what brings you to Oklahoma?" she asked, moving back around her desk to take her seat.

"I got a call from Angelo a few weeks ago about doing an investigation," he said, placing a briefcase on his lap and opening it.

She lifted a brow. "An investigation?"

"Yes. It seems a number of people were getting sick from drinking water and you believed Gallant Chemicals was responsible."

Peyton was surprised Angelo had hired Alex to pursue the matter any further. She nodded. "Yes, that's right."

"Well, I discovered the drinking water was tainted with harmful chemicals, but not from Gallant. And to make sure, we brought in a team of experts from Madaris Explorations. Gallant agreed to let them come in and conduct their own series of tests on the water supply."

That was another surprise for Peyton since she knew Gallant was under no legal obligation to do so. It showed their willingness to uncover the truth.

"Once we were sure we could eliminate them as the culprit, we began investigating other businesses in the area whose water supplies were linked to Pembrook Pines," Alex said. "All of them were in compliance except for one. In fact, we were able to capture on video the person actually dumping harmful toxins in the Arvada Lake."

Peyton sat up straight in her chair. "You're kidding. And what company was it?"

"Conyers Print Shop."

Peyton nearly fell out of her chair. "Conyers Print Shop?"

"Yes."

"But that's owned by Seymour Conyers. He and I went to school together. He knows a lot of the people who live in Pembrook Pines."

"Well, that might be the case, but Mr. Conyers was caught on video illegally dumping industrial waste from his printing press facility into the river just last week. All the evidence was handed over to the police this morning, and I got word that he was picked up an hour or so ago. And I understand that after thorough questioning he's admitted to it. Frankly, there was little else he could do after being caught red-handed."

Peyton closed her eyes and rested her head back against her chair. She couldn't believe it. Seymour had been at that hearing, sitting there watching as she tried making a case against Gallant. He knew about the people getting sick, yet he had dumped illegal chemicals in the water supply again as recently as last week? What on earth could he have been thinking?

She opened her eyes and met Alex's gaze. "Did he give a reason for what he did?"

Alex nodded. "I understand he said business had slacked off, and he couldn't afford to get rid of all those chemicals the way he should have."

"So he risked people's lives instead?" she said angrily, shaking her head, unable to comprehend how Seymour could have done such a thing. He was one of the South Side's success stories, and he repaid the community this way?

Alex stood. "Here's the full report, Peyton. Angelo wanted me to make sure I personally delivered you a copy."

Angelo.

She inhaled a deep breath, realizing what that report meant, especially when she remembered all the things she'd said to him. She had been wrong on all accounts. "Thanks," she said, taking the file from Alex. It was thick, and she intended to read every page of it.

She stood, needing to change the subject as she thought things through. "I understand Gina and Mitch are expecting again," she said, smiling. Gina and Mitch Ferrell were close friends of the Madaris family, who Peyton had gotten to know through her friendship with Mac and Sam.

Alex chuckled. "Yes. Christy spoke with Gina last night, and she and Mitch are happy about it. We've been telling them for years that Cameron needed a baby sister or brother."

He smiled. "And Rasheed and his wife are expecting again as well," Alex added. Rasheed Valdemon was a sheikh in a Middle Eastern kingdom and another close friend of the Madaris family.

An hour later, after Alex had left, Peyton had finally read the last of the report that Alex had left with her. He had been thorough in his investigation, and to bring Madaris Explorations in to oversee the analysis had been brilliant. Their reputation was stellar, not only in Texas but around the country. Reese Madaris was the foreman, and he no doubt had a number of important projects on his plate. Yet he had taken time out of his busy schedule to assemble his team to investigate the drinking-water contamination.

At that moment, her cell phone rang. It was then that

she noticed how late it was. The office had closed a half hour ago. She checked the caller ID and saw that it was Ms. Lora. No doubt she was calling to let Peyton know what had happened with Seymour.

"Pulling another late-nighter, I see."

Angelo looked up from the papers he'd been reading to observe his mother's face. He saw concern and understood why. He had returned to the law firm and immediately began working longer hours when he'd sworn he would cut back.

He tossed his pen aside. "Yes, I need to familiarize myself with this case I might be taking on."

Kayla Di Meglio nodded as she entered and took the chair across from his desk. "Do you want to talk about it?"

He lifted a brow. "The case?"

"No, what's really going on with you, Angelo. Namely, what's going on with you and Peyton?"

Do you want to talk about it? He leaned back in his chair and recalled he'd asked Peyton that same question a couple of times before she'd finally told him that he had a habit of asking Sam that whenever he was in a brotherly mood. Now he knew where he'd gotten it from.

He wasn't surprised that his mother was aware of his relationship with Peyton. He'd learned over the years that when it came to their children, his parents rarely kept anything from each other.

There was no reason to pretend he didn't know what she was talking about. It wouldn't work with his mother anyway. "I can tell you what's going on in one statement. I've fallen in love with a woman who doesn't trust me to do the right thing."

"And that hurts."

His mother's simple statement pretty much summed it up. Hell, yes, it hurt. And over the past couple of weeks he'd had time for that hurt to fester into one agonizing and painful ache. And the sad thing about it was that he knew there was no cure. How could he go about changing something as deep-rooted as misplaced convictions? She knew his family, knew they considered her to be one of their own. Yet, Peyton had this fear that they were like all the others—people with money—and were no more than a bunch of snobs.

He met his mother's gaze. "Yes, it hurts."

His mother didn't say anything for a moment. "I've been married to a Di Meglio man long enough to know how quickly that hurt, when untreated, can become anger that can consume you, eat you up inside."

He chuckled coolly. "I hate to tell you this, Mom, but it's already eating me up inside. I'm mad because, of all the women out there, I fell for one who doesn't give a damn about my feelings. I told her I loved her, and she tells me that she doesn't love me back."

"So what are you going to do?" his mother asked in her concerned voice.

He raised a defiant Di Meglio chin. "Get over her."

"That probably won't be easy."

He couldn't agree more. "No. But not impossible."

His mother didn't say anything for a moment. "There has to be a better way. Sam has told me about Peyton's fears and what that guy did to her years ago. I remember the first time a guy I thought I loved broke my heart. It made things hard for your father, so I can understand how she feels, Angelo."

"Well, I can't," he said angrily. "I am not *him*."

"No, you're not," Kayla Di Meglio said softly. "I know the Eltons, and they can be snobs at times. And I think that one day Peyton is going to realize you aren't anything like their son."

He shrugged. "Maybe, maybe not. And probably when and if she does, it will be too late."

His mother stood. "I hope not. I can't imagine any other woman who would compliment you more. Don't stay too much longer. You need your rest."

He watched his mother leave, closing the door behind her. He gathered his papers together, deciding he would take her advice and leave, too. It had been a long day.

He stood to put on his jacket when his cell phone rang. He glanced down at it and saw it was Peyton calling again. He knew Alex had delivered the results to her so she was calling to apologize for thinking the worst of him. She had called twice already that day, but he hadn't taken either call, since he wasn't ready to talk to her. Honestly, there really wasn't anything to say.

What she didn't understand was that she hadn't just questioned his judgment, she'd questioned his character. And the latter hurt worse than anything, since love, trust and faith were a package deal. But he could plainly see in her eyes, he didn't have any of the three. Until he could deal with that and move on with his life, he'd rather not have any contact with her at all.

Chapter 27

Peyton hung up the phone knowing Angelo was deliberately avoiding her...like she'd been doing to him the past couple of weeks. She couldn't really get mad about it, just annoyed.

She stood up from her desk and walked over to the window and glanced outside. It was night already and she was still at the office. She had read the report again and at the end had called herself all kinds of fool. Gallant would have had a lot to lose had they been found guilty of disposing of chemicals in the water supply. And even Ms. Lora hadn't wanted her to lean too heavily on Gallant, because of all their good works in the community. But she had been so convinced it had merely been a snow job, and just another example of what she deplored in corporate America, where Goliath always beat the little guy, that she hadn't taken a good hard look at the facts. And that had been her first mistake.

No, in all honesty, her first mistake was not believing in Angelo enough to know he would never have taken a case without first making sure those he represented were worth it. He would never sell out. Yet she had all but accused him of doing so.

She turned when she heard the knock on the door and was surprised when Mac stuck her head in. "What are you doing here? I thought you left hours ago," Peyton said.

Mac smiled. "I had. In fact, I didn't even return after my appointment with Judge Crawford at three this afternoon. I went home and surprised Luke with dinner."

"Then why did you come back at this late hour? Did you forget something?"

Mac shook her head as she entered the office. "No, I got a call from Sam after dinner. She had talked to Angelo and he told her everything, and I figured you'd still be here."

Peyton pulled away from the window. Yes, she was still here. "By everything you mean Alex's report that pretty much proves I made a fool of myself by not taking what Angelo said at face value," she said. "He has every right to be somewhere gloating, but I know he's not. He's probably too angry to do so."

"Angelo wouldn't gloat anyway. Not about you and not about this. He loves you too much…although from what I hear you're the last person he wants to talk to."

"I'm not surprised. I've tried calling him three times today and he's not taking my calls."

"Just like you weren't taking his?"

A wry smile touched Peyton's face at the harsh reminder. "Yes, like I wasn't taking his." A moment later she said, "I guess you can say I'm getting what I deserve."

Mac tilted her head a little. "Yes, I can say that, but I won't. And just so you know, Sam talked to her mother an hour or so ago and Angelo is not in a good mood and your name is practically mud about now."

"I can understand him feeling that way."

"And you're going to accept that?" Mac asked.

Peyton threw up her hands. "And just what am I supposed to do about it? I can't force him to take my calls."

A sneaky smile touched Mac's lips. "Why waste your time calling when you can hop on a plane and get a direct flight to New York? Unless, however, you're afraid to face him and admit how wrong you were, how sorry you are and that you love him more than life itself. And that he's worthy of all the groveling you need to do."

Peyton frowned. "Groveling?"

"Of the most serious kind.... It's reserved for men who're most deserving and only in dire situations."

Peyton nibbled nervously on her bottom lip. "I think that this is one of those dire situations and he is most deserving."

"I agree. And I suggest you go home and map out your strategy. And remember he's part Italian. He's not going to make it easy for you."

She'd figured as much. "I'm going to be persistent," she warned her best friend.

"I understand. A woman's got to do what a woman's got to do. And with a man like Angelo, you might even have to go the extra mile or two."

Undaunted by the possibility, Peyton began clearing off her desk. "I have a court hearing at nine in the morning, and after that I'm outta here."

Mac nodded. "I understand."

Peyton glanced up. "What about Sam?"

Mac grinned. "She understands as well. Remember,

she's married to Blade, and she didn't make things easy for him either."

Mac crossed the room and gave Peyton a hug. "We just want you to be happy, and we believe Angelo is the man to do that. You just need to get that chip off your shoulder and believe that you're worthy of any man, no matter who his family is and no matter how much money he has in his bank account. The only thing that matters is that he loves you and you love him."

Peyton wiped the tears from her eyes. For the second time in nearly ten years, she was crying over a man. But she knew that DeAngelo Di Meglio was worthy of every tear she shed.

"I might be taking some more time off, too. Possibly another two weeks."

Mac smiled. "Your calendar is still clear. Take as much time as you need. FDR is working out quite nicely around here," Mac said of the attorney who'd joined the firm last year when Sam had married and moved to Houston. "We'll be able to handle things. We just want you to be happy. So go make up with your man."

Her man. Peyton grabbed her purse off her desk, liking the sound of that. "And I will, if I can get Angelo to forgive me."

"And you will try to make that happen, right?"

Peyton nodded as they both headed toward her office door to leave. "Yes, with all my might."

Chapter 28

Angelo glanced up at the knock on his office door. "Come in."

It was Mike from security downstairs. "A package was delivered to you, sir," the younger man said, setting a box on Angelo's desk.

"Thanks."

"I see you're working late again tonight, Mr. Di Meglio."

"Yes, Mike. I'll be here for a couple of hours longer."

"All right. If you need anything just buzz."

"I will."

The man left, and Angelo stared at the box and then opened it. Inside there was a smaller box, prettily wrapped in white paper with a red bow on top. He noticed there was no card attached. He started to push it aside, but curiosity got the best of him so he opened it. Some of his clients sent him thank-you gifts on occasion, and he wondered who had sent this one.

He pushed back the tissue paper to reveal a wooden shim. He frowned, wondering why anyone would send him a gift like that. He put the top back on the box and pushed it aside. He stared at it for a minute, but was still clueless.

He wondered when and how the package had arrived, since there weren't any postmarks on the box. Glancing at his watch, he saw it was close to eight o'clock. Most everyone had left for the day. His parents had a dinner date and had left a short while ago. They had invited him to join them, but he had declined their invitation, deciding in his present mood he wouldn't be good company. He was thinking about making plans to join Lee Madaris in Dubai. Lee had returned there a few days ago with Mitch Ferrell to finalize the plans for the hotel.

Deciding it was time for him to call it a day, he was pushing the papers on his desk aside when there was another knock at his door. Thinking it was Mike again, he said, "Come in."

He glanced up and his breath caught at the same time as his entire body stiffened. Peyton stood there, in the doorway, her face as beautiful as he remembered from the last time he'd seen her, although she'd been pretty damn angry then.

"Hello, Angelo."

He slowly stood to his feet. "Peyton? What are you doing here? How did you get past security?"

She entered the office, closing the door behind her. "I'm here to see you. I called earlier and talked to your mother. She gave me clearance with security."

Angelo nodded. His mother hadn't mentioned anything to him. He decided to sit back down. "Okay, you see me. What is this about?"

She strolled closer to his desk, and he watched her

as his heart ticked up a beat. She was wearing a pair of dark brown slacks and a pretty mint-green blouse. The outfit looked totally feminine on her.

She came to a stop and then perched her curvaceous bottom on the edge of his desk, almost knocking the breath out of him when she did so. She pushed a few wayward locks of hair back from her face. "I would think my gift would have explained it all," she said, pointing to the box in the middle of his desk.

He arched a brow. "You sent this?"

"Yes."

"Why? Why would you send me a piece of wood?"

She chuckled, and it was so soft it set off a sensuous quiver within him. "It's not really a piece of wood, although I can understand you thinking so. It's that chip I've been carrying on my shoulder for years now. I thought it was time I finally got rid of it."

He swallowed. "Have you?"

"I think so, but there're a few little splinters I need to take care of…with your help."

He released a frustrated sigh. A part of him refused to get caught up in whatever game she was playing. He wanted no part of it. He loved her. Had told her so, yet she didn't want his love, so why should he care about any chips she was dealing with? "Not sure I want to help you, Peyton."

He saw a flash of something in her gaze and his heart caught. She was beginning to feel out of her element, and he could tell. Hell, what had she expected? He was a man with feelings, strong feelings. Feelings that ran deep and she hadn't considered any of that, which let him know after all this time she really didn't know him.

She tilted her head back and licked those lips he enjoyed so much, with that tongue he longed to taste again. Fighting back the urge, he shifted in his seat.

"I really wish you would reconsider," she said.

"Any reason why I should?" he asked coldly. Even he could hear the frosty bitterness in his tone.

She eased off his desk, and he tried not to notice how the fabric of her slacks stretched across what he knew were a gorgeous pair of thighs. "Yes, I can give you plenty of reasons," she said, drawing his attention to her face. "But I prefer dealing with the most important ones first, since I recently got to discover a few things about myself. Although I never admitted it, I was carrying around a lot of baggage."

"Were you?" he asked, watching her as she nervously began pacing in front of his desk. She stood still a second to answer his question.

"Yes. It was a lot more than I thought, too. I've worked my way through a lot of it, and I'm proud of myself for doing so. I feel better, more confident and more secure."

"Are you?"

"Yes."

If he sounded aloof, detached, unemotional and unsympathetic it couldn't be helped. He had put his heart on the line with her, something he hadn't done with any other woman. And instead of believing in him she had thought the worst.

She stopped pacing again and stood still and met his gaze. "Another thing I've figured out, Angelo, is that I love you."

Shock slammed into him, and he drew in a deep breath. Those were words he hadn't expected her to say. They almost did a jumpstart to his heart, but he refused to be moved by them. How could a woman who claimed she didn't love you all of a sudden say that she did?

"Really?" he heard himself ask. "And just when did you realize that you loved me, Peyton? I can clearly remember you telling me just a few weeks ago that you didn't."

She began pacing again, not looking over at him. Instead, she was studying the floor as if she was trying to get her thoughts together, a tactic he often used in the courtroom just before he presented a final argument.

She stopped in the center of the room in front of his desk and held his gaze again, and he felt a stirring of desire that he forced back, but it was hard when she was so damn desirable. "I could say I fell in love with you the night I turned thirty and you gave me the perfect orgasm at the perfect time. But you'd only think I was getting love confused with great sex."

Yes, he probably would, he thought.

"Or I could say it was when you took me to that lagoon, and I remember how special I felt being there with you. But then again you'd only question my feelings."

She was right again.

"Or I could say it was during the times we shared at Dunwoody, but I won't bother because you'd only make excuses. But I will say that time I got to spend with you at the resort made me see what a great guy you were, how much fun you were to be with—in and out of bed. That was a great start."

"Was it?"

"Yes. And it continued when you showed up in Oklahoma. I had fun that weekend."

So had he. Probably more than she would ever know. Definitely more than he would ever tell her now.

"But it was when I returned to Chicago and had a

chance to visit places that meant a lot to me, places and people in my past, who helped shape me into the person that I am, that I began wishing you were there, sharing it with me. And I began missing you like crazy. Then I knew what those funny little flutters were that I would feel at times when I would look at you when you weren't aware I was looking. Those times when I would catch you watching me, those times when you were inside of me and I wished you would never have to leave. I knew then and planned to tell you that Thursday night we were to spend together at the hotel."

Something within him stirred again, and he tried fighting it to stay calm, but he couldn't. He wanted to hear more. He needed her to explain more. "Then we faced off in the courtroom, and you suddenly thought this guy you supposedly loved was the scum of the earth?" he said in a sneering tone. "A guy who would forget about his values, his beliefs, basically his self-respect, not to mention discount the lives of good people—just to do what? Best you in court? Suck up to a new client? Just because I'm an asshole?"

She shook her head. "None of those things," Peyton pleaded. "It wasn't about you, Angelo. It was about me and my insecurities. It was about that baggage I was referring to earlier. It was about me. I know that now, and whether you believe it or not, I was realizing those flaws even before Alex showed up. He merely solved the puzzle."

He leaned forward in his seat, his gaze pinned directly on her face. "So just what do you want from me, Peyton?" he asked, hearing the edge in his voice.

"Your love."

His love? He'd given it to her, lock, stock and barrel. He'd planned to get to know her, court her. But courting her was like courting justice. At least her form of justice. She had been the judge and jury deciding his integrity and honesty. He hadn't stood a chance. It hadn't been justice, but injustice.

"What if I said it's too late and that I'm no longer in love with you?"

She quickly turned her face away, as if his words had been a slap in the face, and a part of him immediately regretted saying them, because he of all people knew he might be upset with her, angry as hell, but he still loved her.

She turned back to him, met his gaze. "If you were to say that, Angelo," she said softly, interrupting his thoughts, "the first thing I would think is that in that case, you never loved me at all if you could so easily fall out of love with me. But then I think I know better. You love me. I might have had my doubts at first, but that weekend after spending time with you in Oklahoma, I believed you. You said it often, and you said it each and every time with conviction and purpose, with meaning. I began believing you. But then I was afraid because I knew you were the one man who I could and would lose my heart to. And I wasn't sure I was ready to do that."

"And you think you are now?" he asked.

She nodded. "Yes. I'm not going to say being a part of my life is going to always be easy. But I promise to try and not cause too many problems."

He lifted his brow, skeptical…which prompted her to say, "I said I would try. So the decision is yours. You can believe that I love you, forgive me and we go from there. Or you can tell me to walk away and I'll go out that door and accept that it's over between us."

She paused for a moment. "So tell me what you want it to be, Angelo."

He heard the impatience in her voice, heard the uncertainty of what his answer might be. He knew what his answer would be. Probably had known when he glanced up and she stood there at the door. Could he really risk the heartbreak he might find with her?

He held her gaze and in a clear, distinct voice, he said, "Walk."

Chapter 29

At that moment, Peyton fought back the urge to burst into tears. She had come here and had given it her best shot. If he no longer wanted her then fine. But she wouldn't give up on him. He still loved her, she knew it. She felt it. But if he needed more time, then that's what she would give him. He had been patient with her and now she would be patient with him.

Squaring her shoulders and lifting her chin, she met his gaze. "Fine."

She turned and headed for the door. When she reached it, he said, "Now lock the door."

She glanced over her shoulder. He had stood and was stripping off his tie and unbuttoning his shirt. She stared.

"Peyton?"

His voice, once again clear and direct, almost made her jump. "Yes?"

"Lock the door."

"Oh." She twisted around to lock the door and then turned back around. He had tossed his shirt aside and had come around to sit on the edge of his desk to remove his shoes and socks. His gaze was glued to her the entire time.

"It might save time if you started taking off your own clothes," he said, standing. She watched his hands go to the buckle of his belt as he removed it from his slacks. It was then that she saw the size of his erection. *Oh, my.* Her palm automatically went to her throat as she felt her pulse beating erratically.

She somehow found her voice. "What do you think you're doing?"

By now he was sliding his slacks down a pair of muscular thighs. "I'm about to make love to you. Here in my office. Do you know how often I've sat in here daydreaming, fantasizing about doing that very thing? I could envision you stretched across my desk, legs open with me between them."

An image popped into her head, and she almost lost control of her breathing as a surge of desire raced through her. "Ahh, don't you think we need to talk, Angelo?"

He looked at her; a crooked smile touched his lips. The smile extended to his eyes. "We've talked. At least you talked, mostly. I heard you and the most important thing you said was that you loved me."

"And you believe me?"

"Yes. You have no reason to lie about it."

He began walking toward her. Naked and in a purposeful stride that was as sexy as anything she'd ever seen. "However, there will be ground rules that we will cover later. And there will be a wedding, which we can discuss later as well."

She lifted a brow. "Wedding? I don't recall you proposing."

He reached out and caressed her cheek with the back of his hand. "I will, sweetheart, after stripping you naked. When I ask you to be my wife, I want you as naked as I am."

And then, with an expertise she found amazing, he removed her clothes. She saw the hunger in his eyes and felt it all over. Since becoming involved with him, she had been taken in ways most women couldn't even imagine.

He stepped back and his gaze raked over her naked body, leaving heat in its wake. She could hear a low growl forming in his throat as he reached out and touched the hardened nipples of her breasts with his fingertips. "If I say it once, I'll say it a thousand times," he whispered raggedly. "You are beautiful, Peyton, so much so that my entire body is smoldering with a need to feast on you like a starving man."

She thought that he could say some of the most amazing things in a way that could stimulate her just hearing them. And when she felt his fingers slide away from her breasts and down her stomach to the curly hair between her legs, a shudder passed through her.

"Peyton Mahoney, will you marry me?"

She raised her eyes to meet his gaze. "You can ask me something like that at a time like this?" His fingers worked their way inside of her and were moving back and forth across her clit.

"As good a time as any...."

"What happened to the old-fashioned on-your-knees kind of proposal?"

He chuckled. "Hey, that'll work."

Slowly Angelo knelt down, getting up close and personal with the juncture between her legs. He leaned in close and touched his tongue to her feminine mound. "Is this better?"

If only he knew, she thought, trying to hold herself together while his tongue skimmed her, igniting fires everywhere he touched. Every so often, she heard the words...*delicious, hot, mine*...flow from his lips.

When she closed her eyes, he whispered, "No, keep them open. I want you to watch me, see me take you this way. Make love to you."

And then he was back on his feet and sweeping her into his arms. He moved across the room and placed her bottom in the middle of his desk. She shook her head. "You were really serious about this, weren't you?"

He lifted a brow. "Why would you think I wasn't?"

Yes, why wouldn't she? "I've never been taken on a desk before."

"Then consider it done."

She sensed the intense need in him even before he moved between her legs, and when he leaned down and captured her lips in an open-mouth kiss that sent her nerves reeling, she moaned out his name. He lifted her hips, tilted them toward him to receive his entry. She moaned deeper with the penetration of his erection as he slowly delved deeper into her eagerly waiting feminine muscles.

He pulled his mouth away from hers when her inner muscles clamped down on him with a force that tried to limit his forward progress. "Let go," he said in a rough tone.

"Not yet," was her reply. She clamped down on him, then eased up, then clamped down again on him, extracting and contracting with an urgency that had him gasping with every breath he inhaled.

"What are you doing?" he asked, his voice deep and tortured.

"What does it feel like?"

She knew he was powerful enough to push beyond her boundaries. She was holding him hostage, but he wasn't resisting. That meant he was enjoying her brand of possession.

And then he threw his head back and screamed her name at the same time he broke loose and pushed deeper inside of her, touching her womb at the exact moment his body burst into an explosion. She felt it, the very essence of him, his hot release, flooding her insides.

And then he arched upward and began pounding into her. She exploded on impact, wound her arms around him and entwined her legs with his. He leaned forward and took her mouth, his tongue tangling and mating with hers.

Each thrust into her body became more demanding, and when he came again, she, too, gave into rampaging desire and passion a second time. It was then that she realized, he had proposed but she hadn't given him her answer.

Hours later, Angelo remembered she hadn't responded to his proposal.

They had redressed and left his office, and he'd driven straight to his place. They had ordered pizza to satisfy their hunger and then stripped again to satisfy another hunger, one that just wouldn't go away.

He was holding Peyton in his arms in his bed. "Before you doze off, you never gave me an answer to my proposal," he said, looking down at her and pushing locks of her hair back from her face.

She smiled up at him. "Sure I did. You just didn't hear it with all those moans."

That was a good possibility. "So tell me again, so I can hear it."

Her eyes, he noted, appeared bright with mischief. "We could just live together for a few years and—"

"Not on this planet so don't even think about it."

"Um, I see the Italian side of you is coming out," she said, reaching up and placing a hand against his cheek.

"Whatever. So give me an answer."

She shifted her body to stare directly into his face. "Yes, I will marry you."

And then he leaned down, captured her mouth to seal their proposal with one earth-shattering kiss. And he knew at that very moment that he had helped to slay her demons of the past and together they could look forward to a perfect future.

Angelo glanced down at his fiancée and smiled. The room was filled with people in the Waldorf Hotel Ballroom in the heart of Manhattan. "Tired?"

Peyton chuckled. "I didn't know your parents would be inviting half the country. I don't remember this many people at Sam's engagement party."

Angelo shrugged. "Mainly because Sam took control of the guest list. However, you, my beautiful wife-to-be, made Mom happy by letting her handle things any way she wanted. Now you see what happened? You'll know the next time. Hell, I don't know half of these people."

Peyton nodded as she took a sip of her wine. She and Angelo would be getting married in five months on Valentine's Day, followed by an extended honeymoon in Dubai. She was looking forward to it.

Peyton had glanced back up at Angelo to suggest they go missing in action for a while when she felt a presence beside her. "Peyton?"

She jerked her head around and met the gaze of a man she hadn't seen in close to ten years. A man she figured she wouldn't see again. "Matthew! What are you doing here?" She felt Angelo stiffen beside her.

"My parents are friends with the Di Meglios so my family was invited." He then glanced up at Angelo. "I'm Matthew Elton. Peyton and I attended Yale together years ago."

Angelo took the hand offered and said in a curt voice, "I know who you are."

Matthew nodded. "When my parents got the invitation, I had to come to see if it was really you."

Peyton frowned. "Why? You didn't think the Peyton Mahoney you knew would be good enough to marry someone with the last name of Di Meglio?"

"No, it wasn't that at all."

"Wasn't it?" Peyton glanced up at Angelo. "Do you mind giving me a few minutes with Matthew?"

Angelo's eyes narrowed. "Yes, I mind."

She knew the man she loved with a passion was trying to be difficult. To ease his ire she leaned up on tiptoe and placed a kiss on his lips. "Please be nice."

"All right. Five minutes and then I'm coming for you," Angelo warned. He then hardened his gaze at Matthew before walking off.

Peyton forced a smile at Matthew. "Come this way. We can step out on the balcony."

"Okay."

Peyton knew it wasn't a coincidence that the Eltons

had been invited to the engagement party. Angelo's mother had done so with a purpose—and it was a purpose Peyton understood from the talks they'd had. Closure was important.

She was glad they were able to find a private spot on the balcony. She glanced at her watch. "We have five minutes."

Matthew arched a brow. "He was serious?"

Peyton smiled. "Yes, he was serious. Trust me."

Matthew nodded. "All right, then. I think you owe me an explanation as to why you left Yale without keeping in touch. I thought—"

"What did you think, Matt? That I would continue to be gullible and believe all those excuses about why you couldn't take me home to meet your family? You knew they would think I wasn't good enough."

She saw the blush of embarrassment that tinted his face. "You knew?"

She shook her head. "Not at first, but I overheard you tell someone and that was okay, but as you can see it wasn't meant for anything to last between us."

"Is that why you left school?"

"Doesn't matter. That was ten years ago. And now I am marrying a man who appreciates me, and neither he nor his family give a royal damn where I was born or to whom. I'm happy, and I hope you are, too."

He shook his head. "No. I ended up marrying the woman my parents picked out for me, and we were divorced within four years."

"A pity," Peyton said, not really caring. He was someone in her past, and she was glad for him to stay there.

"Time's up, Peyton."

It seemed Angelo had appeared out of nowhere and

then he was by her side, where she knew he would always be.

Matthew looked up at the both of them. "I hope the two of you will be happy."

Angelo spoke up before she could. "We will be." And then without saying anything else, he swept Peyton off her feet and into his arms to carry her back inside to the party.

Epilogue

At the wedding reception, when Angelo tossed Peyton's garter into the crowd of single men, it landed right on Lee Madaris's shoulder. He tried pushing it off, but it wouldn't budge an inch. Nolan Madaris glanced over at him and snickered. "I guess that means you're next."

Lee frowned and made a move toward Angelo to give him back the garter, when a feeble yet strong hand stopped him. "Enjoy this year."

He tried not to frown at his great-grandmother. "And what year is this, Mama Madaris?"

"Your last one as a single man." Then she walked off.

He watched as she slowly maneuvered her way over to where her youngest son, Jake, was standing with his wife, Diamond. Leaning on her cane, she glanced back at him, nodded and smiled. A shudder ran through him. Two things you could count on: his great-grandmother dreaming about fish when someone was pregnant, and her being a busybody when it came to her grands and great-grands, trying to marry them off.

"Hey, why are you frowning, Lee?"

He glanced up and met Angelo's grin. His frown deepened. "Why did you hit me with this?"

Angelo's grin widened. "It wasn't intentional. My back was turned, and I just tossed it. I guess it had your name on it."

"Don't try and get cute with me," Lee said, shoving the garter into Angelo's hands. "My grandmother thinks she has everything figured out, but I intend to beat her at her own game." He then walked off. Shaking his head, Angelo grinned, thinking that he wished his friend luck, and placed the garter in the pocket of his tuxedo jacket.

Angelo was still grinning when Peyton joined him a few moments later. In a few hours, they would be leaving for Paris to begin their two-week honeymoon. Before returning home they were flying to Dubai to check on the progress of the Grand MD Hotel, a Madaris–Di Meglio joint venture. He couldn't wait to get Peyton alone in Jake's Learjet, which was flying them to Paris. He was eager to give Peyton her wedding present.

"It's time for us to cut our wedding cake, Angelo."

"Okay, sweetheart," he said, smiling down at her. She looked beautiful, absolutely radiant, and when he'd seen her walking down the aisle to him on the arm of Mac's cousin, Marine Colonel Ashton Sinclair, at that moment he knew he couldn't love her any more. But he was wrong. He was falling deeper and deeper in love with her each and every time he saw her.

They were still working out the logistics of where they would live and practice law. More than likely they would both be practicing law in New York and Oklahoma for a while.

"I can't wait to get you alone," he said, leaning down and whispering close to her ear.

She smiled up at him. "And I can't wait to be alone with you."

They both got what they wanted a few hours later as Jake's pilot flew the plane away from JFK. They had given in to his parent's desire to have a lavish Di Meglio wedding in New York.

Cuddled up in Angelo's lap in the private jet, he handed his wife a sealed envelope. "This is your wedding gift, sweetheart, and it comes with all my love."

She opened the envelope, and her eyes widened. "You bought me the lighthouse?"

He chuckled. "Yes, and that's not all."

She read further and her breath caught. She looked back at him, astonished. "And the lagoon?"

"Yes. Both are ours and I plan for us to make a stop there after leaving Dubai."

Peyton couldn't hold back the tears that flowed down her face. "I love you, DeAngelo Antonio Di Meglio. Thank you for being the man to knock that chip off my shoulder."

She leaned closer and kissed him with all the love in her heart and realized that dreams do come true. She had the man of her dreams, and he wanted as many babies as she did. Life was good, and she knew with a man like Angelo it wouldn't be just good, it would be incredible.

* * * * *

Two classic Westmoreland novels in one volume!

NEW YORK TIMES BESTSELLING AUTHOR

BRENDA JACKSON

DREAMS OF FOREVER

In *Seduction, Westmoreland Style,* Montana horse breeder McKinnon Quinn is adamant about his "no women on my ranch" rule…but Casey Westmoreland makes it very tempting to break the rules.

Spencer's Forbidden Passion has millionaire Spencer Westmoreland and Chardonnay Russell entering a marriage of convenience… but Chardonnay wants what is strictly forbidden.

"Sexy and sizzling." —*Library Journal* on *Intimate Seduction*

Available July 2012 wherever books are sold.

KIMANI PRESS™
www.kimanipress.com

KPBJ4760712

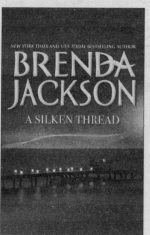

REQUEST YOUR FREE BOOKS!

2 FREE NOVELS
PLUS 2 FREE GIFTS!

KIMANI ROMANCE™

Love's ultimate destination!

YES! Please send me 2 FREE Kimani™ Romance novels and my 2 FREE gifts (gifts are worth about $10). After receiving them, if I don't wish to receive any more books, I can return the shipping statement marked "cancel." If I don't cancel, I will receive 4 brand-new novels every month and be billed just $4.94 per book in the U.S. or $5.49 per book in Canada. That's a saving of at least 21% off the cover price. It's quite a bargain! Shipping and handling is just 50¢ per book in the U.S. and 75¢ per book in Canada.* I understand that accepting the 2 free books and gifts places me under no obligation to buy anything. I can always return a shipment and cancel at any time. Even if I never buy another book, the two free books and gifts are mine to keep forever.

168/368 XDN FEJR

Name	(PLEASE PRINT)

Address	Apt. #

City	State/Prov.	Zip/Postal Code

Signature (if under 18, a parent or guardian must sign)

Mail to the **Reader Service:**
IN U.S.A.: P.O. Box 1867, Buffalo, NY 14240-1867
IN CANADA: P.O. Box 609, Fort Erie, Ontario L2A 5X3

Not valid for current subscribers to Kimani Romance books.

**Want to try two free books from another line?
Call 1-800-873-8635 or visit www.ReaderService.com.**

* Terms and prices subject to change without notice. Prices do not include applicable taxes. Sales tax applicable in N.Y. Canadian residents will be charged applicable taxes. Offer not valid in Quebec. This offer is limited to one order per household. All orders subject to credit approval. Credit or debit balances in a customer's account(s) may be offset by any other outstanding balance owed by or to the customer. Please allow 4 to 6 weeks for delivery. Offer available while quantities last.

Your Privacy—The Reader Service is committed to protecting your privacy. Our Privacy Policy is available online at www.ReaderService.com or upon request from the Reader Service.

We make a portion of our mailing list available to reputable third parties that offer products we believe may interest you. If you prefer that we not exchange your name with third parties, or if you wish to clarify or modify your communication preferences, please visit us at www.ReaderService.com/consumerschoice or write to us at Reader Service Preference Service, P.O. Box 9062, Buffalo, NY 14269. Include your complete name and address.

Harlequin *Desire*

ALWAYS POWERFUL, PASSIONATE AND PROVOCATIVE.

**A BRAND-NEW WESTMORELAND
FAMILY NOVEL FROM *NEW YORK TIMES*
BESTSELLING AUTHOR**

BRENDA JACKSON

Megan Westmoreland needs answers about her family's past. And Rico Claiborne is the man to find them. But when the truth comes out, Rico offers her a shoulder to lean on…and much, much more. Megan has heard that passions burn hotter in Texas. Now she's ready to find out….

TEXAS WILD

"Jackson's characters are…hot enough to burn the pages."
—*RT Book Reviews* on *Westmoreland's Way*

Available October 2 from Harlequin Desire®.

HD73198K